ALSO BY CLAIRE McMILLAN

Gilded Age

THE
NECKLACE

CLAIRE McMILLAN

TOUCHSTONE

New York   London   Toronto   Sydney   New Delhi

Touchstone
An Imprint of Simon & Schuster, Inc.
1230 Avenue of the Americas
New York, NY 10020

First Touchstone hardcover edition July 2017

TOUCHSTONE and colophon are registered trademarks of Simon & Schuster, Inc.

For information about special discounts for bulk purchases, please contact Simon & Schuster Special Sales at 1-866-506-1949 or business@simonandschuster.com.

The Simon & Schuster Speakers Bureau can bring authors to your live event. For more information or to book an event, contact the Simon & Schuster Speakers Bureau at 1-866-248-3049 or visit our website at www.simonspeakers.com.

Interior design by Kyle Kabel

Manufactured in the United States of America

10 9 8 7 6 5 4 3 2 1

Library of Congress Cataloging-in-Publication Data

Names: McMillan, Claire, author.
Title: The necklace : a novel / Claire McMillan.
Description: First Touchstone hardcover edition. | New York :
Simon & Schuster, 2017. | A Touchstone Book.
Identifiers: LCCN 2016053165 (print) | LCCN 2017003290 (ebook) |
ISBN 9781501165047 (hardback) | ISBN 9781501165054 (paperback) |
ISBN 9781501165061 (ebook) | ISBN 9781501165061 (eBook)
Subjects: | BISAC: FICTION / Historical. | FICTION / Contemporary
Women. | FICTION / Literary.
Classification: LCC PS3613.C58539 N43 2017 (print) | LCC PS3613.C58539
(ebook) | DDC 813/.6—dc23
LC record available at https://lccn.loc.gov/2016053165

ISBN 978-1-5011-6504-7
ISBN 978-1-5011-6506-1 (ebook)

For Sandy, again and always

. . . and I thought how unpleasant it is to be locked out; and I thought how it is worse perhaps to be locked in.

—Virginia Woolf,
A Room of One's Own

THE
NECKLACE

THE BLACKBUCK

Before it all begins, Nell looks up at the arched gables, hesitates at the heavy front door. Everything here is a test. No Quincy, not even a peripheral one, knocks unless she aggressively wants to announce herself. A true Quincy would bound in, secure in her welcome. But Nell creaks open the door and silently slips through like an intruder.

Lighted by the wavy leaded glass windows, a taxidermy antelope head gazes down with hazy glass eyes. An Indian blackbuck—she thinks someone told her this as a child. The ears show patches, as if something's been nibbling them. Bits of fur and dust fuzz the floor beneath it. A time-warp feeling settles over Nell like weather. She sneezes.

Her cousin Pansy looks over from the living room and mouths "Gesundheit," then turns back to the small group of women Nell should recognize but doesn't, no doubt in conference over last-minute details for Loulou's wake tomorrow.

What does one call Quincys in multiple? A clutch? That's eggs. A murder? That's crows. A judgment? That's perfect. A judgment of Quincys brings to mind her ancestor Increase Quincy and his infamous verdicts at Salem, and makes her wonder if judgment is encoded in the Quincy double helix.

She feels an arm around her waist and a kiss on her cheek. "Nell-bell." Her cousin Emerson, Pansy's younger brother, is Nell's age and adheres to the male Quincy uniform of dark suit and tie. Despite this, he's rumpled. His tie with a pattern of tiny clocks is fraying at the wide end. He smells like he's been here for at least a few Old Grand-Dads.

"Hey." She gives his waist an extra squeeze, and lets it go that he knows she hates that nickname. She hasn't seen him in years. Then again, a few years is not particularly long between her and the Quincys.

Her parents preferred living in Oregon, where they'd met, and where Nell lives now. They'd put a country between themselves and the Quincys reflexively sizing them up. Despite this removal, Nell's mother would insist they make a pilgrimage here most summers. She'd instruct Nell for the length of the car ride from the airport to use her best manners—please, thank you, pass the hors d'oeuvres before taking one for yourself. She'd turn fully in her seat, lean over the armrest, and inspect Nell's fingernails for dirt while her father drove.

A transformation would come over her parents here. Her mother would become brittle, short with everyone, even Nell's father, whom she adored. Her usually witty and erudite father would go silent. They'd both drink bourbon at lunch, something Nell never saw them do anywhere else. And Aunt Loulou, as her mother called her, would lead everyone into that big dining room for luncheon. She'd seat herself at the head of a table that gleamed with silver and yellowing brocade and proceed to dominate the conversation with the self-assurance of a favorite child who had never been told to shut up. It was here she'd dish out what Nell's father witheringly referred to as "Loulou Lessons."

"Only wear fur between Halloween and Valentine's Day," Loulou had said once when Nell was seated next to her. An unusual honor. Loulou had a confidential, chummy tone in her voice that day. Nell had been conscious of her table manners and had taken miniscule bites. She still can't remember what she ate. The glamour of the statement had delighted her, though now she wonders at imparting this lesson to a ten-year-old. Her mother's lips grew tight across the table. She volunteered at the wildlife animal sanctuary. No one they knew in Oregon wore fur. But this piece of advice seemed important to Nell if she were to become a Quincy-type grown-up. One would have furs, and of course one would follow the rules for wearing them.

"Red shoes should really only be worn by very small children and prostitutes," Loulou said to Nell's mother once when she thought Nell was out of earshot. "Don't you think she's getting a little old for those?" Though Nell didn't know what a prostitute was, she was no baby and she'd refused to wear the red patent Mary Janes after that, much to her mother's exasperation. Until then, they'd been favorites.

And the one she could never remember without a hot flush, even now, happened on the same day as the fur instructions. "Picking one's teeth should be done in private, dear," Loulou had stage-whispered loud enough that everyone at the table heard. "Like most pleasurable things."

She'd turned to Nell's mother. "Really, she should know the basics, shouldn't she?" As Nell's ears reddened, she'd watched in baffled delight as her mother stuck her finger in her mouth, aiming toward a back molar. Her father had choked on his bourbon, silently laughing.

Today, Emerson steers Nell by the arm into the flower room, which has always served as the bar, and tries to get her to drink whiskey with him, though it's only lunchtime. She accepts a glass. It's easier than openly refusing.

"Is Vlad here?" she asks. Emerson's partner, Vlad, works in the conservation department of the Met and is a great favorite of all Quincys. He'd come close to walking away after demanding that Emerson stop being ashamed and come out to the family. Nell still couldn't believe Emerson had manned up and brought Vlad to the farm. "This is a farm?" Vlad had asked. Emerson had explained to his Czech lover, product of a communist childhood, the concept of a gentleman's farm.

"No, he's not," Emerson says now, sadly. "Work. But he wanted to come. They were buds, you know."

Nell did know. Vlad had managed to charm Loulou with his European manners and wide knowledge of art.

"I'm not a hayseed," she'd scolded Emerson after Vlad's first visit. "Why have you kept him away?"

"So that's why you've started early," Nell says now. "If he were here, he wouldn't allow it."

"If he were here, I wouldn't need it."

Nell's wishing she also had someone with her, a plus one, a partner, a human shield. Lately, she's been accepting of her single fate, embracing of it even, and it didn't chafe. But it's days like today that she wishes she had an effective distraction at her side—a charming and successful husband maybe, or a cherubic and precocious child.

Glad of her little detour with Emerson, Nell has a chance to take it all in. The Canaletto over the living room mantel is hanging next to a calendar from the local arboretum Scotch-taped to the wall. The carved jade emperor's bowl sits side by side with a plastic candy dish in the shape of a cow, which moos when anyone reaches for a treat. The two-foot high stack of *National Geographic*s from the sixties still stands in front of the bookshelf that holds a complete set of first editions of Ralph Waldo Emerson's essays and poems—her cousin's namesake and a distant Quincy relative. It's a tableau from her childhood preserved intact—from the highball glass sweating and leaving rings on the marquetry table to the Ritz crackers and cheddar cheese on a chipped demi porcelain dish. She's underestimated the impact of seeing it again. And the scent of the place—mildew mixed with Windex—sends her neurons firing down a wormhole that strips away decades so she is a girl again, self-conscious and bewildered and filled with a fraught desire to belong.

She'd been careful never to let on to her mother that she was intrigued by this side of the family. Since earliest remembering she has known where her loyalties should lie. Despite her mother's efforts to impart her own reticence, Nell's feelings for the Quincys have always been tinged with never-admitted longing and a secret pride.

As she walks into the living room now, her uncle Baldwin is sunken into one end of the loveseat listening to the preparations for tomorrow's services, an untouched glass of something amber at his side.

"Saved a place for you right here," he says, inclining his head without dropping a stitch as he works on a painted needlepoint canvas depicting an elaborate buckeye tree. Needlepointing allowed him all sorts of cover at family gatherings. He could sit in the corner and pretend he wasn't eavesdropping or didn't hear a question, or exit a conversation by concentrating on his work. And damn anyone who dared to so much as raise an eyebrow at his traditionally "feminine" hobby. It was just the sort of eccentricity born of privilege that Baldwin enjoyed flaunting.

"Why, men make the best stitchers," he'd say, his blunt fingers flying over patterns of sailing flags or hunting dogs. There was a wink in it, an acknowledgment that unless you were a Quincy, you probably wouldn't know about such things.

He'd sent Nell's mother a pillow one Christmas depicting what was supposedly the family crest.

"Good Lord," she'd said when she'd opened it, setting it aside quickly and barely looking at it. Though she'd send a gushing thank-you note, Nell knew. Nell had squirrelled away the pillow in her room, blending it in with her menagerie of stuffed animals. She has no idea where it is now.

Nell settles in next to Baldwin, glad for his rapid-fire questions about her life, which cover any awkwardness.

"Still working so hard or have you found time to hike? Isn't that what you Oregonians do out there? Go hiking in the forest? Do you eat the salmon or have you become one of those vegans?" He is too restrained to nose around in her romantic life. Whether it's good breeding or because his wife, her aunt Sharon, ran off with a fly-fishing instructor a decade ago and now lives in Wyoming, she couldn't say.

Pansy and the female relatives have stopped talking about their plans for tomorrow, listening in on Nell's debriefing.

Nell can't help but feel that Baldwin's faux chumminess and the room's silent spotlight marks her as the outsider, the guest. "We don't actually belong there," her mother would say with a little relieved sigh when they'd settle into their seats on the plane back to Portland.

When the wireless doorbell rings, a quotidian digital buzz that replaced the old chimes years ago, Nell's relieved. A true non-Quincy has arrived.

From the formal tone of his emails inviting her to this meeting, Nell expected someone older. But the estate attorney, Louis Morrell, is about her age. His boring suit and subdued tie contrast with his shaved head and corded neck, which indicate he might spend some regular time at the gym. The effect is of a Mafia don's right-hand man, a true consigliere, and not at all the sort of lawyer Nell imagines Loulou hiring. A homegrown boy, Nell's guessing, but she reminds herself about books and covers.

He removes his suit coat and throws it on the long bench near the fireplace, as if he's home from a long day at work. "Louis," he says, pronouncing it "Louie." "Like the song." He walks toward Nell with an arm extended, welcoming her as if he owns the place. "Great to see you, Nell. You're the only one I haven't met yet." A heavy gold link bracelet shines next to his shirt cuff.

She shakes his hand and cuts her eyes to Pansy for confirmation. ("Really? *This* guy?")

Pansy's knowing smirk gives Nell a reassuring sense of coziness—a judgment of Quincys, indeed.

Pansy doesn't pull her punches for anyone. Even as

kids, she often duped the gullible and ditched the slow, including the younger Nell. Uncle Baldwin had given her the name Pansy thinking it old-fashioned—harkening to some long-dead aunt and a flower. The name had made it a virtual certainty Pansy would grow up to be a badass. Five feet ten inches of marathon-honed control, her Patagonia fleece and practical running clothes, even at a meeting like this, convey her complete comfort in her surroundings and telegraph that she's up for anything coming her way—a run, lifting heavy objects, combat. Next to her, Nell feels conspicuous in the tailored clothes she bought especially for this trip, hoping they'd convey an air of easy appropriateness.

Emerson stands. "Great to see you again." They do that one-armed man-hug thing.

So, clearly Louis has been around awhile.

Baldwin manages to stop needlepointing long enough to raise three fingers and shake Louis's hand, but he doesn't get out of his seat. It gives Nell pause, considering her usually gregarious uncle. And then Louis makes his way around the room, greeting Pansy's companions in order of importance, clearly in on the Quincy family hierarchy.

By unspoken cue, they leave after greeting Louis. None of them are invited to this meeting. Nell dives a hand into her purse for a piece of nicotine gum, but pauses. "Never chew gum," Loulou would say. "You look like a cow with a cud."

Pansy's smile disappears as she closes the front hall door behind the exiting relatives. "I'm the only one around here who's planning anything. I'm, like, the matriarch now, or something." She throws herself on a low sofa and puts her feet up on the butler table, mindless of the loose hinges.

"You're the one in town," Emerson says. "Settle down."

"Really?" Pansy asks. "You'll want to be nicer to me. Connie Rensselaer is making those spinach things for tomorrow. I told her they were your special favorite."

Emerson groans. Connie Rensselaer's mini spanakopitas were a bland and soggy mess, which isn't surprising, given that the Rensselaers aren't Greek and none of them have ever cared a whit about food despite having "hot and cold running help," as Loulou used to say.

"You did not."

"No, I didn't," she admits. "But don't tempt me. I told her the caterers were taking care of everything, but she insisted."

If Louis hears this sibling back and forth, he doesn't show it, and Nell recognizes a fellow pro. She's honed similar political skills in depositions and courtrooms and knows exactly how much effort is required to make this look natural. As she watches his finesse, she decides that if one of the most expensive firms in town, plus Loulou— who'd been a notorious snob—can trust him, then she'll keep an open mind.

"I'm so sorry for your loss," Louis says, calling this meeting to attention. Tactfully dealing with death is a requirement in his area of law. He sits on an overstuffed chintz loveseat, the bottomed-out springs forcing his knees up to his chest as he roots through a document bag, un-packing clipped stacks of paper onto the floor until Pansy clears the coffee table.

Emerson slumps in his chair, the caning long ago busted out on the sides. He scrolls through his phone, so big it's like a piece of toast. Emerson works for one of the big New

York banks, a fact Baldwin enjoys strategically wedging into conversations. He's taken a hit in the downturn, but managed to save his job by working twice as hard. His phone is now an appendage.

His slumped posture and distracted manner say "I don't see why we have to do any of this." His attention to his phone says "We all already know what's in these documents." And Nell feels that familiar mix of envy and yearning she's often felt when confronted with Emerson's place in the family.

Louis's email had said he wanted the three cousins, Emerson, Pansy, and Nell, here to go over procedure and process since they'd be in town already for the memorial service and wake. He'd have private meetings with each of them later.

He passes out copies of the will. In her reply email, Nell had requested to be given a copy as right at this meeting and the others had followed on. She'd probably annoyed this Louis lawyer with that, but the pro shows no inkling of it as he hands her a stack.

As a warm-up, he walks them through small gifts to the nurses first, then moves on to a few charities where Loulou had long served on the board, followed by token legacies for well-remembered godchildren. She had about a half dozen of them. It's not something they need to go over, and Nell recognizes that he's leading them in slowly. After a diplomatic amount of time, and proper mutterings about the propriety of all this, Louis continues.

"The firm has been privileged to work with this family. This is just going to be a preliminary discussion about the timelines moving forward." He passes out more papers, which are flipped and shuffled in earnest.

"And as you know, the firm has a long track record with families such as yours—"

"Nell's the executor?" Pansy's voice is calm, her back ramrod straight, feet on the floor now. "Daddy, did you know?" Like a jailhouse lawyer who's picked up enough law to advocate for his fellow inmates, being an old-line WASP means Pansy's picked up enough legalese to read a will. She looks at her father. "What does that mean?"

They've all zeroed in on Nell's status first. Nell feels the effort they've been putting into appearing friendly while they were controlling their curiosity. She rifles the papers in her lap for something to look at, shock and a slight edge of excitement racing through her. She can feel Baldwin's eyes on her.

He leans back. "I did, honey. Your grandmother and I discussed it."

"You'll see," Louis says, cutting off this topic, "she left very specific bequests to each of you."

The prized Canaletto goes to Emerson, along with the first-edition Emersons, which is only fitting.

To Pansy she's left the jewelry in a safe-deposit box downtown. Louis hands Pansy a tiny key and a printout of passcodes and PINs.

And to Nell she's left a necklace.

"We haven't managed to find it yet," Louis is saying to her. "But I'm sure it's here somewhere. I apologize," he says, perhaps noticing Nell sit up straighter as her lawyer brain kicks into gear. "But your grandmother—" Nell starts at the word; she was Aunt Loulou to her. "Sorry, your great-aunt was easily upset at the end and it was decided it was best not to have a bunch of strangers in the house looking for it." It's then that Nell's lawyer armor fully slips on, because if he were her associate, he'd be getting a dressing-down right now. As the lawyer for the estate, he should be on this. He should have made sure someone found it, whether or not Loulou was acting cranky.

"She was pretty loony tunes at the end," Baldwin says to Nell, and then turns to his children and says, more loudly, "She was hoarding scrap silver."

"We did manage to clean out the basement. We had a team that was very sensitive," Louis says directly to Nell, as if she is already in charge.

"Found a whole room filled with nothing but quart mason jars filled with rancid water, like a typhoid version of an air-raid shelter," Baldwin is saying. "And then the scrap silver, of course." He nods his head at Louis. "Bins and bins of it. There was a shoebox with some gold Krugerrands, too. Couple of cases of Chartreuse as well."

Nell's picturing Ali Baba's cave in that dirt-floor basement, but filled with gold formerly under international sanction, tarnished flatware, and liquor that tastes like a Swiss cough drop.

"The gold has been valued and included in the statements," Louis says, trying to sound thorough. "The silver is going to be dicey."

"She was concerned with the collapse of Western civilization, like, legitimately concerned with a coming Armageddon," Pansy says, and Nell can't tell if Pansy shares this belief or is just protective of her grandmother.

"Like the zombie apocalypse?" Emerson says, eyes still on his phone. "You guys couldn't have had her in some blue chips or something?" he says to Louis, who holds up both hands in defense. Lawyers don't handle investments, and it was Loulou's money to do with as she liked, however ill-advised. They all know this.

"So who knows if that necklace is real," Baldwin continues, turning to Nell. "I never saw Mother wear it. Not once." He stops stitching when he looks up and says, "I think she said it was cursed, but that could just be more bats-in-the-belfry stuff. Seems like you got the delusional gift."

His quick dismissal of her single legacy makes her feel like this should be expected. She didn't really think she was here to receive anything legitimate, did she? Nothing besides some leftovers or a mix-up should be expected, even if she is executor.

She can feel Louis watching them all.

Baldwin, of course, gets the house. As the last surviving member of his generation, and Loulou's sole heir, this is expected. Nell's mother, who has been dead a decade now, is not mentioned. Nor is her father, which is understood. Loulou claimed he was never a true Quincy, and, as an in-law, he wasn't. Nell had called him in Italy, and he had refused to come. "Come see me afterward," he'd said. "You'll need it."

"'And the residue of my estate,'" Pansy reads out loud. "'Keeping in mind the provisions I have made for my son, Baldwin, and his children in subsequent bequests and gifts, both in this instrument and throughout their lifetimes, blah-blah-blah to be divided and blah-blah by my grandchildren and my grandniece Cornelia Quincy Merrihew.' Translation?" she says, looking at Louis.

"You split the contents of the house in thirds, notwithstanding the enumerated gifts, of course. The structure itself goes to Baldwin."

Louis passes around another stack of papers without meeting Baldwin's eye. "The trusts, and the money therein, remain much as they were when they were established during her lifetime. You'll see little change there."

Louis turns to Baldwin. "And you remain executor of those."

Emerson is scanning his copy, mumbling to himself.

"There's a bit of money left," Louis says, nodding toward a stack of paper in Emerson's hands. "That's the most recent trust statement from the financial advisors that you asked for."

"It was intended for her to live on," Baldwin says, a touch defensively, as Emerson flips to the last pages containing the totals.

"She went through it like spaghetti," Emerson says under his breath.

"Son," Baldwin says with a shake of his head.

Pansy turns to her father. "Did you know about this, too?" She rises, unfolding herself in the lanky, double-jointed way of an athlete. "About the contents?"

Baldwin only shrugs at Pansy and then turns to address Nell, though she's not asked any of the millions of questions whirring through her mind. "If you must know, she asked me if I wanted it all. And I couldn't lie to her. I don't. I have everything I need, and I don't need a bunch of Mother's old things." At Pansy's look, he says, "What? I thought she should do what she wanted with it. I have to say, I never thought she'd gift it to all of you equally." He turns to Louis and says, "But that was silly of me—"

"As it stands, I know she took a long time considering her options," Louis interrupts, ready to move this along.

"She always did feel guilty about your mother," Baldwin continues to Nell in the magnanimous tone of someone secure that he's gotten everything he wanted.

Nell's neck feels hot, and she decides to opt for the nicotine gum, even though she'd really like a cigarette, an old habit she's been able to fend off in times of stress with the gum. What she'd really like is a few moments to step outside and breathe. Even breathing in noxious poison would be better than sitting in this atmosphere.

"She had one of the nurses call very late on a Saturday night," Louis is saying to Emerson in response to some question about the date of the will. "If you look you'll see we had the nurse on staff as a witness. I couldn't come until Monday morning, so she'd even had a few days to think about it, and she was quite clear." Here he looks Pansy in the eye. "And she was quite lucid when she requested the changes. For good measure, because I knew—" Here he clears his throat. "Because I knew she'd want it done properly, you'll see the affidavit at the end, signed by two doctors, stating that she was in sufficient health, not in pain, and not suffering under any mental deficiency when she requested these changes."

"One of them's Dr. Kelly, her old bridge partner," Emerson says, looking up from the page. "He's almost as old as she is."

"I think you'll find Dr. Kelly is still a practicing member of the AMA. And the other affidavit is from his younger partner in the practice, Dr. Chin."

Louis is then met with a barrage of questions; no one

waits for him to answer before firing another. What does this mean for taxes? Who's to take care of the day-to-day? How does this affect the generation-skipping trusts? What do we do next?

All the questions secretly ask the same thing: do you know what you're doing?

Nell watches as the chummy rapport with Louis fades away, suspicion falling into place quickly. She reaches into her bag for another piece of gum and adds it to the wad in her cheek, feeling the nicotine hit her bloodstream.

"Can I have one of those?" Pansy asks.

"It's nicotine gum." Nell mumbles her confession.

"Okay," Pansy says. "I'd like one."

"Seriously?"

"I'm open to all experiences."

At that, Nell hands it over. She never has been able to say no to Pansy. No one has.

Pansy raises it in toast before popping it in. "Sorry to hear about you and Paul breaking up," she says as she chews. Meanwhile, Baldwin and Emerson drill Louis on provisions she doesn't care about.

Nell has to think for a minute about how to respond to a kindness from Pansy. Things have been over with Paul for months, but Nell recognizes the gesture. And there are other factors to consider. There's Pansy's smugness, backed by her seemingly successful marriage to Brian, a management consultant who travels constantly. There are their two boys, who are enmeshed in soccer and lacrosse. And then there is her job as a holistic life coach and intuitive guide, which seems to be doing well given the elite pricing Nell had seen when she'd stalked the website yesterday.

This is all in contrast to what Nell suspects is the Quincy view of her life, as ingrained as it is retro: a spinster with no kids, a sucking black hole of a career, and a wastrel father in Italy.

"But I never liked him. No one did." And this is classic Pansy, thinks Nell, nodding her head at the predictability, but looking like she agrees. Pansy's digs are not traditionally the type of thing you can call her out on without looking crazy or defending an untenable position. Paranoia hits Nell in the chest at the thought of a Quincy cabal discussing the wretchedness of Paul, of her life, only now letting their opinions be known. It's one thing to suspect, quite another to confirm.

The shimmering glamour-spell of the Quincys is fading, as it does when she's around them long enough, reminding her that her mother did know best and a wide berth is required. She cracks her gum in response to Pansy.

"I've got a new chanting group for healing you might like," Pansy continues. "You should try it while you're here."

Louis is packing up his much slimmer document case. Paper is strewn around the room as if he's detonated a bomb. Nell tries to catch his eye as he moves toward the door, but he won't look at her. She has questions, and she wants to ask them away from Pansy. She gives up any pretense of disinterest and follows him to the front hall, ditching her gum in the wrapper and stashing it in her empty glass.

"You don't know where this thing is?" she asks his retreating back.

He turns and holds up his hands, as if to say "Search me."

Nell doesn't want an enemy, so she won't challenge

his handling of the inventory. "Did she have any other messages for me? As executor, maybe?"

His forehead furrows and lines crease the corners of his intelligent eyes, drawing them down and giving him a competent look, as if he can handle anything thrown his way. She suddenly wonders what he thinks of this whole business, if he finds them all ridiculous. "She was sure of what she was doing, if that's what you're asking." He places both of his bags at his feet and widens his stance, bracing for an inquisition.

"I'm glad *she* knew what she was doing. I have no clue."

"She didn't really confide in me," he says. "I mean, beyond the professional." Nell doesn't doubt that. Loulou confided in few people. "But you being a lawyer certainly had something to do with her choice of executor. She did mention that a few times."

"Loulou was a Libra," Pansy says, coming up behind them, and not even pretending she didn't overhear. "The scales, you know." She holds her hands up with an imaginary set of weights. "They have an acute sense of fairness." She addresses Louis as if Nell isn't there. "As they define it, of course." With that, she walks out to retrieve something from her car.

"She was kind of an outcast, my mom." Nell tries to feel normal as the intricate gears of her family are revealed to him. But she shouldn't feel uncomfortable. In his role as estate attorney, Louis's already had an eyeful.

"From what I can tell, your mother was very much on Loulou's mind," he says generously.

"Are you staying?" Pansy asks, coming back from the car with a saddle leather tote. When Nell doesn't answer, she says, "Brian's out of town and I've scheduled sleepovers for the boys. You really should, you know." She breezes past as if she is Lady Bountiful distributing largesse.

After Pansy passes them, Louis trains his blue eyes on Nell, so light they're almost gray. "Yeah," he says, not unkindly. "Shouldn't say it. But even the little exposure I've had to your family, I've gotta say—I'm glad I'm not you right now." And with that, he hefts his bags and leaves.

THE BOOTLEG CHAMPAGNE

May insisted on throwing Ambrose a party at the farm, as if she were auditioning for the role of wife, showcasing her skill as a hostess, trying to change his mind about leaving on his trip. He wanted to tell her that her strategy was obvious, and that no one doubted her abilities, least of all him. But he wouldn't say that to her now; tomorrow he'd be gone.

She'd arranged it all perfectly, yes. The food was supposedly Chinese. The guests were avoiding it. She'd even found some recipe for milky Indian tea with spices, which everyone ignored in favor of illegal champagne. Little maps hung off the portico and fluttered in the hot breeze—Japan, Korea, all of Africa. A large poster shaped like a postage stamp, with "Bon Voyage, Ambrose!!!" written on it in May's girlish looping script, was propped against the bandstand—the three exclamation points at the end like jabs.

Given that she wanted a real party, and that meant cocktails, she'd convinced his brother, Ethan, to throw the shindig at his newly built country place instead of her parents' house in town.

Ambrose settled an arm across Ethan's heavy shoulder as they watched the guests on the lawn. Ambrose felt a sudden wave of anticipatory nostalgia. He'd invited his brother on the trip only once, and Ethan had declined with certainty. But two brothers off to see the world, really that made such an engaging picture, didn't it? Standing there now, Ambrose felt he should have pressed. His brother should be coming with him. He'd have taken their sister, Loulou, with him if she'd been older. Poor thing was dying for adventure and had been a willing audience as he planned his trip, living vicariously through his many choices as if they were her own.

"Wonder what Father would think of this." Ambrose joggled his glass. The smell of the sharp pine water Ethan used for shaving mixed with the astringent bubbles from their champagne in the heat.

Their father, Israel Quincy, would not be pleased to see them drinking. He was a well-known teetotaler, a throwback to his Puritan ancestors, and a man who publicly supported Prohibition despite his two sons sitting at the hub of the young social whirl, which included illegal liquor.

"Sober mirth and controlled rapture," Ethan said.

"More like ecstatic piousness and wanton boredom." Ambrose enjoyed needling his older brother, something he'd been doing since they were boys. Teasing Ethan made him feel closer to his brother, as if they were on the same team. And today Ambrose wanted to confirm that they were still on the same team. He'd never outright thank Ethan for the party; that would only make them both uncomfortable.

"He disapproves of excess of any kind," Ethan said, reflexive in defense of his father, in defense of anyone, really.

Yes, the teetotaling made Israel seem fussy and, Ambrose hated to admit it, a bit feminine. Temperance was a women's issue.

"Except excess money in his bank account," Ambrose said, and nodded deeply in mock solemnity.

"And your bank account," Ethan said, clipped. "Your travel accounts."

The brothers sipped their drinks in silent acknowledgment of their father's munificence.

"It looks good," Ambrose finally said, gesturing toward the house. "All it needs is a moat."

Ethan kept his eyes on the house across the lawn, but Ambrose knew his brother recognized the olive branch in the backhanded compliment. It was the only type of compliment tolerated between the brothers.

It was then a third joined their group, shouldering into Ambrose, and sloshing a good amount of his drink on the lawn.

"Looking forward to those pearls of the Orient?" Richard Cavanaugh, or Dicky, as he was known, was dressed as an Indian dancing girl—complete with kohl-rimmed eyes and swathed in pink silk shot through with gold thread.

"Get ready now," he said, swiveling his hips in a faux seductive dance. "They're supposedly ruinous." Dicky's exuberance was his calling card and his fondness for costume the stuff of legend. Months ago, he'd come to the Union Club's formal New Year's Eve party clad only in an enormous costume diaper, though it was snowing, wearing an immense frilly bonnet and holding a gallon-sized baby bottle full of rye in his hand—a horrendous Baby New Year. He'd attended that debutante ball in Baltimore in a tuxedo with a Pied Piper hat on his head and set loose one hundred white mice on the dance floor, smuggled in a writhing tennis valise. The club had sent him the extermination bill.

"I prefer Ohio girls," Ambrose said. "Buckeyed beauties."

"Bucktoothed is more like it." Dicky was frequently embarrassed by Ambrose's penchant for the flowery. "I'll pass."

"Best to pass on the buckeye, they have poisonous nuts." Ethan smiled.

"Nuts are not fearsome," Ambrose replied.

"*You're* a nut." Dicky did the hip swivel again, and Ethan backed away in exaggerated defeat, hands up as if at gunpoint.

Ambrose knew this was when his brother felt best, welcoming people like a paterfamilias in training, though he was still a bachelor. Ethan preferred the beginnings of any party, those he attended or his own—before someone spilled a drink on his shirt, before the flowers wilted, before the champagne ran out—and why not? Ethan had built his house for parties.

Finished only last month, the faux Cotswolds mansion was meant to impress with its scale, its grit stucco and stonework, its leaded glass windows. Country, yes, but large enough for house parties with a half-dozen couples in the guest rooms and a small herd of bachelors sleeping on camp cots in the open third-floor dormitory. Ethan imported the coffered ceilings in the front hall from some monastery in Italy, and the library was paneled in black walnut milled on-site from trees felled on his land. The architect ordered all the furniture in one day from a Grand Rapids cabinet-maker—a different color and theme for each bedroom. The green bedroom furniture was painted with flowers and vines, the blue bedroom suite with a geometric Moorish pattern, the white bedroom with gilt and French curves. The rest of the house was styled in popular reproduction Tudor and fake Jacobean befitting a magnate in training.

"Come on now, you two." Dicky rounded on them, linking one arm with Ethan, the other with Ambrose, and marching them out on the lawn, mindless of their drinks. "Form a brother team. Can't have a race without the host and guest of honor."

On the grass, Dicky organized pairs for a three-legged race. Men leaned forward, drunkenly tying their interior legs together with silk neckties.

"Really, I don't want . . ." Ethan started. But before he could finish, Ambrose had loosened his orange and black striped tie, pulled it over his head, and leaned down, knotting it around their knees.

"Defend the Quincy name," he said as he rose.

They put their glasses down and put their arms around each other. Someone to the side snapped a picture. At Dicky's "go," the contestants stumbled, some with glasses in hand, to the cheers of the onlookers. Ethan took off at a swift hop, rearranging his arms and hefting Ambrose with a forearm under the ribs. The brothers stumbled once. Ethan insisted Ambrose match his rhythm. Ethan huffed them across the grass so quickly that Ambrose felt like he might fall face-first. They were neck and neck with the Rensselaer twins when Ambrose's foot slipped. They fell to the sound of tearing silk.

As the Rensselaers crossed Dicky's makeshift finish line, May rushed to them and awarded the winners a ragged bouquet of late summer flowers ripped from a nearby garden bed. Each twin tucked a posy behind an ear and, with a mincing pose in their white flannel knickers, smiled for a photograph, their lady victory between them, laughing.

Pale in white chiffon with a bunch of violets pinned low in her dark hair, May played the hostess well. A sheen of excitement covered her heart-shaped face, her huge doll eyes alight. She was usually languid, carrying a sense of easy dreaminess wherever she went, but she brought her full attention to a party.

Ambrose unknotted what was left of his shredded necktie and swept the grass from his knee. He stood, fumbling in his pockets for a cigarette, which he lit, and then exhaled a plume of smoke through his nose. Shading his hand above his brow, he watched May walk toward them, her swinging gait mindless of two full glasses in her hands.

She's happy, Ambrose noted, though she'd been arguing with him for the last week. She reached up and kissed Ethan's cheek in greeting and handed him a coupe of bubbles. Ambrose watched his brother blush and look away and felt a lightning flash of pride. May charmed most anyone. Then she turned and landed a loud smack near Ambrose's ear, saying, "They're all drunk." She reached for his low-burning cigarette.

He took his silver cigarette case out of his shirt pocket and nudged it into her elbow. "Come on, May, have your own," he said, taking her offered drink.

She shook her head and lodged his cigarette in the side of her mouth, talking around it. "Nuh-uh. Nice girls don't smoke in public. Just steal little bits here and there."

"Since when are you a nice girl?" he asked, surrendering his cigarette to her and repocketing his case.

She laughed. It was one of the things he liked about her, that she could laugh at herself. She hip-checked him, and to hear her laugh again he purposefully fell down on the ground and rolled forward in an exaggerated somersault, as if she'd really toppled him. He spilled his drink in the process.

Righting himself and brushing his white flannels, he said, "Now look what you've done." He reached for his overturned glass and picked bits of grass off it. "'Waste not, want not' is the motto of all Quincys."

A look of annoyance crossed May's face, and then she resettled it into its usual bright social arrangement. "How was it down at the mines?" she asked, handing Ambrose back his ashy cigarette and surveying him through a haze of smoke. "Saying good-bye?" She turned to Ethan and, in an exaggeratedly confidential tone, said, "He was down at the mines this week."

Ambrose's eyes widened; he hadn't told anyone he'd been out there. May had a way of finding out all his secrets.

"You can't possibly accomplish anything down there," Ethan said to his brother, ineffectively masking his irritation.

"Who says I'm trying to accomplish anything?" Ambrose threw the cigarette to the grass, grinding it under his foot.

Ambrose was leaving his job at their father's iron ore and shipping company on the Great Lakes. He'd been an undergraduate when the US got into the war, and he'd immediately wanted to enlist, along with half his class at Princeton. His father tried to convince him that finishing college was more important than dying in a trench in Europe. Such a justification might be fine for others, but Ambrose knew what his conscience told him to do. Action, that was the only basis for judging a life, or so he'd decided after declaring a major in philosophy. When Ambrose revealed that he intended to refuse officer's training and enter the army as a private, he delivered the news with a pert lecture to his father on Rousseau and the veil of ignorance.

But Israel was nothing if not a seasoned strategist. Appalled, he promised his son a trip around the world after the war, if he'd only graduate college before enlisting. Ambrose couldn't resist the lure. In this way he was weak; he'd admit it. But then the war ended quickly, with most of the men Ambrose knew barely finishing their training before the armistice was announced.

He still wanted his trip, even more so since he felt he'd been cheated out of fighting. But after graduation Israel lagged on his promise, insisting Ambrose come home and work first.

If Ambrose was going to work, he had thought he might at least be useful. So he'd taken his Kant and his Kierkegaard and his Nietzsche down to the mines and talked to the men about their lives. After a few trips, his father asked to have lunch with him at the Union Club downtown. The men were uncomfortable with him in the ore yards, his father explained. The manager at the mine was complaining. You have to respect their work, his father told him. Ambrose had quoted St. Augustine to his exasperated father, who patiently explained that such things were fine for study, but one didn't live one's life based on them.

"He just gets in the way when he goes to the mines," Ethan said now, turning to May as if Ambrose weren't there.

"It doesn't matter," Ambrose said. "Thank you for the party." He put an arm around May's waist, wanting to bring her close, wanting to change the subject. He was leaving to see the world, his dream for years. He didn't want to think about the mines. He landed a kiss in May's hair, which he'd meant for her cheek.

"Just don't come home with some tropical disease," May said, elbowing him. He kissed her again, this time at the corner of her mouth.

"Come home with a bride," Ethan said, and Ambrose held May a little more tightly into his side. Ethan could sometimes blunder.

"Corrupting a spinster?" Ambrose said, trying to cover his brother's faux pas.

Ethan fumbled with his glass and then drained it. "Some maidenly sister of a British officer stationed out in God knows where." He said it in a hearty, joshing tone, trying to cover up his suggestion, in front of May, that Ambrose come home with a wife. "Even you could land a girl like that."

Ambrose had a moment of mercy for his brother. Could Ethan be blamed for saying what everyone else thought?

Ambrose's travels would have him gone for at least a year, perhaps longer.

"No corrupting," said May, joking and clearly not upset by this topic, to Ambrose's surprise.

Ethan cocked his head, as if hearing something far away. Then he held a hand out to May and said, "I seem to remember that you like this song."

Ambrose watched his brother lead her off, wishing he'd thought to ask her first. May did like the song, how attentive of his brother to remember. A sour note echoed in Ambrose's head like a faint memory. He watched Ethan take her in his arms, watched them begin to sway on the dance floor—parquet over grass in a corner of the lawn surrounded by summer phlox and asters.

Ambrose had met her first. He'd been intrigued from the start, lots of men were. And he'd spent a good amount of time trying to unravel why. May was lovely, yes, but so were lots of other girls. She was smart, but not uncommonly so. Ambrose had finally decided, after a good amount of contemplation, that what May had was an appealing underlying hunger. An appetite that peeked out at him through her varied reading, her smoking, her love of movement and music. She radiated a constrained want, glimpsed tantalizingly, but fleetingly, since they'd been going around together. She was the only girl in their set who knew the passwords to the hidden speakeasies he and his friends liked to frequent downtown. Really, most of those back rooms were grimy. May would order herself a lime-based cocktail and polish it off with a smart licking of fingers. Her subtle watching of the world, a lying in wait, as if given an opening and a blind eye, she'd grab the biggest piece of cake, the costliest jewel, the rarest prize. It was part of her allure—an appetite that matched his own.

Now, in a patch of afternoon sunlight, watching May laugh at something Ethan said, sweat dampened Ambrose's collar. Their social circle was small, and he and Ethan went to all the same parties. In this way, May had become Ethan's friend as well. But that laughter, it lit an unfamiliar feeling in Ambrose, a tiny spark of anger, fanned with a breeze of envy. He noted how close Ethan was holding her, and how quickly she'd agreed to dance. But this laughter between them—it was as if he'd caught them doing something much more intimate. He tried to remember the last time he made May laugh like that.

He felt his sister, Loulou, at his side before he saw her. She had the habit of stealth. "Are you already gone?" she asked. "You look a million miles away."

Though only fifteen, she'd begged Israel to let her come to May's party. It was both a testament to his father's fondness for May and to his general cluelessness when it came to raising a daughter that he let her, imagining an afternoon of punch and cake under supervision of the faultless May. It was not the sort of thing a girl with a living mother would be permitted.

Loulou singsonged in his ear, "You love her."

"What do you know about love?" Ambrose noted a Rensselaer twin had tried to cut in on May, but Ethan had rebuffed him.

"I know you two belong together. And don't think it escaped my notice that you didn't deny it just now. Or ask me who I was talking about, for that matter."

He turned to focus on her then, noting she was almost

chest-height now. "I suppose there are little bluebirds circling my head? Or is it the stars in my eyes?"

Loulou watched May's feet while ghosting the dance steps, practicing.

"Longing glances across the dance floor, lots of sighing?" he continued.

"Make fun, but I know the truth."

"Tell it to Sweeney."

"Maybe I'll tell it to May," she said, starting for the dance floor.

Ambrose grabbed her forearm, stopping her.

"See," she said, looking where he'd grasped her arm. "Proof's in the pudding."

"You can't embarrass me during my own party," he said, trying to deflect.

"You should never be embarrassed by love, brother."

"That's older brother to you, and I swear I am talking to Father about your reading habits, Louisa. It's made you soft in the head."

"My head's fine. It's yours that needs examining. You might be older, but you're hardly wiser. Why don't you just marry her and spend the honeymoon traveling?"

"I'm not in love with May. We're not getting married."

"Sure you're not. I just hope she'll wait around for a wet blanket like you. She's so popular, you know."

"Everything you know about love you've read in those novels. Jane Austen was a spinster." Ambrose signaled to a passing waiter for a drink.

She flushed, and Ambrose realized his harshness too late. She was addicted to those books, to the entire notion of romance, really, and she wasn't even out yet.

Ambrose tried to think of something kind to say, glad for the waiter with his tray of new drinks. Loulou also took a stem, raising her eyebrows at him over the rim, daring him to stop her. And because he didn't want to be harsh twice, he didn't.

Ethan and May parted at the end of the song. Ethan silenced the orchestra with a wave, and then cupped his hands around his mouth, announcing loudly to all, "Shoe dance." He picked up a willow laundry basket he'd stashed next to the band's dais for just this purpose.

Tittering girls removed one dancing slipper and put it in Ethan's basket, while the wallflowers waited for him to come by with his cajoling before they gave up a shoe.

Loulou leaned her drink on Ambrose's arm and slipped her foot out of one kidskin slipper, watching her brother's face to see if he'd object.

"Lou, I didn't mean . . ."

"Save it," she said. "You always could be a jerk."

Chastened, Ambrose was silent.

"But I love you anyway," she said lightly, dropping her shoe in Ethan's basket as he gave her a wink. Fondness for their little sister was one of the few pure things the brothers agreed on unobstructed by competition or self-protection. That alone was simple.

"Probably because you're a romantic," she continued. "More so than you think. The true definition of one, actually."

"Now, Prince Charmings," Ethan called. "No elbows and no pushing." The orchestra started up a drumroll. "Wait until I say, 'Go,' please, before you find your Cinderella." He dumped the shoes in the middle of the dance floor

33

in an untidy heap and stepped back gingerly, as if from dynamite.

Ambrose spotted May's gold T-strap with the curved Louis heel and started to edge toward the side of the dance floor nearest to his target.

At Ethan's "Go!" Dicky Cavanaugh skidded headfirst into the pile with a flourish. May's shoe landed at Ethan's feet. But Ambrose sped up and snatched the shoe by the beaded strap at the last minute. Ethan looked his brother in the eye and then put his hands in his pockets. "You're leaving soon."

Men huddled around the dance floor flourishing shoes on bended knee, or enacting exaggerated tug-of-wars over particularly delicate prizes. Dicky pretended to faint from the smell of a satin pump, much to the red-faced humiliation of Gretchen Van Horn, who stormed across the grass, slightly limping on one stockinged foot.

Ambrose found May chatting with a group of friends at a distance from the hilarity. He swung her shoe by the strap.

"Have you tried that on others?" she asked, barely turning from the group. "Are you sure it's mine?"

"Course it's yours," he said, kneeling down and balancing her calf as he helped her slip her foot in, indeed the match. May bent down to adjust the buckle.

"You make a handsome retriever. Good dog." She patted the top of his head before he'd had a chance to straighten himself, then she turned back to her friends.

"That means you dance with me," he said, holding out his hand.

"Dance card's full," she said, flourishing the little tasseled book with a drawing of a pagoda on the cover that hung from her wrist. He removed it by its thin silken cord and briefly scanned it, noting the many crossing outs and overwritings of men's names.

"What dance card?" he asked, tucking it into his back pocket next to his hip flask. "It's my party, isn't it? And I want to dance," he said, leading her to the dance floor. "With you."

She felt lavish in his arms as he brought her close in the afternoon heat.

"You're a luxury," he said, overwhelmed by the realness of her. Her pale white dress hinted at paler delights beneath. "An extravagance. Anyone ever tell you that?"

She socked his arm. "I'd rather be a necessity."

The band leader launched into the popular song they'd been dancing to all summer, "Down by the Ohio." She smelled of the violets at her neck.

"Don't give me the absent treatment." He jostled her elbow. "I've rescued your shoe. Shouldn't you be trying to captivate me?" They rounded the edge of the dance floor.

"Capture you?" she said, mishearing him. "You're leaving. Why would I waste my time?" He could feel her hand on the back of his neck, palm facing out, waving to a friend across the dance floor.

After they'd made one full circuit without speaking, she finally said, "Maybe if I were a necessity, you wouldn't be leaving." She tugged at his collar.

He pulled her closer yet. He'd put off his dreams once for his father. He wouldn't do it again. "Come with me," he breathed in her hair. This was his familiar line in their drama.

May nodded to a couple dancing next to them, smiling. "You know I can't. Don't tease me." Indeed, he'd asked before. Each time, she'd refused. Each time, he hadn't expected her to say yes.

"Just come." Ambrose had stopped them now. They stood still on the dance floor. "With me." He understood he was being outrageous. All the other times they'd discussed this had felt hypothetical. He'd used it to tease her, to create distance before their separation. But in this moment, he felt the primacy of the truth that had been there each time. He wanted her with him. He could see her hesitate this time, could feel it in his arms.

"I'm supposed to travel overseas alone with you for months at a time, and then just come back and what?"

And there it was—floating between them was the knowledge that of course May would go with him, if only he'd propose. Yet even under those circumstances— traveling together while affianced, not married—there'd be incredible scandal, as much as if they'd eloped. To May's credit, he guessed she was ready to buck convention just that much, but no farther.

They started moving again, dancing in a circle. They'd argued on the periphery of this all week. Bickering about music, people they knew in common, even ice cream flavors. Never discussing the real issue before them, or, more precisely, before Ambrose. He could propose and endure what he knew would be immediate excitement and instantaneous pressure from both their parents. A round of frantic parties and planning that would tie them both to social expectation and derail his plans for a second time. He refused to be thwarted again. This time he'd be free, and he wanted May to share that feeling, that high so close to liberation. If he could just get her to see that one brave decision was all that was called for. After that they'd be free, both of them.

Ambrose always wanted something more, something extreme, the impossible. People had been telling him this since he was a boy.

She avoided his eye, slipped her hand in his back trouser pocket, and pinched his flask—a practiced move, meant to shock. She stole a quick nip of his gin with a little wink, never losing her footing. This had the stale feel of show to Ambrose, something she'd done before with other dance partners to establish herself as modern. These hackneyed moves sometimes disappointed him—small sneaking re-bellions that never amounted to much. It gave him the tiniest glimpse of one possible future for her, as a debutante who'd been on the scene too long. And it made him more panicked that she come with him, that she avoid that particular fate by choosing daring and desire now.

"We'll arrange to meet distant relations all along the way," he continued, her swig of gin bringing him back, spurring him to push her, to make her see that it was possible. "And of course, Dicky will be with us."

She put the flask back in his pocket with a scandalous pat. They'd stopped moving and now she started pushing against his arms, trying to get him dancing again.

"Dicky would be a wonderful chaperone," she teased once they were moving. "My parents would be so reas-sured."

He wished then that May would stop hiding behind what others thought—whether it was her parents or her friends. If she didn't want to go because of what people would think, at least she could acknowledge that this was her conclusion and not hide behind her parents. He knew May thought for herself; when would she speak for herself, too? "Dicky's so . . ." Ambrose trailed off, thinking of his friend's joie de vivre. Though maybe not the deepest thinker, Dicky did as he pleased.

"Feckless," May said.

"Unbound," Ambrose corrected. "And kind. Look at him with a real Mrs. Grundy like Gretchen." Gretchen Van Horn laughed nearby while Dicky pushed her around in a fashionable fox-trot. Of course he'd managed to charm himself back into her frumpy good graces.

"Perhaps," May said. "But it's easy for him to be unbound by convention. Young, all the money in the world, and . . ."

"And what?"

"And a boy, a man, I guess. Entitled to his pleasures."

"Entitled?" Ambrose balked at the judgment in the word.

"He gets to do what he wants, anyway," May said, turning her attention to the band.

Ambrose felt a tap as someone tried to cut in. "I believe I reserved this dance."

Ambrose swung May around so that his back was to his rival, blocking her from him, as he said, "Buzz off. Should have got her shoe."

May reached out and patted the intruder's arm. "Next one," she said.

Ambrose increased his grip on her, thinking of what it would be like for her in his absence—men circling.

"He probably wants advice on some girl," she said, as if hearing his thoughts.

"Come with me," he said again.

She stopped and drew back. "You're leaving," she said, quietly. "You chose that."

"Choose to come with me." Trust me, he was thinking. Trust that we belong together.

Perhaps his sister was right. Perhaps he *was* a romantic.

He saw Ethan step out of the French doors and scan the party, no doubt looking for them. Ambrose took care that May's back remained to Ethan. Really, he didn't know why he had to do that. He felt overwrought, and just before he swung her off the dance floor and into the grass, he saw Loulou take Ethan's arm and lead him back inside. Did Ambrose imagine the tiny wave from his sister?

Ambrose clasped May's hand and led her out of the garden and down a narrow path mown through an idle pasture that was filling in with saplings—locust and poplar and sassafras—a leftover from when this had been a working field.

"What are you doing?" May asked.

He tugged her along with a smile, heading for the pond on the other side of a meadow. Ethan had convinced their father to send his ballistics team, used for blasting out quarries, to come out to the farm and blast a pond into the back of his land. After the extensive dynamiting and dredging, the pond covered twenty-five acres and was a consistent sixteen feet deep, more lake than muddy swimming hole. To get in, one had to jump from a diving board jutting out from a stone walkway set between two bathhouses used for changing. There was no gradual wade-in on a silty floor of muck. This pond required strong swimmers.

"Nobody will see," he said. "Nobody will care."

"Am . . ."

He turned and kissed her then, her familiar taste mixed with spice from that ridiculous tea she'd been forcing on everyone. He was lost in her until he stopped, eyes closed, and took her hand and turned.

"I love you," he said to the air in front of him, walking.

"You don't. You're only saying that now." She stumbled a bit over a root in the path.

"I think I know who I love," he said, and turned back to smile at her.

"Then stay with me. If you love me, stay." With both hands she pulled him back, leaning her whole body toward the party.

"Come with me now," he said, dropping her hand, which made her stumble backward, but she didn't fall.

"This is all new to you, right?" she asked his back. "That's why you're being so cruel?"

The word "cruel" gave him pause for only a second, and then he kept walking, willing her to follow him. He wanted a piece of her that he could take with him. If she'd say yes to this now, perhaps there was hope for them when he returned.

He was two paces in front of her, not far at all, and yet he had to look back, compelled to know, right then, if she'd give in to him.

When he glanced over his shoulder, her smile was beautiful.

"Trust," he said, as he tugged her into the little clapboard changing house. The women's side had a fireplace hewn of river rock so ladies could warm up if the water was chilly. The inside smelled of moss, dark water, and dust. He laid his linen jacket down on the floor, and pulled her into his lap, her back to his chest. "You should trust me."

"I do."

"You don't," he said as he kissed her ear and hummed under her hair, taking in the musty smell of crushed flowers, her pale neck skin mixing with the violets wilting at her nape and the scent of the cool pond. "You don't at all. That's the problem."

"You're the problem," she said quietly.

He ignored this as she turned and kissed him. Whether she was becoming eager or more confident, he couldn't tell, and quickly didn't care. He was lost in sensation.

"Want this," he said. It was his statement.

She turned again, giving her back to him. She swallowed and nodded, looking straight ahead, not at him. "Yes." She'd taken it as a question.

He felt her breathing stop as he undid the first glittering button on the back of her dress and placed an open-mouthed kiss at the top of her spine. He thought she'd stop him then, as she had before. But she exhaled, shifted against him, and then leaned forward, closing her eyes in surrender, or was it resignation? He undid each of the buttons down to her waist, each time smiling as he revealed more skin and lace. He realized that when no one was looking she'd give him everything. She'd give him the impossible.

"You can stop me," he said, though he knew she didn't want him to stop. His hands roamed the silk at her waist. "One word will stop me."

"I know," she said, turning around to sit sideways. She kissed him then, her hands in the hair at the nape of his neck, her tongue in his mouth.

"I've wanted . . ." he said, but he lost himself in the electricity zinging through his veins.

"What?" she asked, though she knew.

"Just wanted."

She looked ladylike, sitting sideways in his lap, but also like a siren with the back of her dress open, a new fire in her eye. "Tell me." She ran her hands down his shirt, across his chest, and started undoing the buttons. "Tell me what you've wanted."

"You. This. Everything," he said, lying back and taking her with him.

THE POND HOUSE

Nell exits the men's pond house and throws her cigarette in the water, immediately regretting it and hoping no one will see the butt marring the pristine dark surface. Back in Oregon, she allows herself one cigarette a week, agonizingly rationed. But as she lights a second and makes her way back to the party she thinks, Screw the gum today.

After the meeting yesterday with Louis Morrell, Pansy and Emerson arm-twisted her into staying at the farm for the wake. Nell wishes now that she'd insisted on going to a hotel; at least then she'd have an escape hatch.

At that thought, she veers off the trail to the house and heads for the old stucco tennis pavilion. She tells herself she's not hiding, tells herself that this is the part of any party she likes best, whether attending or throwing. The sounds of the guests loudly chatting wafts across the field to her, punctuated by bright bursts of laughter as the drinks go down, and the clatter of food prep in the kitchen comes muted but clear from across the lawn.

As a girl back home, upstairs in her bed during her

parents' dinner parties, drifting off to sleep to the murmur of adult conversation below, the yellow light from the front hall would cast a warm, dull glow in her room. She felt encompassed, protected, as if nothing was getting through that group of jolly suburban revelers and up the stairs to her room. Today Nell wishes she could lie down upstairs and listen to this party without having to attend; perhaps she'd feel safe again.

She sits down on an upside-down five-gallon feed bucket, crosses her legs at the knee, and kicks her foot out at nothing as she finishes her toxins. Detox and retox, it's how she copes when she's back here.

In the sixties Loulou had let some farm manager convince her to pen sheep on the clay tennis court. An ingenious way to save on fencing, he'd told her. Nell remembers running through the field with Pansy, who'd shown her how to cram tufts of grass through the fence to entice the sheep. Then, mustering all their young bravery, they'd snuck in and cornered one, daring each other to touch its rank woolly fleece.

Now the old clay court was submerged under three feet of petrified sheep shit, well-fed weeds, and blooming wildflowers. Virginia creeper had long ago pulled down the fence.

From the direction of the kitchen she hears Pansy directing the caterers with confidence. "They need more of those little BLT things out there. Please check the ice in the flower room. And where is Nell?"

Nell has just enough time to stub out her cigarette and bury it in a nearby bag of potting soil before Pansy steps out on the lawn and takes the path to the sagging pavilion.

"You really shouldn't be out here. They're not sure if the roof'll hold." Pansy wrinkles her nose. "Do I smell smoke?"

"It's the bacon from inside," Nell says.

"Thought you were sticking to gum," Pansy says, sniffing again. "Come join us." Pansy, always the insider. Nell, always in need of an invitation.

Nell shoulders past her cousin, making for the mown path in the grass toward the kitchen.

"Any ghosts out here?" Pansy examines the rafters of the little tennis house. "What. You remember that story Loulou used to tell."

Nell does remember. Loulou's favorite story was of a deadly key and forbidden locks. It was outrageously scary for children and told with a certain sadistic glee.

The first night they'd heard the story Pansy had begged their parents to let them sleep in the same room. The adults couldn't resist her charming request for a cousin slumber party.

Nell had lain awake listening to Pansy breathing, trying to decide if she was asleep or not. In an agony of fright, Nell had finally given in and whispered into the space between the twin beds in the Moorish room, "It can't be true, right? That story?"

She'd felt relief when Pansy hissed back reassuringly, not even making fun of her, "No way." She'd heard the rustle of Pansy getting out of bed, the scrape of her narrow twin bed.

Then she said, "Here, push yours."

Nell rose at once, relieved. They shoved the beds together until only the width of the spindly rails remained between them.

This, of course, brought the warning steps of an adult up the stairs. The heavy tread down the corridor gave them more than enough time to dive under the covers and feign sleep.

"What are you girls doing up here?" Her mother had been the adult sent to check on them. She squinted into the darkness, a glass in her hand. After taking in the scene she said, "Go to sleep now, or we'll have to separate you."

She'd closed the door, but turned back with a mother's instinct and left it ajar so a beam of light fell across the foot of their beds.

"Here," Pansy had said, reaching her hand toward Nell.

Nell put her hand in Pansy's and squeezed. They'd stayed like that until they'd fallen asleep, neither one remembering who'd been the first to let go.

Now, Pansy overtakes her on the mown path back to the house. Pansy's the first one through the door and lets it swing back in Nell's face. Their girlhood gone, Nell can never pinpoint exactly when the end began. College and careers had made Pansy competitive. It's been ages since either of them would bother to hold the door open for the other.

The kitchen is small for a house as large as the Quincy farm, because it was meant for staff. Loulou had never so much as brewed herself coffee, had always employed a cook. A housekeeper was given free rein to remodel it in the sixties and had chosen the pressboard cabinets, the harvest gold Formica counters, and the avocado linoleum floor where plywood now shows through a few scuffed holes. Today the kitchen is hot and cramped with caterers.

"I'm so sorry about your grandmother, honey." One

of the caterers offers a hand and then pulls Nell in for a surprise hug. "A great lady."

Nell smiles, but the woman has gotten it wrong. Nell isn't the representative of the family. Why don't they ever hug Pansy?

"She was a handful, you know what I mean?" The caterer releases Nell and busies herself garnishing a Meissen platter with ham salad sandwiches. What was the woman's name again? Carol, maybe? Carol wipes her eyes, actually tearing up. Nell braces herself for what's coming.

"Got so mad at me once over something. A roast not hot enough, I believe. I thought she was going to smash the whole platter on the floor. Instead she slammed it on the counter, chipped it. Expensive thing, I think. Just like this here. Didn't tip me that night, either. She was a stickler."

Nell keeps her smile. She's heard stories like this before, everyone in the family has, and she never knows how to respond. If she defends Loulou, Nell seems approving of her bad behavior. If she sympathizes with the speaker, it usually boomerangs, with the aggrieved party coming to Loulou's defense, saying something admonishing like "With the elderly, they get a little cranky at the end. God bless, hope I live as long."

Nell pats the woman's arm and makes a mental note to tip her double at the end of the afternoon. As executor, she'll be shepherding the bills for all of this.

Pansy walks Nell through the warren of rooms—kitchen, cold room, food pantry, butler's pantry, warming room, and finally out into the main hall of the house, where the wake is in full swing.

Someone has cranked up the ancient stereo and dragged

the speakers into the front hall. "Help Me Rhonda" is playing, distorted and scratchy. Children take pictures with their phones as their parents do an ironic twist, while tiny cousins jump and squeal, delighted to see adults dancing. College-aged Quincys inspect the turntable, now chic in Williamsburg and Silver Lake. One of Pansy's boys plays a violent game on a cell phone, slingshotting birds into pigs. The young parental generation drinks gin in the corners, wondering if this sort of thing is okay for a wake. Does one dance? Rensselaers and O'Brennans, Van Alstynes and Cavanaughs from every generation have turned out, lured by old kinship and friendship connections.

"She would have hated this. Don't you think?" A Cavanaugh aunt is standing next to Nell. She's slim in heavy gold jewelry, with liver spots on her arms, which speak to an impressive golf handicap.

Nell hums, unsure. Loulou had loved a party, but famously hadn't cared for California. Nell had been surprised to find the Beach Boys record in the stack. "Nothing west of the Mississippi is worth a damn," Loulou used to say.

"I've met your new Van Alstyne cousin," the golfing Cavanaugh aunt continues. Nell has only just met her, too. A lawyer who does complex transactional work at a big firm in Manhattan; at least they'd had something to talk about for a few minutes. The new bride seems nice enough, smart, and on her best behavior.

"She seems very sure of herself," the Cavanaugh aunt says in a conspiratorial tone. "Very confident."

It was just the sort of comment her mother would have mocked for months when they got back home.

Before she'd left Portland, Nell had vowed to be proactive, to ask someone, and directly for once, about her mother's rift with the family. Her mother's mother, May Quincy, had died in childbirth. Loulou had stepped in when her widowed brother had proven too grief-stricken to care for a baby. It wasn't surprising that her mother had felt like an outsider being raised by her aunt, and then Baldwin came along. Baldwin was Loulou's born child, a boy, and the baby. He'd been a favored prince. Nell supposes it's a straightforward enough story of rivalry once removed and amped up by circumstance.

Nell had questioned her generation about it, but they were as clueless as she was about advanced family politics. Asking her uncle Baldwin had seemed an insurmountable task when she was younger, and her father is a dead end. She's tried him a few times, and he gives her the same answers about the Quincys every time.

"That's not something you need to worry about," he says. He blocks her attempts with "That's not something we need to get into." And once he even started to explain, "With her gone . . ." but didn't finish.

She sets herself the challenge of asking Baldwin about it during this trip, and she won't wimp out. You're a grown-ass woman, she reminds herself, and a trained lawyer at that.

Reflected in the cloudy haze of the aged front hall mirror, she sees the back of Louis Morrell talking solemnly with an elder O'Brennan in pearls the size of gumballs. The whole O'Brennan family has been longtime friends of the Quincys. She wonders what Louis knows. From the way he was talking at the meeting, he has his own views of the family. From this angle in the mirror, Nell is free to contemplate him. She's struck by his ease, his casualness, and his complete self-possession. She's seen men who try to win the room with backslapping and men whose air of aloof reserve hides a trembling neurosis. But she has to admit that Louis seems comfortable in his own skin, chatting with the power dowager as he sips cold coffee.

She has a perfect view of his broad shoulders, his lean runner's build. When the woman moves off to talk to another guest, Louis looks up and catches Nell's eye in the mirror, and she realizes he's been watching her check him out the whole time.

"Busted," he mouths at her in the mirror.

THE TRAVEL LETTERS

Tokio

Dearest May—

I made it. You didn't think I would, did you? It is a wondrous sight here. When I arrived, I called on my aunt Clara's friend Mr. Rockhill at our embassy. He gave me lunch, put a horse at my disposal—a villainous little pony with a painfully punitive saddle—and told me the best things to see in town. Then he invited me to supper on Sunday. I've been taking photographs every which way and feel my eye improving daily. I found no word from you here and admit this makes me feel low. Please let me find a letter from you in Singapore. You know I most fervently wish you were here.

Ambrose

o   o   o

Singapore

Ethan—

I am stalled up in my room without any clothes, waiting for the washing. Dicky has decided to be unencumbered and has gone off

51

into the city wearing a man's kimono and Japanese trousers, the same things he's been walking around in for the last week since we left Tokio. You should see how the locals react.

We hiked the side of a volcano the day before we sailed. Mount Asama, which is still active, sends out clouds of sulfurous smoke and ashes. For a moment, it seemed I was back home in the steel yards.

I am chomping at the bit to get to the shooting. I hear it's good, though all assure me that the jungles are thorny and thick as well as swampy and unhealthy. Never fear, I have citronella to ward off the ticks and carbolic acid and gaiters for the leeches. Loulou made me pack it all, of course, along with the snake venom antidotes.

Do write me and tell me news of home.

Ambrose

o   o   o

Mandalay

Darling May—

My last night here before I head into the jungle, and still no word from you. The Van Alstynes are here and convinced me to go to the hotel ball. We left for the riverfront after only two songs and sat under the full moon and drank champagne and spun yarns. The Van Alstynes are most pleasant company, but through no fault of their own they make me feel wistful and melancholy and missing you. They're very much in love, and sitting with them out under that pale moon and hearing her weave tales for him full of hidden meanings and places special to the two of them fills me with longing for you. She's his Scheherazade. Sitting with their example, I started to think that maybe I was a fool for not having proposed to you, married you, and started out on this adventure with you at my side. Loulou said as much before I left—out of the mouths of babes. I fear I've made a mistake, darling. Could I come back to you now and take you off with me? Or perhaps you'll finally agree to come and meet me. I have this dream that you might turn up somewhere along the way. I've been sticking very close to my itinerary. Perhaps you will materialize somewhere.

Ambrose

o   o   o

Rangoon

Dear Father—

I'm just back from shooting in the jungles, and I'm going to take up some matters from your letters that awaited me.

Firstly, as to my observance of Sundays—maybe I haven't been as careful as I should have been. This is because I have not been able to arrange it without considerable machinations involving train schedules, boat leavings. I suppose I will have more options when I move on to Delhi.

Secondly, as to the matter of splitting with Dicky. There has never been the least bad feeling about it because we understood all along that it was something that would inevitably occur and would enhance our differing interests. I've found I like walking and riding in the mountains and jungles more than I like the cities. Though I've immersed myself in the culture and squeezed out every drop of experience, not to worry. Dicky, as I'm sure you've guessed, jumps right in the swim of things in any port where we call, but he lags and complains so much when we're in the field that it dampens my enjoyment.

You needn't worry about me. This trip has been everything I've ever wanted.

Your loving son,

Ambrose

Jeypore

Dear Darling May—

Despite your paltry letters, I'll continue to write to you. Did your mother never tell you it's rude to ignore a suitor? I am still a suitor, aren't I? A suitor in absentia? I am counting on absentia to make the heart grow fonder. Perhaps when I return you will be very fond indeed.

While you have not come to find me, I have found Dicky in a Rajput city. Found is not the right word. He cabled me to come north to Jeypore, and so I have. You would laugh, as he is ensconced in a small palace fit for a prince, with walls inlaid with mirrors and a dancing girl who visits him at night. It's true. Tell no one. He told me about her yesterday at tea and I had a glimpse of her as I was leaving at dusk—a true beauty. Dicky claims she speaks French—can you imagine? But I suppose you can, as that's so typically Dicky. I suspect they have not one word in common, but maybe they don't need words.

As I walked back to my hotel through the streets, all I could think was how I wish you were with me to see it. Grim fortresses crown the hills, and the deserted capital of Amber with its temples and courts and halls spun me back to a very different vision of the medieval period, filled with the glories of Akbar the Great and Shah Jahan. I was tempted to run back and get my camera kit, but the light faded.

I leave in three days to shoot in Cooch Behar with the maharaja's son. The prince extended the invitation at Lord and Lady Minto's, who live here near the palace. We struck up a friendship as we stood on the sidelines during the after-dinner dance. I've found I've completely lost interest in dancing anymore if it's not with you. For something to say, I mentioned I found the shooting hard. He insisted I come with him to a distant relation's palace in Cooch Behar, and I thought only a fool would refuse such an invitation. Dicky promises to come meet me in Delhi after I'm done, and we will carry on together from there. I half expect to find he's deserted me and decided to stay with his maharani forever. I can't say I blame him. If there's one thing I've learned on this trip, it's that only a fool turns his back on passion.

Please write to me. Yet again you have reduced me to begging. Do you ever think of me? Do you miss me? It's the gem capital here and every bauble I see makes me think of you—your hands, your ears, your neck . . .

Ambrose

o   o   o

Cooch Behar

Ethan—

We are only just out of the jungle. Thank you for the case of shooting shells. I fear the ones over here, as I've heard stories that they're shoddily made and prone to exploding in the chamber. The shooting has been beyond my imaginings. I shot at a blackbuck, convinced I'd missed—that's how fast they are—until one of the coolies spotted a blood-covered trail in the wooded area and we were off after it. It was hard, as the antelope trampled things up pretty well and a light rain started, which washed away most of the blood. The men were constantly retracing their steps and making casts in all directions. We did find him though, dead in his tracks, and took his skull and horns. I am not keeping any skins except two buffalos and this large antelope.

I already shipped them home via an import and export company here. Father will receive notification when they arrive, and the customs must be paid in Cleveland. Please don't let him open all the bundles. They're full of gifts, and I'd like to have the pleasure of bestowing them myself.

In my downtime, I've been reading about those terrible old rascals and warlords Genghis Khan, Tamerlane, Akbar the Great, and Shah Jahan. If you can get your hands on any of their biographies, I urge you to read them.

I'll write more in the next post, as I am dead tired despite being housed in splendor at a palace with my friend, the Indian prince. His uncle, the maharaja, makes our father look like a pussycat.

How is May? I haven't received a letter from her in weeks.

Love to all there,

Ambrose

o   o   o

Delhi

May—

Please expound on the events in my father's short telegram of today. Though my questions will likely be answered in the telegraph station before you get this letter, the telegrams give me only the bare facts. I can get no news over here. Please write to me in detail.

When I arrived back at the Taj Palace Hotel, a stack of telegrams was waiting for me about the fire in Sandusky. How badly has Ethan been injured? I don't mean to be brutal, but Father's telegram was vague. How bad was the fire? Which mine was it? Were miners injured? How many? Is it out now? I could not tell from Father's telegram. I am heading to the telegraph office now to await some news, and then to the embassy. Even though I will find out more today, please write me with details whenever you get this letter. I feel very far away.

Ambrose

o o o

Delhi

Dear Father—

I only just received your wire reading "Return at once." The telegraph station wasn't open last night or this morning. It took some doing, but I had it opened that I might hear from you. Am looking into arrangements now and heading to Bombay, which is the most logical port for passage.

Ambrose

o o o

Bombay

Ethan—

What ho, hero! You of the derring-do! I've just had a letter from Aunt Clara telling me of your running into the mine fire in Sandusky. What courage! What mettle!

Everyone writes to me that you have been injured as a result, and I am grieved to hear it. Please know this letter sends you all my best wishes and brotherly love for a quick and painless recovery.

Father writes that I should return home at once. Of course, I shall if needed, but I wonder at Father's prejudice in the situation. I thought I'd go straight to the source and hear what you think from your own mouth, or pen as it were.

If needed I will return at once.

I remain your loving brother—

Ambrose

o o o

Columbo

Dear May—

I apologize for my silence. Things are easier now that I am in Columbo. My hotel, the Galle Face, is supposedly the finest in the East outside Cairo, and the embassy here has been helpful. I was having a hard time securing any routes out of Bombay that made any sense. And I figured coming here would give me more options.

Thank you so much for your letter that found me here with details of the fire in Sandusky and Ethan's recovery. I am glad to hear he's better, though I read of his accident with sadness. I sent along a package of trinkets to him from Bombay in hopes they might amuse him while he convalesces. Ganesha is the elephant god of new beginnings and fresh starts. Please tell him the significance of the little statue when it arrives. He progresses well? At the risk of sounding crass, what is the extent of his injury? I've written to him, but received nothing back. I suppose this is to be expected.

Ambrose

o   o   o

Columbo

Dear May—

I didn't hear from you yesterday but got your two cables today and one from my father, which reads: "Prefer you return home. Answer." I haven't answered yet. My funds are running low. I used a good portion in India, and Father is refusing to augment them, given this tragedy. I know he wants me there. I still haven't decided what I'll do. I've written Ethan, wanting his honest opinion concerning my return. Please encourage him to be frank with me. I've waited so

58

long for this trip, as you know. To come home with it cut so short, I don't think it's best for me, or for anyone there. You, more than anyone, know how I was before I left. But if needed, I will return.

Ambrose

o   o   o

Columbo

Dear Ethan—

By now you all have had my telegram and know of my decision. As I mentioned, I'm of two minds about this, but in the end your gracious letter let me know what I must do. (How well your dictation is coming along. Now that you're a dictator, should we find you a little country to rule over?) I trust that you will soften the blow for Father.

Since you seem to so completely understand my thinking, if you can, please help Father see that I can't return home just now. The need to complete my trip is not something I can completely justify, even to myself. I know I should come home and maybe I could shoot in the Rockies and see the Grand Canyon and Yellowstone after I've come back to help with work. But you've reassured me there's no need.

May told me before I left that I was like living with a caged tiger, frustrated yet half-asleep and swiping at things unpredictably. I was unable to see anything clearly. But I'm starting to understand now, both my place and my purpose. And I know if I returned with this thing half-done, I'd be of no use to anyone.

Especially not to you, I'd only be in the way. From the sound of it, May has become your Florence Nightingale. She's kept me informed about your paraffin treatments and iron supplements, and writes that everyone is encouraged that you can already tolerate the complicated massage and X-ray regimen to keep you from contractions. I hope it

59

is not too painful, and I'm glad to hear you're healing quickly. This has also eased my decision, though only slightly.

I can't return home without seeing more, doing more, being more. Father has told me he won't forward me any more money and so I must ask you for a favor to forward money to me. I will, of course, repay you once I get home. I'm pained to ask this of you with everything else you confront in your current health, but you've assured me you're no invalid. Father has made it impossible for me to withdraw from the corpus of Mother's inheritance without some legal wrangling, and I'm afraid I've spent the interest. I will sign any promissory note you wish in connection with this. Please see your way to doing me this favor. I can't come home yet; I'll only long to leave. I've lived that way before, and I can't do it again. You've seen me that way, and you can't wish it on me.

Before you send a party out to drag me back, let me say that I am in my right mind. I am not losing my wits. I only think that now I cannot return without fulfilling my dream.

I am your loving brother—

Ambrose

o   o   o

Columbo

Dear Ethan—

Your cable arrived yesterday, and the bank draft as well. I cannot tell you how grateful I am to you as my brother and now my bene-factor. Thanks to you, I am heading on a steamer to the Philippines and will be out of touch for a number of weeks. From there I will go to Siam. Your generosity has caused me to consider both northern China and a glimpse of Korea as well. How can I thank you?

Your loving brother,

Ambrose

o o o

Siam

Dear Ethan—

Your generosity astounds me. Thank you for encouraging me to go to China and for understanding my desire to completely see this trip through. Thanks to your additional funds I will be able to push through to Korea as well. I will forever remember the brotherly kindness you've shown me.

Ambrose

o o o

Peking

May—

My father's telegram with news of your engagement to my brother reached me only today. I suppose congratulations are in order. He tells me the engagement is to be a short one. Perhaps the thing is already done. Forgive me if I don't return home for the wedding. I know you understand my reasoning behind this choice, though I can hardly begin to understand your reasoning or your choice.

Ambrose

THE DRESSING TABLE

After Louis catches Nell in the mirror, he moves toward her with his quick assured step, his blingy watch, his blinding smile, and suddenly Nell starts to feel weary. She tells herself it's jet lag, that she's not running away when she heads upstairs just to lie down, just for a minute.

After she'd agreed to spend the night at the farm, she'd poked through the bedrooms, but her cousins had already camped out in the cleanest of the guest rooms.

"You know . . ." Pansy had said to Emerson when they found her wandering.

"You're totally right," Emerson had said in their sibling shorthand as they led her into the master bedroom.

She'd had to ask if Loulou had actually died in there. She couldn't help it. Looking at the draped tester bed, she had to know.

"She died in hospice," Pansy had said in the dull tone of disgust one uses with a hysteric. "She needed that type of place at the end."

"Right," Nell said as Pansy checked the bathroom for clean towels like the proprietor of a country inn.

Now Nell rounds the corner into Loulou's dressing room. The elaborate vanity table still winks with her silver-backed brushes and cut crystal bottles that had always attracted children like foil-wrapped sweets. When Nell was little she would sneak in here during epic games of hide-and-seek while the adults had cocktail hour below. Now, Nell's phone and charger and less glamorous accessories are nestled in with Loulou's loot. She'd felt like a trespasser last night. But now, with the noise of the party downstairs, this feels like her sanctuary.

She sits on the chic little bench in front of the mirror and instantly feels she's not alone.

"Oh hey," she says, rising when Emerson emerges from the bathroom. "I didn't know anyone was up here."

"Sorry. Was looking for aspirin." He opens his palm and displays two ancient-looking chalky pills. "Think they'll kill me?"

"Sketchy."

"Liquor's quicker." He shrugs off the doorjamb to reveal a bottle of Jack Daniel's in his other hand. "Want some?"

She can never say no to a drink with Emerson. Yesterday at noon was only the most recent example. It'd started the time he'd snuck rum, kept for guests, in a thermos and told her to meet him down at the pond.

"Fair warning, Quincys don't drink rum," he'd said as he passed the drink to her. "But I like it." It had been her first taste of alcohol, and it'd tasted like fruitcake on fire. Emerson had stealthily pilfered from each of the dark, light, and spiced rums in the farm liquor cabinet so as not to be detected by adults—a vile concoction. She didn't pull a face, though, wanting to seem cool in front of Emerson. "Yet another reason I'm a misfit," he'd said.

She knew that he was on the school newspaper and the varsity swim team at his fancy school. And from the picture she'd spied on Uncle Baldwin's refrigerator, he'd taken a pretty girl to the prom. "Right," she'd scoffed. "Total misfit."

"I am." He'd taken another swig. "There's no way I'm going to live up to any of this shit." Emerson was the only boy in his generation, and even then Nell knew living with Baldwin's ideas of Quincy grandeur had to be rough. It wasn't until later that she'd understood exactly why Emerson had beat himself up like this.

"You're not a misfit," she'd said. "You're an unfit. That's what my mom calls it. I am, too, I think. There's a difference."

"Your mom, huh?" he'd said. "Like, unfit for human consumption?"

"Unfit for Quincy consumption. I've heard her say that to my dad."

"And who would want to be consumed by this stuff anyway?" She'd seen him smile as he'd passed her the thermos again.

They'd eased into the pond that night. Too big a splash would have woken everyone in the house. They'd spent the midnight hour trying to stay afloat in the warm top layer of inky black water, only rarely diving down to the chilly depths below.

Today he goes back in the bathroom and returns with a toothglass etched with flowers at the rim. She accepts the drink as he comes and sits next to her on the bench.

"You look for it?" he asks.

She'd thought about hunting for the necklace last night, but rifling through Loulou's things by moonlight had felt creepy. She nestles her glass of unwanted whiskey in with the sparkly things.

"Here," he says, opening the top drawer with a harsh tug. "I know I would."

It's all tins of old powder and glass pots of hand cream, a dried-out tube of Revlon Cherries in the Snow lipstick, and a stack of ironed handkerchiefs with a scrolling L on them.

As if he's satisfied there's nothing worthwhile in there, Emerson gets up and heads back into the bathroom. She can hear him rustling through the cabinet and tells herself that he isn't looking for leftover pain medication.

She opens the next drawer, trying for stealth so Emerson doesn't hear her, though she doesn't know why. He seems okay with her snooping. It's filled with bobby pins, a strand of good, yellowing pearls, and many pairs of costume earrings. This isn't the serious stuff. That's all been residing in the downtown safe-deposit box waiting for Pansy for more than a decade. Loulou had put it away when she'd stopped going out socially, when a rotating band of nurses had started inhabiting the house with her.

Sitting there, Nell has an idea for her first act as executor.

"Hey, Em," she calls.

"Yo." He rounds the corner, visibly swaying as he accidentally bumps into the side of the dressing table.

"I was thinking I'd put some of this stuff out and let people take a little token." She watches as his eyes narrow and his lips grow thin, the sway gone.

"As a remembrance," she says at his silence. "It's all bound for a thrift store anyway."

He suddenly sounds sober. "You know I hate to get in the middle."

"What middle?" Nell feels the unseen ice of family dynamics shifting under her feet.

He pauses, looking at the sparkly heap. "You might give Pansy some of it."

Nell lifts up an old compact. "She can have whatever she wants." Nell waggles the tarnished thing. "I mean, of course she can."

He sighs, coming into the room. "You know she's still a gigantic pain in the ass, right? It's not like she's changed."

Nell says nothing. A brother has a right to criticize, but she knows he'd take umbrage at her piling on.

"And she was kind of shitty to you the other day." He's opening the door of the narrowest closet, recessed in the wall with hidden hardware, meant to store something valuable.

She hadn't thought Pansy was particularly shitty to her. She'd thought that given the state of things, Pansy was pretty generous. But maybe Nell doesn't know what shitty looks like, always happy with crumbs, with merely being included. Maybe if you were Emerson, you'd know from shitty.

He hauls out a disturbing fur coat that looks like a dead bear and dons it, doing a lurching Charleston on the faded rose-colored rug. Rhythm is not a Quincy family trait.

"It's disintegrating," Nell says, as bits of fur fly around the room.

"Raccoon." He sneezes heartily. "It might have fleas, though."

67

There's a gray astrakhan with a pale pink lining hanging next to a glossy floor-length sable that's shedding in the heat.

"Surprising," Nell says.

"Oh, this wasn't hers," Emerson says, lifting a sleeve that shows the cracked hides underneath. "The good stuff never is. These have got to be theirs," he says, referring to Ethan and May Quincy. "G-Lou was so upset, you know. Everything landing on her head. She couldn't deal. I mean, the stuff," he says, "it was nice stuff, but it was an avalanche. Plus, she wasn't even twenty. That's pretty young to be in charge of a kid." He pauses only now, remembering that he's talking to Nell. "Dad says that's why she married Granddad Dicky. He stepped in and took control, protected her, I guess. Before they started fighting like *gatos y perros*."

"I don't think she really threw any of their stuff away," Em continues. "Just pushed it to the back of the closet and put her stuff on top. Amazing, when you think of it. That she loved her brother that much. Imagine feeling that way." Emerson stuffs the coat back in the closet. "Pansy would have my shit on the curb and hauled away chop-chop if I bit it unexpectedly."

"She would not," Nell says, smiling.

"Who are you trying to fool?" Emerson asks. "But you should do what you want," he calls as he heads back into the bathroom. "Don't you call the shots and stuff now?"

Nell crosses the room and opens Loulou's closets with a deep sense of trespass, tempered by having Emerson in the next room to make her feel like everything's on the up and up. He's running the taps, washing his hands. The

closet smells like the inside of an alligator handbag mixed
with faded gardenia. Thin chiffon and dangling silks hang
in organized rows, a crunchy lavender sachet tied to the
top of each hanger. Loulou's handbags neatly line the top
shelf—some glossy, well-tended clutches and a Chanel in
the classic style. There's a tidy stack of silk scarves as well.

Nell gets it all down and spreads it across the bed, trying
to make an enticing display. This will show how fair she
can be, how magnanimous. It's only a symbol, yes, but
symbols are important, she tells herself as she essentially
merchandises Loulou's old things.

Back at the dressing table she opens the final drawer to
find it packed almost exclusively with cards and letters. Nell
unfolds them, thinking they might make for a nice token,
too. She's admiring a fancy dance card with a pagoda on
the cover and a silken cord for the wrist when her hand
grazes a dust-furred lump.

It gives her a shudder and, thinking it's a dead mouse,
she steadies herself. She takes a sip of warm Jack and,
almost pulling the drawer out of the runner, sees it's an
ancient and faded Crown Royal whiskey bag.

When she finally gets the triple knot undone she steels
herself to look inside, bracing for unknown horrors, but
instead sees a glint of gold and sparkle.

A clear blue stone of immense size is set amid a surrounding circle of nine different jewels. She knows immediately that it's the necklace from the will, her necklace.
And yet it's not at all what she'd imagined. She'd been
expecting something refined, a bit more traditional. This
is tribal and chunky, dull and totemic, with a spirit of its
own. She spots a pearl, what looks like a diamond, coral,

and other stones she's unsure of surrounding the main stone, as big as any she's ever seen. She flips it over and finds exquisite enameling on the back—so detailed against the skin, it's a crime only the wearer sees it. Brittle metal ribbons are attached to the sides, and she spies an artlessly rewoven spot. "Condition issues," that's what Baldwin calls damage. "Makes it less valuable, but more sentimental," he'd say, as if Quincys preferred it that way.

Without thinking too much about it, she props it under her chin and ties the cords at the back of her neck. Through the grime, a high shine sparkles, and even Nell can recognize that it looks good. It might be the first piece of jewelry she's ever put on that actually feels right, that feels like she doesn't want to take it off.

"That's some hippie shit, right?" Emerson asks, coming into the room, toweling his hands. "Imagine old G-Lou in a sixties mode." And then he seems to check himself, remembering that this is Nell's inheritance. "It's nice, though," he offers.

"From Ethan and May?"

"Who knows?" he says, eyeing it suspiciously. "From what I've seen, most of their stuff is more understated." Of course, thinks Nell. Of course, between now and yesterday he and Pansy have already been down to the safe-deposit box to check out her loot—the art deco diamonds with jade and onyx, the Edwardian emeralds set in platinum with pearls. Nell knows she would. "But I can't imagine G-Lou ever buying that," Em says, inclining his head.

Thinking some action will make her feel better, she takes it off before turning to go downstairs and invite everyone up to choose something.

She's met with surprised quick nods, which indicate a desire not to participate. Never mind, once there's a small exodus up the stairs, the rest begin to follow.

A small crowd of women gathers around the bed, looking at Loulou's things, commenting on her taste, remarking on her penchant for quality. No one wants to go first.

When Pansy walks into the room she takes a slow stroll around the bed and then sidles up to Nell. "Can I speak with you?" Everyone averts their eyes as Nell follows her.

Pansy drags her into a ramshackle bedroom across the hall. "You're giving stuff away now?"

Nell reminds herself that in a time of upheaval it's best to give people the opportunity to adjust. "It's just some odds and ends, nothing either of us want. I thought it'd be a nice gesture. Sentimental."

"So this is—what? You're starting already as the one in charge?" Nell's sure the women in the bedroom can hear them. She sees a few of them come out into the hallway and head back downstairs.

"I was trying—" Nell fades off, realizing how it's going to sound.

"To be generous?"

"To be accommodating, I guess."

Pansy's tone shifts. "I understand this is new to you. And I want you to know that I'm here to help. So you might want to ask first. That's pretty basic, right?" With that prim reprimand, Pansy heads back into her grandmother's bedroom, and Nell can hear her mutter, "I don't know how this is going to work."

Tension is palpable as Nell crosses the hall. The awkwardness when she enters the room is nearly unbearable.

And to make a gesture, to relieve some pressure, to prove she's not out of line, Nell picks up the necklace before she can think it through. "Here," she says handing it to Pansy. "Get a load of this. Crazy, isn't it?" The room is silent, watching them.

"Is this the . . . ?"

"I think so," Nell says. "Try it on."

"It's yours," Pansy says, pushing it back to her.

"I think it'd look best on you." She pushes it, a little forcefully, into Pansy's hands. "You're the jewelry girl, right? You should have it." There is a desire to please, a desperate wanting, yes, but it's edged with just a bit of "fuck you." "You think this is all so wonderful? Watch me give it away," she wants to say, letting her actions speak for her.

Pansy takes it, with a snatch, into the dressing room, holding it in front of her chest. It winks in the light. With her height almost anything looks good on her.

"You could definitely pull it off." Being generous with Pansy makes Nell feel less like a gate-crasher, a little bulletproof, even.

"You think?" Pansy asks, raising and lowering the necklace against her sternum, and Nell feels a slight panic at the thought of Pansy actually calling her bluff, actually taking the necklace. Nell, you groveling idiot, she thinks. What have you done? She only wanted to have offered. With everyone watching, it'll be incredibly awkward to backpedal now.

"Yeah, I mean, it would make more sense, right?" Nell says, a bit weakly.

Pansy walks back into the bedroom and tosses the necklace onto the bed. "I'd never wear it." The unspoken being that it's gaudy, tacky, clearly costume.

Pansy picks up the Chanel handbag and swoops it over her shoulder. "But this. Vintage 2.55? Don't make 'em in this type of leather anymore." And with Pansy having made her choice, the others feel more comfortable diving in.

Scarves are unfurled and chosen. The elder O'Brennan in the pearls goes for a twill Hermès in a pattern of lilacs. The alligator bags go fast. The new Van Alstyne cousin by marriage looks pained as the Cavanaugh golfer insistently encourages her to select something. The new bride finally picks up a canvas tote bag that has "Shop Till You Drop" printed on it in blue script. Well played, thinks Nell as the young wife heads downstairs with her irreproachable choice.

In the end almost everything is gone except the rhinestone brooches from the fifties, tarnished and out of fashion, and the hefty Crown Royal necklace, as Nell has taken to calling it.

"Guess it's yours after all, much as you tried to wash your hands of it," Pansy says, tossing it lightly toward Nell's side of the bed, and Nell checks the twist Pansy's put on her attempted generosity.

Since Pansy's passed on it, Nell doesn't feel illicit slipping it over her head. Before she heads back downstairs, she catches a glimpse in the dressing table mirror, an outsize sparkle against her plain black clothes, making them look almost chic.

And in the vein of her illustrious forefathers, she does what generations of Quincys have done to gain courage and to gird themselves, to shore themselves up in the face of good news and bad. She heads downstairs to fix a drink.

THE JEWELRY BOX

Walking into his father's house, the smell of wool rugs and lemon furniture polish convinced Ambrose he was home. Israel Quincy's heavily gabled and turreted house loomed three stories above the street that the locals referred to as "Millionaire's Row," which made Ambrose cringe. Israel's house was draped in cornices like a wedding cake groaning under a layer of butter and sugar. The family insisted it was "Italianate" in style. But now, having seen much of Italy, Ambrose could only think of it as American—garish and gaudy, with a domed glass observatory on top of the mansard roof and an ornamental portico over the front door.

He'd stayed at the Union Club in New York for two weeks. Increasingly frequent letters and telegrams from his father only made him linger in the city. He'd spent his time wandering the park alone or sitting in the club's silent reading room smoking and staring into space. The quiet of the place, men enjoying the solitude of their newspapers and their cigars, was all he could stand after traveling alone for so long.

In the end it was a letter from May that motivated him
to take the train.

She'd been short; terse, really. She'd said she was happy,
that he couldn't stay away forever, and that they were family
now. She didn't apologize. He supposed that was correct.
She shouldn't apologize for marrying his brother.

He reread one part of the letter so often that he had it
memorized, though he's sure May didn't give it nearly as
much thought when she wrote it, likely tossing it off without
realizing how much she was revealing. "I've been thinking
that life shows us who we are, our actions wrap us up in
the end like nothing else. Everything is how it should be."

It was her tone mostly, her familiar directness echoing
his own thoughts; this convinced him. Because what would
he do, really? Never go home again? Never talk to them?
Make some big dramatic statement? As appealing as those
options were, they had the whiff of something else—of
defeat, of acknowledgment that he was brokenhearted.
And in the spirit of getting a dreaded deed over with, he
bought his train ticket.

He'd forgotten what it was like to stand in the front
hall of his father's pile, where the windows were covered
by crewel curtains to keep out the soot from the steel yards
miles away. But Ambrose carried the ease of the world traveler now; he was a man of perspective and broad horizons.

The driver brought in his trunks, thumping them on
the gleaming floor and likely scratching the tiled foyer.
This brought Mrs. Gilder, the housekeeper, clucking out
of the kitchen asking that his things be taken up right
away. The commotion managed to flush out his father
from the library.

Ambrose felt his two years away when he saw his father. Israel Quincy's lean, flinty face resembled his Scottish ancestors. His clothes were impeccably starched and spotless per usual, but he stooped forward now on his cane, a new paunch around his middle.

"I see you've become a bohemian," his father said with no hello.

"It's a beard," Ambrose said with a laugh, and stepped toward his father, who drew himself up on his cane and extended his hand, precluding a hug. Ambrose shook it, both his hands grasping his father's. Israel grunted at this show of enthusiasm and led his son into the library, muttering, "It's a bushy one."

The cut glass bowl of the peppermints his father kept in the library sat where it had since Ambrose's boyhood—his father's sole vice, sugar. The minty scent mixed with the decaying smell of his father's Moroccan leather–bound volumes—a smell from childhood, from being called to the library and scolded for some misdeed. That sameness—as if he'd never left town, never left this room—should have comforted.

Israel lowered himself into an armchair next to the cold fireplace and began a nearly impenetrable monologue about business—a discrepancy in accounting, a concern over a recent acquisition in the Upper Peninsula, a diatribe about labor relations at the mines.

Ambrose took deep draws of Mrs. Gilder's overly sweet lemonade as he listened. His father's wall of speech required him to respond little. It wasn't until Israel had been prattling on, never mentioning the mine fire, that Ambrose realized the source of his father's chatter. Israel was nervous.

Ambrose's time away had given him the power to make his father uncomfortable.

"The fund for the widows and orphans now that the fire's out in Sandusky—how does that work?" Ambrose decided to try his hand at getting them on a topic of interest. He had ideas for how the fund should be structured, about the appropriate level of help for the families. He didn't want to overstep bounds early, but having worked for his father before his trip, he knew how the company compensated the unfortunate.

"That's a bit premature."

Ambrose's brows furrowed. "They must know who's . . . affected," he said, reaching for delicacy.

"Premature you being concerned with it. But I'm sure you've read in the papers, the fire's still burning." His father grazed the tip of his mustache with his fingers. "They sealed the shaft. It was your brother's decision, and it seemed the least . . . the least I could do. It has to burn itself out. Unfortunately, it has a nearly endless supply of fuel."

"It didn't smother?"

"Apparently it has a source of oxygen or it wouldn't still be burning, now would it?" Israel snapped, and then continued. "We made the best decision we could at the time. The temperature readings at the surface, in the non-sealed part of the mine . . . That can happen with seam fires."

Ambrose wondered how many bodies had been trapped inside. By the time they'd made the decision to close it off, there'd have been no chance of survivors. But the families of the dead, surely they'd have wanted the remains?

"I figured you've been reading about it in the newspapers. That you'd want the latest news," his father said. "The local authorities found nothing wrong. But some people are never satisfied, are they?"

"Cleveland news isn't reported in Srinagar."

"Well, I meant New York, when you landed," his father said, annoyed. "Certainly in the weeks you spent in the city, you read the papers."

Ambrose had read rumblings in the New York papers, murmurings that shortcuts had been taken at the mine, that the number-two escape shaft had been poorly engineered.

"How many dead?" Ambrose asked.

"Twenty-six." His father didn't hesitate, certain.

Ambrose leaned back, wishing he had something much stronger than lemonade.

"Your brother," Israel said, following a private train of thought. "He's had a rough time of it since the injury." Israel studied the tip of his shoe. "He's shown incredible resilience, Ethan has." He leaned down to brush a speck of invisible lint from the leg of his trousers. "It's time for seriousness now."

Ambrose felt the implicit judgment in his father's state-ment. Ambrose hadn't returned home when summoned, a definite outrage in his father's mind, and he had yet to demonstrate sufficient responsibility. To counteract the familiar feeling of inadequacy creeping up on him, he told himself it wasn't yet decided that he was staying, let alone joining his father. These were Israel's assumptions based on Ambrose's return. They needn't be facts.

Ambrose had forgotten the exhaustion he'd felt re-sisting his father's manipulations and attempts to control outcomes. Only now, being returned to his father's stifling presence, did he fully appreciate the freedom and ease he'd felt while not constantly guarding against these maneuvers. Ambrose had been right to resist his father's demands that he come home. He'd been right to listen to his brother urging him onward, though now Ambrose knew Ethan's generosity came from self-interest and hidden motives concerning May.

"He's coming with May for dinner tonight. To celebrate." Ambrose reminded himself to appear unaffected at the sound of May's name. "And of course your aunt Clara, too; she's most eager to hear of your trip. She convinced me to invite a few more people as well." His father continued on, giving Ambrose an update on each of the evening's guests.

Ambrose had left his anger somewhere in the jungles of Asia—anger at May, tinged with exasperation at her flightiness; anger at Ethan, tinged with competitive rage; anger mostly at himself. It rarely surfaced anymore, but this was not the same thing as being resigned. Maybe it wouldn't be as bad as he thought when he saw her. Maybe, as May had said, in the end their actions revealed more than any other thing between them—his own actions as well as hers. Maybe he'd had enough time and distance to become comfortable with both.

He wondered how much his father knew about him and May. From the paternal perspective it wouldn't look too unusual. May had known Ambrose first, but had ultimately fallen for Ethan. Such things happened, perhaps more often in his father's day, when social circles were smaller.

Did Ambrose imagine the tension, the judgment in his father's face? Perhaps Ambrose was being uncharitable, always guarding against his father and barricading himself. He'd gained perspective on his trip, maybe enough to engage his father as an adult, man to man. He needn't be on the lookout for slights and disrespect. A man knew how to handle a father. Especially one who, Ambrose now noted as his father shakily rose from his chair with the aid of his cane, was rapidly becoming an old man. Ambrose felt an unfamiliar softening, and he walked to the front hall and rifled through the jacket he'd thrown on the sofa for the leather-bound packet in the interior pocket. He unwrapped the cord.

He was proud of his photographs and thought they held promise. He'd had a great many developed during his stay in New York. He chose one, a unique perspective of the Taj Mahal, and brought it to his father standing behind the carved desk.

"Look," Ambrose said, handing the print to his father. "A true wonder of the world."

Israel gave it a cursory glance and handed it back to Ambrose.

"It's incredible in person. Much more so than in a picture," Ambrose said.

"It'd have to be, wouldn't it?" Israel tapped the photo with the back of an index finger. "I've seen this picture before. We get the world news here." He leveled his gaze at his son. "Unlike Srinagar."

Ambrose felt the challenge in his father's words, and he flipped through a few more pictures of jungles and temples trying to find something his father hadn't seen, something to amaze him.

Israel kept watch over Ambrose's shoulder. He stopped Ambrose at one photo in particular, reaching over to grasp it and bring it closer.

Ambrose had snapped Dicky's Indian princess in profile as she'd come into the room unaware, eyes down and a glossy strand of hair slipping out of her long plait, a surreptitious portrait, taken unasked.

"Loulou will be here soon, of course," Israel said. "She's out with her friends. And I believe May's invited young Richard as well."

Dicky's girl had objected to having her picture taken, but Dicky had pleaded with Ambrose to find a way. Dicky had become so insistent that Ambrose had started teasing him about including the prize in the trunks with the hunting trophies he was sending home. Nevertheless, Ambrose had returned each evening with the camera, each time pretending he was photographing the riotous inlaid mosaics on the walls or the architecture of the limestone turrets outside while he tried to frame her into the picture. He felt guilty for it, but he finally snapped her.

Israel said nothing, carefully lining up the edges of the photo and folding it before methodically ripping it in half, and then in half again. "Your sister has taken quite a shine to young Richard." Dicky had returned well before Ambrose, and had been taking Loulou around ever since. May had mentioned something of this in her letter.

His puritanical father's nonplussed calm as he ripped each quarter into smaller pieces unnerved Ambrose, but he couldn't look away. He supposed he shouldn't be surprised at Israel's knowledge of Dicky's indiscretions. Dicky was a braggart and a gossip. That Israel kept up with such gossip indicated that things between Dicky and his sister were more serious than Ambrose had guessed.

Israel returned the photo to his son in pieces. "Fortunately, young Richard . . ." Ambrose knew Dicky would forever be "young Richard," even in his seventies. ". . . seems ready to nest. And I've known the Cavanaughs my whole life. Your mother and Celeste Cavanaugh were the same year coming out."

Ambrose tried to remember how he'd felt on the train coming home—a world traveler, someone with perspective and ideas. How was it possible that in less than an hour his father had managed to strip that away?

His father turned to the cold fireplace. "I don't pretend to understand your decisions, Ambrose—leaving, not returning after the accident, or for your brother's wedding, which would have been the decent thing to do." And with that phrase, and with the ripped photo in his pocket, Ambrose thought that maybe his father understood a little more of the situation than previously imagined. "Begging from him so you could continue sightseeing and hunting." He said the last two words like "whoring" and "gambling," and in a tone as if Ambrose had robbed a widow. "But now that you're back, I'm sure you'll want to get on with it."

Ambrose's shoulders slumped as a feeling of powerlessness and ancient, sullen despair engulfed him.

"And we must decide which club you'll join," his father continued, turning toward him. "I'm sure you don't want to join mine—full of old men. Ethan's might do, but it's turning into a business club. We'll ask him where the young men are joining these days. The bachelors."

His father walked to the bowl of candies, selected one, and held it out to Ambrose. "You always did like mint," he said.

Ambrose placed the mint in his mouth, a concession

to his father and a small price to pay for finally being able to leave the room.

Upstairs, he spat the candy into the doily-lined trash can.

His childhood room shrouded him in afternoon silence and damp heat. The yellowed shades drawn against the bright sun made his room a warm, dim tomb. His relief in escaping his father embarrassed him.

He opened his valise and rooted through notebooks and papers, searching for his flask. He'd come to his father's dry house knowing he'd need supplies. His hand brushed the cerulean leather jewelry box—longer than a ruler and wider than his wallet, the leather tooled in gilt with lotus flowers and paisley. The box represented a problem he'd been pushing from his mind, refusing to think about or decide. But here it was, clearly caught up with him now. The jewelry case was shabbily made. The glue on the white silk satin inside was already yellowed at the seams. Given the Indian love of all things English, it wasn't surprising they'd copied the jewelry boxes. Ambrose preferred the traditional silk pouches and inlaid sandalwood boxes he'd seen in the markets. He'd been meaning to buy one, though after May's telegram he never seemed to get around to it.

He lifted the lid and a thrill lit his eye, as it had when he'd first seen the jewel—a quickening felt by all knights-errant when first laying eyes on ancient bounty.

A sapphire as big as a robin's egg sat nestled in the middle of a circle of gems. Two peacocks, set with diamonds, supported the dazzling sunburst of stones on their backs. Small emerald drops dangled in their beaks. He'd since learned that peacocks were auspicious and good luck, but given the state of things he doubted it. The peacocks and the sapphire with its constellation around it formed a heavy, chest-spanning pendant, the gold so ruddy it looked like brass. Where, in the west, a chain might attach to each side of the neck plate and clasp in the back, ribbons of blue, violet, and real gold were tied in intricate knots on each side of the collar. These were then tied around the wearer's neck.

It was tribal, exotic, and so large it bordered on vulgar. It was meant to be May's, but he had second thoughts about giving it to her now. Such an extravagant gift would surely be strange for a sister-in-law. Though perhaps no stranger than May actually being his sister-in-law.

He lay back on the bed, the necklace on his sternum, a heavy thing.

She'd be here soon. Though he told himself he had released his dreams, it would be awkward. He planned to smooth things for them both, for everyone, really. Her letter made him suspect she'd help him in this.

He'd considered selling the necklace in New York, and he'd taken it to a few merchants in the Diamond District who'd quoted low prices, claiming it was unfashionable.

But he knew May would like it. He'd been picturing her wearing it.

The thought of her with him at his going-away party had been a well-worn and much-used source of fantasy for months. A force of habit, familiar and effective in its ability to satisfy. Without thinking of it too closely, and with a certain amount of enlivening defiance, his hand found his belt buckle, unbuttoned his trousers. When he'd heard of the wedding, his anger had stopped this practice. In the last few weeks he'd revisited this vision—only a few times, and always with a pang of conscience. His excitement was refreshed by the new taboo of it. He shouldn't be thinking of her like this, shouldn't be thinking of her at all. With a sharp tug up and slower stroke down, he gave himself over to memory. And in the privacy of his mind it was just a memory, an efficient, disembodied daydream. It didn't mean anything.

He was cleaning up, confirmation of his aloneness settling over him as his heart stopped racing. Chimes rang from the front hall. Mrs. Gilder ringing them down for cordials and then dinner.

He crammed the necklace in his jacket pocket without the case and glanced in the mirror. His disheveled clothes telegraphed how little he cared, a reassuring costume and something to live up to. He was not unaware of the effect he achieved on women. Part of the appeal lay in his height, his trimness, but also in his eye and his energy, which now radiated an easy assurance. While there were men more handsome, there were few more daring, a trait Ambrose had learned to leverage in his favor on his trip. It wouldn't suit him to come down in polished evening clothes and their attendant conformity and planning. He liked rolling out of bed with satisfaction on his face, fortified in his own pleasure. He would get this over with and then everyone could move on.

As he came down the stairs, he heard voices on the threshold, which stopped when he entered.

"What did I tell you?" his father said to the room as he gestured at Ambrose. "Won't even dress for dinner."

Ambrose was frozen for a full moment, and then he forced himself to move toward his brother, who was standing with May at his arm, the two of them a complete portrait.

Ethan stepped forward, as if he were the master of this moment, welcoming Ambrose home.

But Ethan didn't offer a hand; he raised his right arm and embraced Ambrose. And it was then, looking down, that Ambrose saw it clearly.

His brain quickly slotted pieces together like a puzzle, reorganizing assumptions and theories, recalculating his father's disapproval and Ethan's generosity. He felt anger draining away, alarm and shame filling their place.

Ethan hugged Ambrose tightly with his one good arm. Ambrose hugged back with two. The brothers were now locked together. Ambrose could feel the force in Ethan, as if he were intent on steering the evening, steering Ambrose in general, where he chose. Ethan finally pulled back after embracing long enough for Ambrose to collect himself.

"Welcome home," Ethan said.

"I didn't know" was all Ambrose could manage, nodding down. While he'd read about it in letters, it was another thing to see the raised lesions, the pale pink scars that wrapped around Ethan's knuckles and disappeared up under the cuff of his shirt.

"Didn't you?" Ethan asked, a brisk sting in his inflection and then a wide smile that looked genuine. "I got your letters and that funny elephant. God of healing."

"New beginnings." Ambrose noted that Ethan already had strategies for negotiating his injury.

They'd said he was still doing his massage therapies.

He was scheduled for additional surgeries. They'd done everything to prevent flexion deformity. They were still trying things. This wasn't the end. These were the thoughts Ambrose held on to now. He cast furtive glances at Ethan's shiny, mottled hand and clearly lifeless arm. It looked painful. It looked permanent, and that permanence was the thing that stunned Ambrose. He'd thought there was still hope.

As Ethan took control of the conversation, chattering to smooth things over, the faint lingering stain of jealousy washed off Ambrose, replaced by a tint of pity and a hit of genuine sadness at the sight of his brother.

May, cool in white and pearls, stood silently beside Ethan.

Ambrose didn't know what he'd been expecting. It had only been two years, and yet she'd changed—her face more angular, and her smile an insurmountable boundary. Her hair was chopped in a precise shingle. The severe hairstyle was so popular, and something he hadn't gotten used to since his return. A few strands of silver sparkled in the part of her hairline. A thin band of diamonds glittered on her left hand.

A quick look passed between May and Ethan, a silent understanding that cut Ambrose deep. Ethan had won. Though looking at his brother's curled claw of a hand, Ambrose was thwarted from feeling outrage.

"Sister." It was out before Ambrose realized his attempt at levity was awkward. The room silenced to watch them.

May gave a little laugh. Her hand came forward, but dropped just as quickly as she fidgeted with a gold bangle etched with vines. Even she realized they couldn't shake hands.

Ambrose stepped to her then, and she was in his arms for the briefest moment. Scent of soap and violets—or perhaps he imagined the violets. She embraced him gently, carefully, so that no part of her actually touched him except her forearms and her cheek, just barely brushing his whiskers. It was a second, an instant, a brief memory of her scent mixed with pond water bringing him back to the days before he'd left, and then it was over.

"Congratulations," he said, his head swimming. The room collectively held its breath.

"Thanks, Am," she said quietly, looking at his face, but not his eyes.

Ambrose turned toward the room. "Everyone's been so busy while I've been gone."

The party silenced at this.

"Especially me, auditioning for my role as the human Roman candle," Ethan said, stepping forward.

Ambrose thought he saw May wince. The rest of the room laughed rather too loudly and then, with a communal exhale, the party moved on. He saw his uncle tidily brush his hands together before reaching for a glass of Mrs. Gilder's ginger cordial.

If Ethan had changed, and May more subtly, too, the change in Loulou when she stepped forward was both alarming and delightful. She'd shot up to nearly his height and she'd chopped her hair, too, which dismayed him. He imagined she'd done it in emulation of May. Her eyebrows were plucked into twin thin arches, making her look older and her eyes look more wide set than he'd ever noticed before.

"Big brother's back," she said as she hugged him.

"Clearly I'm needed," Ambrose said directly to Dicky as they shook hands around her back.

"You made it in one piece." Dicky's wide, panicked smile belied his nerves.

Seeing them side-by-side, Ambrose felt their connection, could practically see it shimmering. And for once in his life Dicky was silent. He wouldn't look Ambrose in the eye, and stepped back, trying to beat a quick silent retreat, when Aunt Clara put a hand on his arm, keeping him at her side. She had a nose for discord and a force of will that ordered the world to her ideas of propriety. She fancied herself a diplomat, but was viewed more like a policeman. She was also a world traveler, having flown into Persia via biplane. She would want tidbits of Ambrose's trip, exotic tastes she might savor. And she'd do it while keeping an eye on "young Richard."

"Mr. Rockhill wrote to me that you met with him in Tokyo."

Ambrose felt the barb in the statement. He hadn't written his aunt once during his trip. He'd assumed his letters to his father would be passed around the extended family. She seemed not to want to scold him tonight, though, and for that he was grateful. He felt an odd sort of sympathy emanating from his usually dour aunt. She shared all her brother Israel's views on Prohibition and the youth of the day, but she differed with him on women participating in civic life. With the new right to vote, she'd even mentioned getting involved with politics herself, which her brother found unspeakable. That she had only obliquely chastised Ambrose's lack of communication was an unusual mercy.

"You would have enjoyed Tokyo," he told her. "Temples in every corner of the city, blossoms every which way."

"I do so enjoy nature." She was swathed in silk and velvet, acres of it, and nodded at him with a look in her eye usually reserved for the very young or very old.

Sweat dampened Ambrose's collar. He realized he stank. His beard started to itch. He needed a bath. He wanted a drink. He needed something to do besides stand here under scrutiny, and then he thought of the crates he'd shipped home.

"Let me show you what I brought back for Ethan. I think you'll especially enjoy it," he said to his aunt.

"What's that?" Ethan asked reflexively at the sound of his name.

"Let me give you your present," Ambrose called loudly over to him, noting May was watching. Giving his brother a gift in public seemed like a good idea, as if Ambrose might adjust the balance of whatever scale weighed above all their heads.

His father called the chauffeur, and Ambrose helped the man bring the largest of the crates into the front hall from the icehouse, where they'd been kept in cool storage.

The whole party followed them out into the hall.

Ambrose called for a crowbar, and after much pulling and prying and huffing, the lid was detached and lifted. Inside, securely packed in straw, lay the severed, stuffed, and preserved head of a blackbuck antelope.

"A beauty!" Ethan said, leaning over and attempting to heft the trophy into the room with one hand, trailing a mountain of sawdust and wrappings onto the floor. Ambrose had to catch the heaviest part of the mount and help his brother carefully lower it to the floor. Admirers pressed forward, wanting to touch the taxidermied beast.

"A perfect specimen," his aunt Clara exclaimed. "No doubt the natural history museum will be envious."

"They must already have one," Ambrose said.

"But not nearly so fine," said Ethan. "Look at these horns!"

"It's macabre," May said quietly.

"You cannot deny the beauty of this animal," Ethan said, flourishing his good hand in display.

"Dead animal," she said.

"Yet no less majestic for it." Ethan turned toward his brother. "It's going to look splendid out at the farm. Probably in the front hall."

"My thoughts exactly," Ambrose said.

May smiled at him, a bit sickly, he thought. Ambrose couldn't help but feel a little sorry for her. She looked so dejected that he decided to give her the necklace right then. Really, what could it possibly matter now?

"I knew this wouldn't be your sort of thing, May," Ambrose said, nodding toward the antelope. He lowered his voice, trying to be confidential, but somehow the room had silenced and everyone listened. He snaked his hand into his pocket. "I brought you something else."

He brought the necklace out like a totem and offered it to her.

He could tell she didn't want to take it from him, didn't want to touch it, and he proffered it more emphatically against the back of her closed fingertips until she really had no choice but to open her hand.

"It's a traditional wedding gift in India. The groom's family gives the bride jewels. Instead of a dowry," he said.

Somewhere in the background his father muttered, "Heathens."

This seemed to jolt May back to her good manners, as reflexive as breathing. The litany of dull platitudes—"Thank you" and "Isn't it beautiful?" and "I really like it"—all landed hollow on Ambrose's ears. All except for the "You shouldn't have"—that one sounded like truth.

"I'll help you," Loulou said, tying the ribbons around May's neck.

"Ambrose, you have an eye," his aunt Clara said with satisfaction. "I wouldn't think it would flatter May, but look at her."

Everyone in the room turned to admire May in the heavy collar with the bright azure stone surrounded by its rainbow of gems. Instead of dwarfing her, the immense size of it suited her, a queen with a proper-sized jewel. The gold set off red tints in her hair; the deep blue enhanced her pale skin.

"It's heavy," she said. "Like a yoke."

Ethan crossed the room and lifted the piece like a doorknocker before letting it fall back on May's chest with a soft thump. "Certainly portable," he said, turning to his brother. "Makes it as easy as possible for the wife to get away. I wonder if that's wise." He turned to his brother. "Thank you."

The words hit Ambrose like a slap. Ethan thanking Ambrose for a present for his wife was the most natural thing in the world. The claim Ethan had on May was both shockingly real and completely casual.

Mrs. Gilder came in then, calling them all to dinner. Loulou quickly detached herself from Dicky and made for Ambrose, as if to save him. But before she got to him and because they were standing next to each other, and because it would be unnatural not to, Ambrose offered his arm to lead May in.

"Where's it from?" she asked, privately, hand touching her chest.

"India. I told you."

She turned to look at him then, no need for the question between them.

"Jaipur," he said more quietly as he pulled out her chair and helped her into her seat. She gripped his arm, giving him the lightest squeeze. That slight pressure reassured him. The past would soon be covered over by a number of new memories they'd make as family, as brother- and sister-in-law. Their past was a silly youthful interlude, quickly forgotten and never to be mentioned in what would be a long kinship. Without looking at her, he felt that. He sensed she knew it, too.

THE GUN RACKS

Nell hears the hubbub from the top-floor landing. Halted at the door under the blackbuck, her father is shaking hands with the old O'Brennan in pearls while a small crowd forms around them.

"Quite decent of you," the woman is saying.

She can hear her father apologizing for not attending the memorial service, can hear him explaining about flight times and time zones, but she notes that he's scanning the room out of the corner of his eye. When he sees her, he makes no pretense of heading right for her.

Living in Italy agrees with him. He moved there right after her mother died, and he's never come back. Nell visits him annually. Dressed in a sharp suit with a sumptuous Charvet tie, his deep tan speaks to the afternoons he spends playing mixed doubles on the courts at the American Club.

"You're looking quite groovy," Baldwin says, coming up to him now. Compared to the sea of baggy khakis and clodhopper shoes in the room, her father's snappy lace-ups look like something from another planet. And Nell knows that his clothes are only one of the many things that have grated the Quincys about her dad. Being younger than her mother, he'd been made out to be an opportunist, some kind of gigolo—an efficient double insult to both Nell's mother and to him, despite his independent money, his degree in classical civilization from Yale.

Her father ignores Baldwin, stepping back to take her in with a paternal CAT scan. He's frowning, and she knows he's about to comment on the lint-covered, shapeless sack dress she's wearing. He's always liked glamour. But instead he eyes the necklace.

"New?"

Before she can answer, Baldwin, who Nell didn't realize was still hovering, butts in. "Mother left her that." He stands between them, refusing to move off, blatantly attempting to control this interchange. Nell's unaccustomed to this much of Baldwin's focus. She notes that he's deduced exactly what the necklace is, despite claiming to have never seen it before.

"Did she now?" her father says.

Nell fumbles with the cords. How can her dad make her feel like she's twelve years old again? "What else did she leave you?" he asks.

"A bottom-line guy, concerned with the nitty-gritty," Baldwin booms to the room. He's always thought her father was grabby, lack of evidence being no obstacle to opinion. "Not like old Nell, here. You can rely on Nell." She wonders how much Baldwin's had to drink, or if this is just his usual bonhomie, goosed by unaccustomed strong emotion. She figures he's excused either way at his own mother's wake.

Her father's eyes narrow. "First a drink, I think," he says.

"Wet the old whistle after all that travel." Baldwin follows him off to the flower room, pattering in his ear. Even from across the room, Nell can see her father stiffen when Baldwin puts a hand on his back, pushing her dad along like he's under house arrest. The crowd parts for them, some giving her father nods, most pretending they don't see him.

"He's always been like that, hasn't he?" Pansy says, materializing at Nell's elbow. "I thought for sure he was a movie star when I was little. I remember being so surprised when I found out you guys lived in Oregon and not Hollywood."

"Clearly it skipped a generation." Nell waves down.

"Yes, well, glamour sometimes does that," Pansy says in a breezy way that hides the knife inside.

Her dad returns with a hug for Pansy, whom he's fond of, she of the stature and presence. And so Nell's a bit surprised when, with only the merest effort at polite conversation, her father puts a hand on her arm, right above the elbow, and says, "Come with me."

He leads Nell into a small office off the front hall, lined floor to ceiling with gun racks. The guns have all been auctioned off, and now the racks hold fishing rods, umbrellas, and tripods for cameras. Everything from the racks to the Palladian fretwork is lacquered in an ancient dull green, the ceiling stained gray from cigars long since smoked.

"You're here," Nell says when he closes the door.

Her father crosses the faded Turkish carpet, a squat glass in his hand, which he puts on the windowsill while he forces the sash up, flaking a good amount of ancient green paint in the process. Her father isn't afraid to adjust things, adjust Quincy things, to his liking. Then he flaps his suit jacket out behind him and sits down on the window ledge like some exotic bird.

"I thought you weren't coming," she says.

He takes a sip of his drink and grimaces. "I forgot how vile this is."

"Used to a nice Barolo?"

"Not this," he says, lifting the glass, but setting it down a good three feet to his side. "This." He gestures around the room and then rummages in the inside pocket of his jacket.

"Don't start," Nell says. Her father's view of the Quincys is familiar and frankly unsurprising; the dislike is mutual. But something about being named executor, the days she's spent here, the necklace around her neck . . . she doesn't want to be the outsider, not today.

"Who's starting?" He pulls out a pack of thin cigarettes and a silver lighter engraved with his twisting monogram.

"You're smoking?" Nell says, horrified, though the irony is not lost on her. She'd love one right now. But even without him here, there's no way she'd light up inside the house.

Her father, though, doesn't have these compunctions as he lights his cigarette, adding to the gray haze on the ceiling. "She made me stop when we got married. We both did. And we agreed we could start again when we turned seventy-five. Young enough to still enjoy it and old enough not to care. I'm just starting a little early." She notes his pack is an Italian brand. "It killed her."

"Yeah, cancer. So how can you do that to her memory?"

"Not this," he says, flourishing the smoke in front of his face. "This." He makes a generous arm sweep. "These people. Their secrets and expectations. Killed her just as sure as this"—he puts the smoke between them, at eye-level—"will kill me." He slides over, as if he's rethought rejecting his drink, and picks up the glass again. "God, I can't wait to see her again."

"See her again?" Nell asks. Already her father's penchant for drama and flair is grating on her.

"I have returned to the Church," he says after a sip. "You really have no choice in Rome. It's incredibly soothing. But I meant at night. I only rarely see her in my dreams anymore."

A return to the church of his childhood is unsurprising, thinks Nell, given her father's love of stage and pomp, art and history. That enjoyment was a source of connection between her parents, Nell knew. No one could fail to notice that her father unabashedly loved beautiful things and pleasure, a stance in the world that was more fraught for her mother. The puritanical streak was inherited both through genes and example. But her dad enjoyed the finer things. He was often her mother's guide and sometimes her proxy.

"Soothing and incredibly bigoted. Gay marriage, pedophile priests, women denied priesthood . . ."

He picks tobacco off his lip and then says, "Don't lecture me, Cornelia. I am still your father." As if he has to remind her of their roles, since somehow he has become the brooding smoker and mystic, and she the uptight defender of Quincys and equality.

"Wouldn't smoking be like a slow suicide sort of thing? Aren't there rules against that?" Nell asks.

"I miss her all the time," he says, ashing out the window into a viburnum, and Nell feels a pang. She misses her mother, too. Though it's been over a decade now, she no longer feels a breathtaking pain, but a constant aching companion. And it's sad to think of her father alone, though she suspects he has female company. He has referenced "a friend" once or twice in the past, which has her picturing some well-preserved, older, Anna Magnani type. Nell can admit there might be women who would find him attractive. He's still lean from all that tennis, and he has a good amount of his salt-and-pepper hair left. Though to her he is just her father, an old man who has recently taken up smoking and religion.

"Don't judge me," he says. "It makes me feel like you're one of them."

"I didn't say a thing," Nell defends.

"But I can feel you censoring yourself." She wonders just how Italian he has become. "And you're not one of them. You never were. Neither was she, thank God."

Seeing that he's feeling wistful and defiant, a promising combination, Nell thinks this might be a good time to move her cause forward.

"You know, I've been wondering . . ." But she's having a hard time finding a place to start. "I've been curious . . ." But this has so often felt like a punishing guessing game. If she poses the correct query, locks will click open, doors will swing wide, truths will be revealed. If she can't find the right question combination, all remains sealed. "Well, you never asked" is the common response when she's managed to finally unearth a secret.

"I know you have," he says, and this feels like an invitation. "Why do you think I'm here?"

"I think it's time you told me," Nell says with the

mounting energy of someone about to be let in on a long-guarded secret.

He sighs as he walks into the little bathroom and throws the butt of his smoke into the toilet with a sizzle.

"I mean, don't you think I should have some answers?" she asks above the flush. "About why Mom hated them all so much?"

He turns on the taps and washes his hands. "Or why you do, now that we're talking about it."

He comes back in and throws himself down on a low loveseat, slumped like a teenager so his head hangs on the back.

"Well?"

"Well nothing. She didn't hate them. I don't either, for that matter," he says.

"No?"

"I wouldn't be here if I did." Nell decides the only way to do this is to wait him out. "She was so untethered, your mother. And they're so . . ." He waves a hand.

"Hearty and rah-rah," she says, reciting the phrase she heard her mother use many times to describe her family of origin.

"She was out of step," he says, looking at the ceiling. "And they really don't make space for that, let alone for someone as delicate as your mother. It wasn't a nurturing sort of place. Loulou was never one to really see other people for who they actually are."

"That doesn't seem like enough reason to barely talk to your family."

"If we're going to do this, you're really going to have to listen," he says.

Nell controls her rising ire at being scolded and wills herself to be still, to listen, even if her father is being sharp.

"Loulou had her problems with your mother—this foundling waif who was put on her. Her niece, yes, but the product of so much loss."

"Israel had died." Nell nods, hoping to move him along by filling in the gaps of the story she's already familiar with.

"Heart attack, yes." She can hear the music coming from the front hall—Motown now. "And I think she was deeply shocked by it. I mean, I can only assume, but Israel Quincy was very religious, very strict, so I'm not saying he brought it on himself."

"But you're going to."

"He was just marinating in shame after that mine fire. It was practically Japanese."

"Then Grandmother May dying while Mom was born, I mean that happened back then, right?"

"Uncontrollable hemorrhaging, yes. In the face of all this it was just too much for Ethan. A father he worshipped, and his wife . . . There was no way he could care for a baby. Loulou was basically raising your mother anyway, when . . ." He falters for a moment here. "It made perfect sense at the time that it became formal. But even though it was all in the family, she felt like an orphan, a charity case, because Ethan left all the money in Loulou's care."

A stone drops in the well of Nell's mind, making ripples through her thoughts and assumptions.

"How did Ethan die?" And as she asks the question, Nell realizes this is a piece of the puzzle she's never had, or even wondered about, until now. Again, the maddening need to ask the right question.

"Ethan? Why, he drowned in the pond," her father says calmly, watching her face. "Right here."

Nell had assumed he'd been sick, but no.

"Incredibly sad. It was almost never spoken of because you kids would never want to swim in it again, now would you? Remember how much Old Lou used to like to swim? It was almost an act of defiance for her."

Nell does remember Loulou in a light blue rubber bathing cap and a matching modest one-piece, swimming until well into her eighties. Quincys have a history of being strong swimmers.

"From what I understand he drank quite a bit, so maybe he was drunk at the time. I've also heard that he was in pain after his injury. So maybe he took something for it and it was an overdose, for all we know. There was no autopsy or anything. Everyone was too sad. Or maybe he panicked or he had a little stroke. He couldn't use one of his arms, but people said he swam like that all the time with no problems. It happened at night, which makes me think it must have been somewhat intentional." For the first time since he's arrived her father's face looks less guarded, looks genuinely sad. "They say the next morning when they fished his body out of the pond, every one of the staff cried." He looks at Nell then. "Of course we couldn't tell you children any of this."

"Well sure, but you never told us even after we grew up."

"That is the danger," her father says, nodding to himself. "First things are known, but not talked about. Then they're not talked about so for long that they become unknown."

"So tell me," she says. "Tell me what I need to know."

He drains the last of his glass, and she can tell he's contemplating letting her in on something.

"There was always something with the money. I think Ethan thought Loulou would know best what to do with it," her father continues. "He never imagined she'd need it for herself after the divorce."

Loulou had famously divorced Dicky for his philandering decades ago, when it became so public she couldn't ignore it anymore. Done at a time when such things were much more scandalous, it was a testament to her social standing that Loulou had managed both to come out on top, and to remain friends with her choice of the Cavanaughs. The split had even provided cover for her to change her name back to the more recognizable Quincy. It was what everyone called her anyway. And while she'd had a bit of money herself, Dicky had never made much, and so they'd been draining her inheritance the entire marriage.

"So when Ethan signed over your mother's guardianship, all the money went with it. He never changed his will after May died to make specific provisions for a child, so with her gone, it all landed on Loulou. The expectation, of course, was that Loulou would give it to your mother, and while your mother was well taken care of, you know as well as I do that Old Lou spent most of it as right and didn't think twice about it."

A knock on the door makes Nell jump and brings a strange panic, as if she should get in the closet like when she was young and playing hide-and-seek.

"Sorry, need to use the bathroom." Baldwin strides in, and Nell wonders at his sixth sense, wonders if he was listening at the door for secrets about to be revealed.

"Why don't you use the other one?" her father says, enjoying kicking Baldwin out of any part of the farm. "We're in the midst of a chat."

"That's just great," he says, with a weak smile. "Some father-daughter time. I'm sure you need it." He shuts the door as he leaves.

Her father watches, waits until the door latches, and then waits a beat more. She almost expects him to get up and check that Baldwin isn't crouched on the other side with a glass cupped to his ear. "Your mother thought you should be allowed to have your own view of things. Your own view of the family. Your family. She never wanted to tell you. Didn't think you should be influenced by her. And the money had messed everything up in her mind. She knew that, and she didn't want that for you. But then again, she absolutely believed what she believed. And that wasn't going to fly around here."

Nell wills herself to be quiet, knowing that urging him to get to the point will only make him drag this out longer. She's wondering what could possibly cause this kind of secrecy, but somewhere in her gut, she's always known.

Sighing and not looking at her, he says, "She thought that maybe Ambrose was her father, not Ethan."

Nell sits down, felled by an assertion both outrageous and obvious. Something known but never spoken of.

"The timing?"

"Is possible." Her father gets up out of his chair and walks to the wall hung with a gallery of Quincy ancestors preserved much like the blackbuck out front. He's searching, and Nell is taking in this news when he says, "And look."

He points to a framed picture of her ancestors Ambrose

and Ethan Quincy, side-by-side, arms around each other, knees tied together at the start of a three-legged race. "She, much more than you, had it. But even you must see it here. These things tend to skip generations, you know." He's gesturing to the picture. "The dark hair, the dark circles under the eyes. Luckily for you, you got some of my Italian, so it blends more on you. But it was quite striking with your mother's pale coloring. Striking to anyone who knew the family." Nell is peering closely at the photograph. "Or even looked at pictures. She looked quite a bit like him. Black Irish, you know. Bit of an adventurer, loved travel and speed, just movement really."

Nell looks at the picture as if hearing something through an echo chamber, pieces and parts of the Quincy family refitting and reconfiguring in her head. "That's my grandfather?"

"It would explain the money. Why Ethan never changed his will. He was hoping for children of his own. Your mother and I were sure of it. Of course, everyone made out like she was crazy, most of all Loulou, who was going to have issues with your mother no matter what. Loulou revered both her brothers, but Ambrose was the favorite. That's what everyone said. To suggest something this tawdry, a love triangle among brothers . . . Well, you know how she was." Nell did know. Loulou had been prim, uptight, and never very interested in any of the sensual pleasures of life except the pleasure of new clothes. "She pretended your mother was crazy, spiteful because she never felt like she belonged and Baldwin got all the attention. Imagine being jealous of an old washout like Baldwin." Her father leans closer toward the photograph, as if contemplating this. "But these things are never rational, are they? It was clear to everyone that Loulou was expecting a level of gratitude your mother never mustered. But how is a child supposed to do that, even understand it, really? It made things strained. The rest, you know."

At Nell's silence he says, "She never had proof, of course. Never had anything but what she believed in her gut. And, of course, me. I agreed with her one hundred percent." He says it with pride that makes Nell wonder if he'd had to convince himself. Maybe he'd done it so successfully that now he even believed it.

"Grandmother May would have been pretty shady," Nell says, and peeking out at her is both the recognition of the truth when one hears it and the realization that she wishes she didn't know.

Because Nell can instantly see it from the other side. What was Loulou supposed to do? There was no proof really, besides a family resemblance—and that was murky evidence. What her mother believed in the end couldn't be corroborated or unequivocally known. And so it was just unpleasant, perceived as a veiled vehicle for a complaint about money or favoritism. Frankly, the more Nell thinks it through, the more impressed she becomes with Loulou and Baldwin and their patience and long-standing attempts to overlook this accusatory "quirk" of her mother's, her insistence on a conspiracy theory of the most unsavory kind. Their efforts to continue to include her, to leave it unsaid, to hope she "grew out" of this belief—really, what more could one do in a family?

And perhaps this made Loulou more comfortable with the money. Let her allow herself to take, to spend. Not that she'd made this calculation consciously. And Ethan hadn't made the money either, really. From what Nell understood, it all came from Israel. Ethan attended board meetings and collected checks and that was the extent of his involvement with Israel Quincy's iron ore concern. It was all just Israel Quincy's money floating through the family, wasn't it?

"And this," her father says, flipping up the necklace to inspect it. It's been a long time since she's been this close to her father apart from a quick welcoming hug. He smells of bourbon and sharp citrus—probably Italian cologne. Since when did her father wear cologne? She imagines it's a gift from his hypothetical lady-friend. "You know Ambrose traveled the world. Went to India, I'm sure of it."

"So?" Nell says, stepping back so the necklace is forced to drop.

"So nothing. But I never saw Old Lou wear this." Her father is shaking his head. "Had a diamond stashed on her at all times, the bigger the better. She would have sported that thing like nobody's business. It had been ruined for her, I'm sure of it. That's the only reason she wouldn't show it off." He's still staring at it and then says, "I'm sorry, sweetheart, but that's the only reason she'd give it to you."

Her aunt-grandmother-whatever, who couldn't stand her mother and was going crazy at the end of her life, left a gaudy piece of costume jewelry to Nell. It's not the end of the world. It's not even unexpected. Yet standing here in the midst of everything that is almost hers, the large gifts going off to her cousins, it makes her eyes water a little.

"It's a serious piece, all right." Her father knows his

way around jewelry. Nell has never cared until now. "You should get it out of here and get it appraised right away."

"I thought it might be costume."

"Not costume." He steps closer with his hands behind his back, examining it. "I'm telling you." He straightens and looks her in the eye. "You should take it to the museum and have someone look at it. You'll need to protect it."

The door squeaks open, and the sound of the O'Jays fills the room.

"Not to alarm you, but you guys probably want to come out for this," Emerson says.

The living room is deserted, as if everyone has taken cover. Pansy is in the front hall trying, with manic insistence, to give away flower arrangements to fleeing guests. It's then they hear the shouting.

Baldwin and Louis Morrell are in the library, silhouetted in the dim lighting.

"I understand you're with a fancy firm." Baldwin's face is red. "But if you can't handle this . . . I've been advised." His voice rises into an uncharacteristic screech. "I have my own advisors!"

"Baldwin," Louis says in a professional voice. Even from across the room, Nell can spot the clench in his jaw. "Why don't we just calm down?"

In the history of the world has anyone ever calmed down when spoken to like that? Rookie move, Nell thinks.

And it enflames her uncle, who looks like he's ramping up for a tell-off. It's then Nell's father steps forward, giving Louis a complete up-and-down inspection before turning to Baldwin and saying, "Why don't we go out for a little air? I haven't been down to the pond in ages."

Baldwin looks startled and then stalls, but her father leans in confidentially. "Everyone can hear you."

Her father steps out on the terrace. When Baldwin follows silently and immediately, Nell's reminded that they've known each other since before she was born. She can hear her father's soothing tones asking after the dilapidated landscaping, watches as he hands Baldwin his cigarette pack unasked, which Baldwin surprisingly accepts, and then they are out of sight.

"That your dad?" Louis asks, skimming a hand over his bare head.

"He is. What was that about?"

"Baldwin's pretty sauced. He was just blowing off steam." Louis is probably used to being an unwitting target, being constantly immersed in dicey family scenarios. But having someone push that much energy at you has to be unnerving, even if it isn't about you. Especially if it's not.

"What was he in a state about?"

Louis puffs out his cheeks and blows. "You, actually."

"Me?"

He sits down on the sagging chenille sofa. "You gave away some stuff."

"I thought I could do that."

"Technically, it's a little early to start giving out the miscellany. That said, people do it all the time."

"Oh God, I'm sorry. It was just a bunch of junk," she says, sinking down next to him, keeping a good three feet between them.

"That comment's not going to calm down your uncle any."

The squishy sofa is already doing a number on her

back. It's really made for reclining. The room's lined in leather-bound books by the yard, burgundy and acid green volumes that are essentially wallpaper. Recent paperback thrillers are wedged next to a complete set of Wilkie Collins and a chunk of Balzac in translation foxed with mold. The dim light makes her feel drowsy. The adrenaline of the day has faded away, leaving exhaustion. A new flat-screen TV sits on an ancient card table, a thick black cord snaking out of the side and disappearing into a hole drilled straight into the middle of one of the wide planks in the floor. She remembers coming down on summer mornings and lying with Emerson and Pansy on the stiff throw rugs, watching staticky cartoons on the old TV propped on the same card table.

"I've been thinking about what you asked me yesterday, if I had any message from Loulou." He sounds stilted. The usually composed Mr. Morrell looks nervous. She's wondering if he has bad news. "You should know she was very certain about what she wanted concerning the gifts. I advised her against it, but she was adamant."

At Nell's furrowed eyebrows he says, "Not about the gifts in particular. I mean, who cares what I think? Against specifying them in the will. I thought it should be distributed through a trust, the whole thing actually, for tax purposes."

Nell hazily remembers this from her one estate planning class in law school. She hasn't thought to question the structure of the estate. This isn't her area of law.

"But she wanted it specifically enumerated. Even more so after I explained the tax and probate consequences. She wanted to make absolutely sure that a judge distributed the gifts as she intended. It's not uncommon to do it this way when there's suspicion of a challenge. I get the feeling she thought it was going to be controversial. She never said anything, but I think she was concerned with your uncle Baldwin monkeying around with parts of it. That's why she made you executor, not him."

Looking at Louis, she wonders if she doesn't have a small glimpse into why Loulou hired him. He's smart, certainly, and employed at an elite firm. But there are lots of lawyers who fit that bill. He's handsome, she realizes. Craggy, you might call it, with none of that boyish thing going on. Perhaps Loulou wanted a piece of eye candy around at the end, and why not? Yes, she thinks, she's sure Loulou enjoyed being called on by Louis Morrell.

"It's taken me completely by surprise. The whole thing has," Nell says.

"It shouldn't. You obviously know your stuff. And she thought you wouldn't be influenced by old family dramas. And there is the lawyer thing, of course," he says. "I was thinking . . ." He's leaning forward now. "I don't know how long you're in town, but maybe we could talk about this over dinner."

"I don't do working dinners," Nell says reflexively, rising. "I think it's so much more efficient to just make a proper appointment and get it all done in an office. Do you want me to call your assistant or something?"

He gets a strange look on his face. "Right, so much more efficient."

It's then that she realizes her blunder. But before she can rectify it, can protest that she'd love to go to dinner with him because it's then she realizes she would, Baldwin and her father come back in. They both stink of smoke. Baldwin sticks his hand out to Louis and they silently shake. "Let me buy you a drink, young man," Baldwin jokes, leading Louis off toward the flower room, and Nell recognizes that signature move for what it is—a very Quincy way to patch things up. No apology. No acknowledgment.

THE CROQUET SOIREE

Ambrose watched Ethan working his way across the lawn—shaking guests' hands, kissing cheeks, slapping backs. Viewing him from only the right side, his brother looked unchanged. Still, there was something in the forward slope of Ethan's neck, something in the tight set of his jaw that telegraphed the injury on his left side, well concealed in the sleeve of his tuxedo.

Ambrose walked into the early evening shade where he'd be hidden for a moment while he took his flask out of his pocket for one quick swig of rye. He needn't have been stealthy about it. May's bourbon punch had initially caused a scandal, but it catalyzed the guests. Tonight she'd put together a black-tie croquet soiree. Multiple courts were laid out on Ethan's lawn in the fading early summer light. Guests had formed teams in a simultaneous elimination tournament.

After the welcome-home dinner weeks ago, Ethan had hounded Ambrose to come stay in the country. Ethan's attempt to force normalcy into the situation only made Ambrose perversely want to thwart his brother. Yet Ambrose

CLAIRE McMILLAN

did understand the desire to move on, move past, to make things stable.

About a week ago a short, very proper note arrived from May, thanking Ambrose for the necklace yet again and extending an invitation to stay for the weekend, starting with the croquet tournament on Friday. A friendly gesture one might make to any new brother-in-law. Very correct. But in the end it was his father who convinced him to go out and stay at Ethan's.

"Don't you want to see young people?" Israel asked him, handing over the unopened invitation at the breakfast table, guessing correctly at its contents. The newspapers lay spread between them. His father smelled of talc, whiskers perfectly trimmed.

"Despite what happens at May's parties . . ." Israel kept his eyes on the newspaper in front of him, proving that while May's parties had become notorious indeed, Israel was not inclined to criticize a daughter-in-law who had married his injured son. "I imagine you'd find the company of people your own age more enlivening than that of an old man."

Ambrose relented after an evening with his father during which the sole topics of conversation had been the price of smelting equipment and a gruesome story about a trolley accident two blocks away, which ended in his father's suggestion that Ambrose become involved in civic regulation of urban railways. It was the next morning that Ambrose agreed to visit the newlyweds. Because after weeks of brooding in his father's house, Ambrose realized he was either going to make things normal or he was going to leave. And what better way to decide his course than trial by fire?

Now, standing in the same spot on the lawn where he'd been two years ago, he wished he'd taken a train back to New York instead. The change in his brother's house was clear.

May lived there now.

The barest hint of her violet scent greeted you at the threshold. A new Canaletto hung over the fireplace in the living room—something his brother never would have purchased. A complete set of the works of Emerson sat on the bookshelves, and Ambrose knew all the pages had been cut by May. Vases of flowers enhanced marquetry tables, scattered anywhere one could possibly anticipate needing them. Even the band setting up in the front hall for later reflected her. These were no part-timers reworking the standards, but an honest-to-God jazz band from Chicago.

A girl he didn't know was swaying, taking practice swings with a mallet that she held like a golf putter. Lots of that dark eye stuff they all wore now, garish lips, a flat body that was unattractive but oddly appealing in her sparkling dress. She was likely some parvenu friend of May's, Ambrose thought. Though she looked too young, even through the makeup, to be May's contemporary.

Watching her, Ambrose felt a subtle loosening in his mind, the perpetual low-grade tension he lived with receded slightly.

He swiped a glass of iced punch off a silver tray and walked it over to her. She sloshed a bit of it as she propped herself against her mallet to take a sip. Faint echo of May as she spilled a little more down her forearm before she drank the rest in one impressive gulp.

"The famous Ambrose Quincy," she said as she ducked

her head to wipe her lips on the back of her wrist with a glitter of diamond bracelets. "So baaaad you didn't even make it back for your own brother's wedding."

"Let's see, I was in . . . Ceylon that week, I think." He picked up an abandoned mallet and positioned a ball to start the game.

"Can't say I blame you." She wasn't listening to him, but watched as he lined up a beginning shot through three wickets. "Brother marries your girl, I wouldn't come back, either. Even if he is a hero and all."

Ambrose's swing and then additional shot sent the ball wide, sailing off course. "She wasn't my girl."

"Oh no?" Her penciled eyebrows shot up, and something in his tone must have told her to move on. "'S good news, I guess. Tell me about where you've been."

They played the game as he told her an abbreviated story of staying at a famous palace hotel in Bombay. Suddenly her eyes got wide. "You were with Dicky Cavanaugh."

Ambrose nodded.

"I mean if the rumors are true . . . How d'you like him with your sister? I know my brothers wouldn't let me near him." May's debauched punch negated prim chitchat. This was clear. What was more surprising was that she even knew about the Indian dancing girl. First his father, now her; Dicky must have been indiscreet indeed.

Ambrose could see her true age, younger than he'd imagined, and his interest cooled a few degrees. "Your brothers have you on a tight leash, do they?"

"Like a choke chain."

"But you seem to get the punch down, don't you? What do they think of that?"

"Why don't you ask them?"

"Do I know your brothers?"

"You don't recognize me?" she asked with a wide smile.

Ambrose looked more closely at her. "Should I?"

She dropped her mallet. "I guess not." She turned heel with a little shimmy. "You've made my whole night." And without another glance, she did a quickstep dance away from him.

It was then May walked across the lawn in a silver dress, dark hair and dark eyes. He was getting over the shock of her now—a real woman and no longer a ghost haunting his mind. In the deep V of her gown, against her skin, she wore his necklace. Though he effectively looked calm, he couldn't be normal, could not yet react to her in an offhand manner like friends. He lowered his eyes from the vision, fiddling with the handle of his mallet.

"Are we going to play?" she asked.

"You first," he said, picking up the green ball, glad of something to do, and settling it next to the post.

She nudged it with her shoe for a more advantageous shot and then gripped the handle.

"Rigging it so you get your way?" he asked.

"It's my party." She pretended to study the course. "Someone once told me rules about that."

She lined up her shot, looking incongruous with a wide stance in her lamé gown. She sent the ball flying with a solid *thwock*. "Nicer without the beard," she said, turning to him.

Was she flirting? Trying to unsettle him? He felt the edge in her voice, a slight defiance, as if daring him to become outraged, to fight her. He hit his ball through the wickets, joining hers. She came and stood next to him; they were touching shoulder-to-shoulder. He wanted to shove her off, shove her away. But he suspected closeness was her strategy, used to unnerve her opponents. For just a moment he felt how difficult things could be.

"Who's that?" he asked for something to say, pointing with his mallet toward his former opponent, who was now encircled by laughing men.

"Don't you recognize Arabella Rensselaer?"

What he remembered of Arabella was a bandy-legged girl with her hair in plaits, younger sister to the twins, Frederick and Michael Rensselaer.

"She's an embryo deb; came out while you were gone. She's having quite the year, so I hear, though someone told me she's angling hard for college. Smith, I think. She'll be lucky if she can swing it. Poor thing, I hear her mother's about ready to ship her off to one of those Swiss finishing schools where you spend all day hiking and eating muesli."

"Do those places still exist?"

"Not everyone's free to roam the world, you know." He felt the sting in her words. "It's where they'll send Loulou, I'll bet, if Dicky gets any more serious." She took her second turn and missed. "What do you think of them?"

"Dicky and Lou? I try not to."

"That is your preferred way of doing things, isn't it?" she said.

"Pretty sure I haven't cornered the market on that. Pretty sure you know all about that."

She blew out a little puff of air as she rose from aiming a shot. "This isn't the way to start." She took a breath, righted her elbows, and stiffened her back, a hand at her chest. "Let's start over. Let's start like this—I love it. Truly. Thank you."

"You already thanked me."

"It means something to me."

This grated, as if he should be surprised, grateful, re-lieved? Of course it meant something. It meant everything. He'd never have given it to her otherwise. "It's a trinket, really. For tourists. You don't need to make a big deal out of it," he said, avoiding her eye.

"Someday I'll hand it down to a daughter and I'll say, 'Your uncle Ambrose gave me this as a wedding present.'" A pause stretched out in front of them and into it she filled, "I'd like to do that. We're family now."

Ambrose said nothing, suddenly enduring the game, taking wild, chancy shots, hoping to get it over with quickly. He'd made the wrong choice in coming here. He wanted to go back to town, wanted to go back to New York, wanted to get on the next ship leaving for anywhere far from here.

"I'm happy now," she said after a pause. "I've wanted you to know that." She twirled her mallet like a windmill, making sure he kept his distance.

"I suppose that's all that matters."

"Aren't you happy? Wasn't your trip everything you wanted?"

"You stopped writing me." He took the mallet out of her hand.

"I could see when you left that it wasn't ever going to work," she said, coming close and speaking privately. "I thought it was just the trip. I mean, I didn't know if you'd even come back, especially after . . . But it was so much

more than that, too. With you gone I could see that clearly."
She went on. "It's so easy now. And nothing was ever easy
between you and me. There was push and pull, too much,
I think. Always keeping track of who was winning."

"You did that?"

She smiled wanly. "Don't pretend you don't know what
I'm talking about. Ethan and I . . . No one has to lose.
You have to see that. And if you don't see it now, I hope
you will. I hope you won't bear me any ill will. I truly did
what I think is best."

Ambrose noted that she'd said nothing about love.

"I want us to be friends, Am. I want to see you happy
and settled."

"Forgive me if that seems a little . . ." He trailed off.
"Clearly that wasn't what you wanted. Not at all."

A red flush on her cheeks traveled down to her jawline.
"You made it clear what you valued."

"You're the one who made everything irrevocable."

"It wasn't me," May said quietly. "You didn't come back."

"He told me not to. It didn't make the trip any longer."

"You let him pay you off," May said.

Ethan appeared at May's side then and stepped in
between the couple. "Pay what off?" he asked May, awkwardly taking the mallet out of her hand. Watching him,
Ambrose wondered if his brother was in pain. Judging by
the glimpse of the long incision scars running up Ethan's
arm there was surely nerve damage, and couldn't paralysis
cause phantom pains?

"Pay you back for my trip," Ambrose said, twisting what
they'd been talking about, hiding it. "But we're settled up
now, aren't we? Or am I going to have to dump a wheel-

barrow full of gold doubloons on your doorstep?" Ambrose had his lawyers take the portion he owed his brother out of his corpus when he'd returned. But the accountant had called him last week. It'd been more than a month and Ethan hadn't deposited the check. Given the size of the draft, the man had been worried it was lost.

"The bookkeeper's taking care of it," Ethan said, and swung the mallet with his one good hand, sending the ball through two wickets and hitting the post, effortlessly ending the game. "What do you make of that?" he asked, rising from a crouch.

"I think our actions show us who we are more than anything else," Ambrose said, while looking at May, the desire to antagonize her not something he fully understood himself.

"I'll say," May said as she stepped to Ethan and took his bad hand in hers. They were a team as they navigated his injury, making it imperceivable to an outsider. It looked like he led her onto the dance floor, but Ambrose knew she was hoisting his hand in hers, allowing herself to be led.

Ambrose walked over to the cut glass punch bowl, needing a drink.

"Couldn't stay away, could you?" Dicky ladled his drink with care.

"I was invited. Where's Loulou?"

"She's here somewhere," Dicky said, as if they'd been married for years. "Off with her nutty friends."

Ambrose took a sip of punch. Dicky criticizing anything about his sister, even her friends, raised his hackles.

But Dicky was perceptive. "Don't know why you're so uptight," he said. "We could double-date together. You and Arabella, me and Lou. They're great chums, you know. And we'd be two brothers in arms."

Ambrose had played one game of croquet with Arabella, and already they'd been paired off, likely by everyone at the party. "You're not my brother," he said. They weren't jointly fighting a war. Against what? His sister? Women?

"No, I'm not. And a good thing, too, given how Ethan's treated you." At the look on Ambrose's face, Dicky continued. "Look, Loulou told me. I said to her that it wasn't that serious with May before you left, but Lou set me straight. Told me she'd talked to you about it at that going-away party May threw. Told me she'd seen some things. I can appreciate you're in pain. You don't have to pretend with me."

Ambrose was appalled at the thought of Loulou spilling his secrets to Dicky, both that he'd been outed and that she was already close enough to Dicky that she'd take him into her confidence. Gone now was the abashed Dicky from Ambrose's welcome home dinner. "I'm not in pain. No one's pretending," Ambrose said.

"Fine," Dicky said. "If that's how you want to play it. But Loulou knows things."

"So you're the expert on Loulou now?"

"Oh, I understand," Dicky said. "She's your little sister, but she's not a kid anymore."

A thundering clap of revulsion shuddered through Ambrose, though he knew that wasn't what Dicky meant at all. Dicky might be a hedonist and a libertine, but he was conventional and a coward. Ambrose would bet his life Dicky wouldn't dare do more than kiss Loulou. Nevertheless, he wanted to tell Dicky to wipe that smug smile off his face, wanted to tell him that his father knew about the dancing girl, that it was the talk of the town. But he had a moment's thought for Loulou. Though perhaps his sister knew about India, too, and that thought hurt Ambrose. That his idealistic sister, lover of Austen and Brontës, should have grown into a shrewd-eyed realist, a compromiser, and all at the hands of Dicky Cavanaugh. Ambrose took a swig out of his flask.

"Have it your way," Dicky said at Ambrose's silence, and then walked to Loulou, taking up her hand and exaggeratedly kissing the knuckles, which made her friends titter and blush. So perhaps he knew a few gestures out of Austen.

Ambrose dumped the remaining contents of his flask in the punch bowl.

After the winners of the tournament had been awarded a little silver dish from May and the runners-up had been given a crying towel, and then jokingly used it to fake-weep; after the band had taken a break and then another again; after the waiters collected empty glasses off the side tables and brought liqueurs or coffee to the last of the guests; after guests started their drawn-out good-byes—Arabella stood leaning against the door, eyes half-closed, skin flushed, no coat. He checked his shock at seeing a girl so young so visibly intoxicated. Such a thing would never have happened before he had left. He liked her the better for it, found it a little appealing even, that lack of control.

"How are you getting home? Need me to rustle up a car?" he asked, taking the tiny crystal thimble of syrupy liquor out of her hand. She'd definitely feel ill in the morning.

"Not going," she said, swaying a bit. "Am staying. Dear May said I could stay upstairs." She laughed. "Look at your face, you old thing. Not in the dormitory. Jeez, where's your mind? Still off in the Orient with harems or something? In a guest room, silly. I sent the chauffeur home to Mommy. Aren't you staying?"

No wonder her parents were sending her to a Swiss finishing school. Though he realized May's invitation to stay probably saved her parents the scandal of dealing with a tipsy daughter.

"Yes, I'm staying," Ambrose said.

"Then maybe you should tuck me in." Even through the worn lipstick and the liquor on her breath, she had a beautiful smile.

"What's required for tucking you in?"

"A nice big old teddy bear, that's for sure."

Ambrose smiled. "I'll see if May has one of those lying around."

She came forward then and grasped his lapels. "I think she outgrew hers." Arabella leaned in farther, so that their lips were almost touching. As much as things had changed, and a visibly drunken woman grabbing his jacket and leaning into his face was certainly new, she stopped a few inches from him. She waited for him to come forward and actually kiss her.

And something about her, a hint of May really, made him duck his head to hers.

Through the faint waxy-rose traces of her lipstick and the softness of her mouth he could hear the guests around them chatting, and then he heard May. Her low, distinct voice saying good night to someone made him pull back abruptly, leaving Arabella's mouth open.

Arabella smiled and actually winked at him and then headed for the staircase, where one of the maids was waiting on the top-floor landing to show her to her room.

THE MOON OF NIZAM

On her father's advice, Nell calls the museum the morning after the wake, closing herself in Loulou's aqua-and-black-tiled bathroom and trying to keep her voice down. Even though her last name is Merrihew, she tells the receptionist on the phone "Nell Quincy," feeling like a fraud. As a girl, Nell had secretly wished the more recognizable Quincy had been her last name—a name with the stardust of Roosevelt or Rockefeller or Kennedy. Not that she's alone. Loulou had hers changed back the moment she had the social cover of her divorce, and Baldwin used Quincy when making dinner reservations to ensure a good table. Her mother had given it to Nell as a middle name. Cornelia Quincy Merrihew was a mouthful, though dignified, and it looked good on the nameplate outside her office door. But it is with sheepish feelings of pretense that she uses Quincy with the museum.

The curator of Asian art returns her call in minutes.

"Could you email me a picture?" the curator asks. Nell's briefly stymied by this suggestion, by the sudden thought of the necklace going out in the world. At her silence the curator rushes on, covering. "It's a bit of a formality. In this case, I'm sure I'd be interested in the piece. Why don't we choose a day for me to come look at it?"

Nell's certain she doesn't want a museum curator coming to the farm, doesn't want Baldwin or Pansy to start asking questions.

"I can bring it in," Nell says quickly.

"It's best for me to come to it," the curator says. "I'd hate for something to happen to it while traveling. And really, it shouldn't be disturbed from where it's resting without a fine art packer handling it."

Where it's resting is around her neck. Where it was resting was stuffed in an old liquor sack and crammed in a dressing table. This woman is probably picturing some sort of buried treasure scenario, a dusty attic, or at least a proper jewelry box. Nell can imagine the woman's white gloves, her pocket loupe, and an LED penlight.

"No, really. I'd prefer to bring it in," Nell says with what she hopes sounds like finality.

There's a long pause and then a sigh. "Of course, Mrs. Quincy." The name makes Nell wince. "If you insist."

The Quincy name must have some magic left in it because an appointment is made for the very next day.

In the same clothes from the wake, the only decent things she's brought, Nell walks through the glass and marble atrium of the Cleveland Museum of Art. She hears efficient click-clack footsteps behind her before she turns.

Reema Patel is wearing a dove gray flannel shift dress, the cut severe, toned arms on display. Though the color would make your average woman look like a corpse, it makes her skin glow and enhances the dark circles under her eyes, adding gravitas in counter to her beauty. Her hair is a glory—black, enviously shiny, and cut in a thick hem at a professionally appropriate two inches past her collarbone. On her feet are a pair of burgundy suede heels low enough to run in.

Nell's relieved there's no one from the development office joining them as she follows Patel to her office. Nell sits in the modern and uncomfortable chair across from the tidy desk. There's a framed diploma from Oxford on the wall, which explains why Patel's accent sounds more English than Indian. Nell notices a diploma from Yale as well before turning her attention back. She doesn't want to appear the snob judging schooling.

They exchange the usual pleasantries, with Patel offering condolences on Loulou's death and an obligatory comment on her longevity, and Nell commenting on the new Pompeii exhibition downstairs.

And then Reema Patel sits back, waiting for Nell to start.

She wonders how many times Patel's been subjected to "treasures" from Granny's attic—reproduction tourist trinkets presented by an eager, slightly haughty face. Nell's suddenly embarrassed, rethinking her visit. Surely if this necklace were real, it'd have been kept downtown in the safe-deposit box that housed all the "good" jewelry, the specific bequest notwithstanding. Nell's pulled family strings that she doesn't feel entitled to use to get this meeting. Patel would probably prefer Nell announce some legacy from Loulou, specifically bequeathed to the Asian collections.

But there is no way around her visit now, and Patel

looks like she'll quash dreams with sensitivity. Nell pulls the whiskey sack from her handbag, wishing she'd thought to put it in something cleaner.

Patel leans over, as if a delicate relic has been placed on her desk. Nell's gratified by this show of deference, and it's effective in conveying Patel's seriousness. As Patel gingerly opens the bag, Nell notices that Patel's nails are short with jagged cuticles, a pleasing juxtaposition with her posh clothes.

When Patel removes the necklace from the sack, a little gasp whooshes between her lips. She places the jewel reverently on the dusty velvet, her head nodding faintly as she tucks her hair behind one ear. She bows closer until her nose is almost touching the sapphire, and it looks, incongruously, as if she's smelling it. Then she raises her head quickly, sneezes violently, and scrambles for a tissue. She turns to her computer, typing quickly on the keyboard with one hand as she blows her nose with the other.

Nell remains silent, though a barrage of questions runs through her mind.

After looking back and forth between the screen and the necklace, Patel swings the computer monitor toward Nell. Nell counsels herself not to beam, not to look greedy, but she can't help smiling; on the screen is a black-and-white picture of the necklace.

"I'm not a gemologist," Patel starts. "But this," she says pointing to the screen, "is the Moon of Nizam, also called the Sapphire of Baroda. It belonged to the maharaja of Baroda. It's been missing since the 1920s."

All that registers is that this is one of those gems that actually has a name, and that it's missing.

"Missing?"

Patel nods. "Maharajas would sell their jewels to the British. They'd never admit it, of course, and once the jewels were out of the country . . ." She leans back, rummaging in her desk drawer. "Also looting during Partition. Sometimes they made gifts." She reaches up to make air quotes and then goes back to searching.

Nell hazily remembers glancing on the case of the Koh-i-Noor, the largest diamond in the British crown jewels, during an international law seminar back in law school. India wants it back, claims it was looted as war booty by the British East India Company and then given to Queen Victoria for her crown. Britain claims it was a legitimate gift, though the twelve-year-old maharaja who bestowed it had just had his territories conquered and occupied by the British army. Pakistan has requested return, claiming original ownership. The Taliban has even claimed rights. Each time there's some summit in London or the Olympics come to the UK, Nell sees the Koh-i-Noor pop up again in the news. She mentions this to Patel.

"India keeps getting shot down on that one," Patel says. "There's little hope there. But they have successfully repatriated some of the jewels of lesser maharajas when they come up for sale or . . ." She pauses here. ". . . things. Tell me about this," she says.

Nell recounts the story of finding the necklace. Patel is nodding and ransacking her desk. Nell considers mentioning the will and that the necklace is hers, but that seems private, still unreal, and oddly boastful.

"A gemologist will need to look at it. There are always

fakes floating around, usually cobbled together from old pieces so the whole thing feels authentic. Ah!" Patel finally finds what she's looking for and pulls out a pair of tweezers. She picks up one end of the necklace's gold tassels. "This could be a crude repair here, or it could be a clue that this is an attempt to pass off a fake." She's pointing to the rewoven spot in the cording that her expert eye had spotted instantly. There is no accusation in her voice, just matter-of-fact professionalism. "A condition report, a gemological grading report . . ." She's dragging the necklace into better light, not looking at Nell while she keeps talking. "Provenance issues for sure, since it's all so mysterious. Do you have any idea how your family got this?"

"Inherited."

"I mean before."

"Ambrose Quincy did one of those grand tours in the twenties. Brought back stuff for everyone," Nell says, thinking of her father's comments, thinking of the blackbuck head in the front hall.

"So it could have been stolen, or sold, or stolen and then sold. You wouldn't have the bill of sale, would you? A customs declaration form?"

Nell's blood rises with defensiveness. Is there a family in history that could find such slips of paper? Have them on hand for immediate inspection a hundred years after the fact? She supposes a clan of robotic bureaucrats could. "My family's had it for coming up on a century," Nell starts to explain, but at Patel's patiently inquiring face, Nell amends, "No."

"Perhaps you should look for one," Patel says distractedly as she flips over the necklace and examines the enameled back. "Exquisite meenakari," she says, gesturing with the tweezers. "Has me leaning toward authentic. It looks well intact, perhaps suspiciously so, which cuts both ways. Sometimes, in older pieces, the enamel chips. The meenakari was never documented, I'm guessing, since it's been missing so long, which is a pity because then we could cross-reference and know for sure." She turns the monitor back toward her, clicking the keyboard, presumably looking for a picture of the back to verify.

Patel using "we" makes Nell feel reassured. "You just said things went missing," Nell says, still mulling over provenance issues.

"Yes," she says looking up, "but not things like the Moon of Nizam. It's said the Moon was the favorite jewel of Shah Jahan." She opens her desk drawer again, rooting through pencils and Post-it pads. "Why can't I find anything today? That's craftsmanship. That's five hundred years. Here it is." She brings out a mini black camera.

The words Shah Jahan echo around in Nell's brain like diamond dust. "So Ambrose could have bought it from someone who stole it."

"Mrs. Quincy," Patel says, looking up from taking a picture of the necklace. She has not asked for permission, but she might be one of those better-to-ask-forgiveness-than-permission types.

"It's Ms., and please call me Nell."

"Nell," she says, her voice softening and her eyes twinkling in a deft smile, meant to reassure. "I don't mean to be impugning your ancestors." She says this with a slight singsong on the gerund, losing that clipped Britishness.

"But if this is the Moon of Nizam, and I'm not saying it is . . ." She clicks off a few more pictures. "It's highly doubtful that it was procured through legitimate means."

"It was sitting in my great-aunt's house in a whiskey sack." Nell laughs, trying to get Patel to join, but she only smiles slightly.

Nell's sure now she's made the wrong choice in bringing it here. She should have asked Emerson to get Vlad to look at it, or taken it to Christie's for an appraisal. Even *Antiques Roadshow* would have been better.

"Yes, well, you have some options," Patel says, back to very British now. "The first one, and I would encourage this, is that you allow the piece to come into the museum on consideration."

Nell nods, trying to keep a bland face.

"This object is potentially an artifact of significant cultural history, and as such deserves to be thoroughly researched by an institution like ours. And if you'd allow it to come here, I'd have the registrar insure it, then we'd sign a conservation service order to examine it to determine the materials. We'd run tests."

At Nell's face, she says, "Noninvasive, of course. I'd do the research personally, and I'm sure I don't need to emphasize the significant international contacts and resources I have at my disposal based on my connection with the museum. It would probably make sense to interview a few members of your family as well."

"What?" Nell asks. "Why?" she says before she can stop herself.

Patel slows, aware she's tripped some wire. "That's a fairly typical procedure in a case like this. It can help with provenance, but also with historical placement of the piece, dating, all sorts of things."

At Nell's pause, she continues. "In the absence of bringing it to the museum under consideration, I hate to suggest it, but you should probably hire counsel."

"Bringing it to the museum?" Nell asks.

Patel turns back to the jewel, examining it again. "On loan, of course, but ultimately, if this is what I think it is, for acquisition."

It's barely Nell's and now the museum wants it. Is she supposed to hand it over? Will they buy it? Is it even real? Patel is cool and calm, but Nell's started to sweat. Nell half expects Patel to sweep the thing up and lock it in her desk drawer.

"This is all my opinion and an educated guess, Nell. You're free to get another one," Patel says in the tone of someone absolutely certain of her facts. "I'm sure I don't have to explain to you that there might be some thorny legal issues." She turns and points down at the necklace. "If it comes up for auction, the Indian government could try to enjoin you from selling it and pursue a right of replevin. Then again, they might do nothing. These things are never clear-cut. And then there's the Mahj."

"I'm sorry?"

Patel clicks around on the keyboard again and then turns the monitor back toward Nell to show her photos of a handsome and clearly inebriated young Indian man appearing to stumble out of a London nightclub, arm in arm with Prince Harry.

"I take it you don't read *People* magazine. The twelfth maharaja of Baroda is young, bit of a playboy, and runs in

Prince Harry's circle. Called the Mahj. His family would be the family that it went missing from."

"Would he have a claim?"

"Who knows?" Patel says in a quick way that sounds like she knows. "But sapphire jewelry of the time frame is rare. Indians, especially the Mughals, considered sapphires bad luck. My grandmother was appalled by this." She wafts her engagement ring, a petite duo of Kate Middleton's. "She was adamant that I sleep with it under my pillow for two nights and if nothing bad happened and there were no bad dreams, then I was okay." They both smile. "Of course I was keeping it no matter what, but that didn't stop me from doing what she said." Nell nods. "Luckily, no bad dreams. But maybe that's why they put the Moon in the Navaratna setting."

Nell digs out her phone and opens the notes application. "The nine-stone setting," Patel leans forward, toward Nell's phone as if she's dictating. "It's supposed to symbolize the moon, the planets, the sun, things like that, supposed to bring good luck." She gestures toward the inlaid stones with her tweezers. "Maybe they thought it would counteract the sapphire."

"Like it's cursed?" Nell's thinking of Baldwin's comment, trying to remember if it's the Hope Diamond that's cursed.

"I wouldn't go that far." Patel turns back to her monitor and is clicking through pictures again. "India's interest in it might hinge on publicity. If a potential sale became notorious, they might feel compelled to act. If the maharaja were involved, say. But you'll also have customs issues; I'm not a lawyer, but I'm sure the legal issues would spin out into a huge web."

This sounds like a threat, and Nell's wondering if Patel can get the government involved if she wants to. If the necklace is the Moon, if it is stolen, does Nell have some kind of legal duty? Does Patel have some kind of reporting duty? Nell's racking her memory of her sole law school ethics class.

She decides it's time to leave, time to retreat, to research as all lawyers do when cornered, and to plan. She rises and scoops the necklace into the little bag and then into her purse.

"Thanks for your time," Nell says quickly.

Patel rises. "Really, we're equipped to keep it safe," she says, shooting a hand forward, and for a moment Nell thinks Patel is going to wrestle her for it. But she's only offering a handshake, a faux-friendly formality.

Nell shakes her hand quickly and is out the door. As she turns into the hallway, out of the corner of her eye, she sees Patel sit and reach for the phone.

THE REMEDY

Ambrose walked into the sunny breakfast room where May sat slumped at a stick-wicker desk facing the wall, the telephone at her ear, an overwatered violet in a cachepot suffocating slowly at her elbow. Arabella was the sole occupant of a ransacked breakfast table, sitting before an untouched dish of gray oatmeal swimming in cream, the sight of which made Ambrose want to heave. Her hair was unkempt, and she had dark rings of old makeup under her eyes. She was unabashedly dressed in her spangled dress from the night before.

"Take this," Arabella said, sliding the dish toward Ambrose. "The smell is killing me."

He was glad that he'd gone straight to his corner room last night and fallen into bed alone. She'd been quite drunk the night before.

May hung up the phone and turned. "Your parents are sending the car. It should be here within the hour."

Arabella stood then in her remarkable state of dishabille. "I know I'm in the way." She smoothed her dress as Ethan came in the room and raised his eyebrows.

"Cousin Ethan," she said. Though no relation, Arabella had known the Quincy family all her life. Her parents had known the Quincys far longer. She waved a hand, her wrist still encircled in diamonds—gaudy now in the morning light. "Thanks for the party," she said, sequins sparkling on her dress with a dull twinkle. And then to Ambrose, so only he could hear, "I'll see you at the club this afternoon." She pursed her lips and blew him a silent kiss, unseen by anyone else as she walked by.

The maid entered the room and set a silver toast rack in front of Ambrose and placed a small pot of homemade marmalade beside it. His brother's favorite, he noted. Ambrose had the briefest flash of desire to get up and follow Arabella, to leave and never come back.

"That girl," Ethan said, fondly shaking his head as he sat down. "A real speed."

"I heard that," came Arabella's reply from halfway up the stairs.

"They're all like that nowadays," Ethan faux-whispered.

"And that," she called.

Ambrose bit into a piece of cold toast with marmalade, bitter and cloyingly sweet at the same time.

Sitting up so straight in May's ladder-back chairs and eating something unappetizing seemed appropriate penance, along with his pounding head, his roiling stomach.

"Not feeling so well?" Before Ambrose could answer, Ethan went on. "I must say I feel great today. I'd like coffee. Nothing more for me, Dorothy," he said, addressing the maid. For the first time Ambrose noted the bluish lines around his brother's eyes, the rigid set of his mouth.

"Also an egg yolk," he was calling. "And Worcestershire and a little cayenne for my brother here. He seems to have caught a bug last night."

"Just tea, please," Ambrose tried to revise the order.

But the maid had disappeared through the swinging door to the kitchen.

May was scratching on paper with a little gold screwtop pencil, instructions for the gardener or perhaps revisions to the cook's daily menu. She was as competent in these tasks as anyone would have imagined her to be, including Ambrose.

She joined them then, sitting on Ethan's left, his bad side.

"What shall we do this morning?" May asked with too-bright cheer as the maid cracked an egg in a glass, separated it at the table, and discreetly put the shells in a bowl for disposal. She added the requisite condiments and set the concoction at Ambrose's place. Her deft delivery of this remedy gave credence to the rumored decadence of May's household. Giving a sly sideways glance at Ambrose, May said, "If you're feeling up to it, doing something, that is."

She was dressed in crisp hacking clothes, fit for walking or riding, and Ambrose was pleased to see his necklace winking from inside the neckline of the starched broadcloth shirt she wore. Her breeches cinched at the waist, and the pale moleskin eased over her hip and thigh. Her dark hair was sharp with water or pomade against her cheek, and her eyes flashed with darkness, too, when she said, "I'd like to get out and about before the gymkhana."

Ethan laid the newspaper at his place one-handed, but the thin paper bunched as he tried to turn the page. May reached over and smoothed it for him, as if she'd done it a hundred times, and then turned the page. Watching them, Ambrose realized she likely did this every morning. "Maybe you can convince Ambrose to go with you on one of your tramps. I'll save my energy," he said, leaning over an article.

"Save it for the bidding," she said.

"May, don't start." He touched his temple gingerly.

"Does your head hurt?" Her tone immediately softened. In a quiet voice she asked, "Do you need your pills?"

"No." Ethan's petulant tone, as if they'd discussed this numberless times, convinced Ambrose more than anything that his brother had been in pain for a while. "But I will if you go on about this."

May turned to Ambrose. "I think he ought to buy all the horses this afternoon, don't you? One grand gesture to help those poor families."

At the gymkhana all proceeds, entry fees, and the money raised from a horse auction would go to a fund for the families of those who had died in the mine fire. May had wrangled most of her friends into donating the horses.

"There's already been money distributed. There's a relief fund, the community chest."

"The community chest!"

"Yes." Ethan's voice was rising. "What's wrong with the community chest?"

"Nothing, if it buys you a little peace of mind," May said.

Ambrose watched his brother visibly compose himself. "I'm not the only one making the decision about that," he said in a controlled voice. "And besides, we don't have room for twenty extra horses, darling." He nodded at the paper and May reached over and turned the page for him.

Then her hand fluttered to her neck, where she fiddled with the necklace, looking sideways at Ambrose as if waiting for him to join the argument. If Ethan did buy all the horses in a show of atonement, the gesture would end up in the newspapers, and not just the society column. Ambrose thought such a public display, his brother buying up polo ponies at the country club, would look more Marie Antoinette than Robin Hood—a tone-deaf gesture. Though he supposed he understood May's desire. Just yesterday there'd been an editorial in the paper calling the fire a slaughter and speculating that shortcuts had been taken in constructing the secondary mine shaft.

"I can't stop thinking about them," May said. "About those families."

Ambrose felt the need to come to his brother's defense, to his whole family's defense, really. "I don't mean to be cruel, but those men, they knew the risk." When she didn't look up, he added, "Their wives, their families did, too."

"Not you," she said to Ambrose, and then turned fully in her seat, edging him out of the conversation so she could face Ethan. "You can give the horses away," she said. "Or we'll give them back to the families they came from and donate the money where it belongs."

"Do I have to keep on paying?" Ethan asked quietly, stopping both May and Ambrose for a moment. "There are better ways to go about helping." He reached up and smoothly turned the page for himself.

"It's dangerous work and they're paid accordingly," Ambrose said to May, wanting her to see reason.

She turned on him then. "They were trapped underground and burned alive. You're telling me it's possible to pay someone for that?"

"No one forced them to take the risk. It's a calculation they made." He hesitated before he added, "They probably went unconscious from the smoke before the fire reached them." Though it sounded hard, Ambrose truly thought there was some consolation in the idea of the men not suffering.

"You sound just like your brother," she said, getting up. "Your father will be so pleased."

Ambrose had seen enough of the world now to know that men took all sorts of risks to make money, to survive. Ditch diggers in India, pearl divers in Japan, tanners, garbage haulers, and every sort of unsavory work, he'd seen it and understood it. Still, it didn't mean he'd changed into his father, or Ethan for that matter.

"Sometimes those are the risks men are willing to take to see their children eat."

"Or to see the owner's son travel around the world, I suppose," May said.

Stunned silence enveloped the table. Even the kitchen was quiet. He didn't know what he'd been expecting— sisterly camaraderie, a joshing, easy sort of intimacy like he had with Loulou?

May rubbed the starched cuff on her shirt. "My comments were made from worry. I apologize," she said from rote, as if she'd had outbursts before on this topic and had memorized an appeasing apology. She rose, her hobnail boots echoing across the hall and out the front door.

Ambrose's head swam with her reverberating acerbity. Ethan managed to fold the last page of the newspaper closed. The egg yolk jiggled in its brown broth when Ambrose pushed back from the table and bolted into the gunroom. He made it to the bathroom just in time to be sick in the toilet.

After he'd composed himself, he returned to an empty breakfast table—no sign of Ethan, and a void left by May.

His stomach felt tender and a headache lingered on the edge of his vision. He'd never felt it more keenly, the desire to flee. Movement, to be going anywhere, calmed him, provided fresh air to blow out the cobwebs from his brain. He decided then that a walk was what he most needed.

His spirits rallied just a bit when he walked under the blackbuck hanging in his brother's grand entrance. Here was evidence of adventuring, not of reading about it in newspapers, but of hunting in general for truth, for knowledge, for a way to live.

Once out the door and on the lawn, he took the small path lined with pea gravel to the edge of the tall hay fields.

The path now led to a tennis pavilion, blindingly white, in the distance. Plunked down, really, in the middle of working fields and the bordering woods. The pale ochre clay tennis court baked in the sun. Since when did either

Ethan or May play tennis? The unnatural gaudiness of the thing made him suspect it was a gift from Israel, who considered exercise wholesome.

As Ambrose approached the little tennis Parthenon, he saw May sitting on an open ledge of the pavilion, in what would have been a window, pondering the open views. He thought he should apologize. He'd been making the reasonable argument, but she'd seen it as callous. He hazily thought she wouldn't have done that before, would have given him the benefit of the doubt, wouldn't have tried so hard to read malevolence into his words. He suspected she'd take offense at anything he said now, as if she were confirming the new slot he'd hold in her life. One booted foot dangled down and kicked out into space, the other stretched out along the length of the ledge.

She didn't see him as he approached, and he found himself hurrying at the opportunity to talk to her privately. They hadn't actually been alone since his return. There were always people around, always someone listening.

Her leg stopped kicking when she saw him, and he watched her eyeing exit routes from the pavilion, but then she must have realized there was no escaping him, unless she blatantly ran off.

"What's wrong?" she called when he was near. "Were you sent after me?"

"Nothing. Get far?" he asked, knowing she hadn't. Teasing had been his familiar shorthand with her when he'd left.

She looked at him sideways and said, "It was fine." He'd need to find a new shorthand between them.

"I wanted to say," he started, but found that somehow

her mere presence had managed to turn the tables. She seemed in the right; he, the crass industrialist. "I don't think it's perfect," he said. "I agree it was a tragedy."

She kept her eyes on the view as she said, "I know you do."

It was quiet, no breeze, a burning, cloudless sky and the sound of cicadas in the trees.

"I snapped," she said, slumping. "It gets to me." He could see her pulse beating next to his necklace. "And I guess I was surprised. You were so above all the grubbing," she said, almost to herself. "I always liked that about you. That you were above everything." Her words reminded him of those days before he left.

Looking back, he could see that in those brief moments everything had been his to judge and choose. He felt a faint beat of that pulse through his blood now. His surety during that time had been the most comforting thing in the world. He'd not realized how fleeting it would be—a moment when he felt a real and tangible certainty. Since coming home, since seeing his father, since May's decision, since Ethan's accident—it seemed like he hadn't known anything at all. To have that firm conviction back for a minute—he'd forgotten how alluring it was. Forgotten how appealing it was to see himself through May's eyes.

"Not that I know what I'm talking about, according to your brother." She said this with no small amount of bitterness for a woman who'd been married so shortly. She kicked off her perch and came to stand next to him. "Double-edged sword, I guess. That you used to think for yourself."

"I did. I'm not sure—" he started, noting she'd used the past tense, but she interrupted him.

"It makes no sense if we're not friends. We—" Here she turned toward him, looking over his left ear, as if intent on something in the field behind them. "We knew each other so well before. It seems a waste for that to all just—" She made a fist and released it, as if to say "poof," and then turned to walk toward the house.

He had to hustle after her.

"I was thinking you and Arabella make quite a good match," she said when he caught up, her hands behind her back like a marching general. "I believe she sees things very much the way you do." Though just last night he would have agreed with her, today the comment rankled. She'd compared him to a flighty debutante, and yet again a line was drawn in the sand. You are on this side. I am over here. "I saw you kissing her last night."

They were at the bottom of the field, about to enter the garden, still a good way from the house.

"Kissed, not kissing," he said.

Just then Ethan, in a light-colored suit, fashionable in the early summer, stepped out under the dark portico.

"Darling, you'll make us late. We're due there now," he called, his voice rising over the lawn.

"May," Ambrose said, taking her hand before they reached the lawn. "I want to be friends, too."

Her arm went limp and slipped out of his grasp. She hopped up into a lilting jog toward the library doors, her boots shuffling in the wet grass, the morning dew just burning off. She reached up to give Ethan a kiss on the left cheek, his bad side. She didn't hesitate. Then she dashed inside and up the stairs to change.

Ethan held the door for his brother, the scars on his hand looking more pronounced against the heavy wood. "She'll be right down." Then Ethan shut all three of them quietly in the house.

THE IMPROMPTU PICNIC

Lake Erie looks brighter next to the Shoreway as Nell's driving away from the museum. She'd put the Moon on in the parking lot right after she'd left Reema Patel, talk of loan and acquisition and the maharaja ringing in her head. It's safer on her. She's convinced of that.

She parks near the service entrance to the farm and checks her hair in the rearview mirror. Even in the shade, the Moon sparkles outrageously, and she's having a hard time hiding it inside her neckline. Now that she knows what it is, her father's advice comes back to her. She heads inside and pounds up the rickety back stairs to Loulou's bedroom, intent on stashing the Moon in her luggage until she can decide on a truly safe place to store it.

It takes Nell one look at her suitcase to realize that someone's been up here, been through her things. The back door slams, and Pansy's shrill, nasal voice calls out, "Yooo-hoooo."

"Hey." Pansy's voice is controlled to the point of suspicion when Nell walks in the kitchen. "Where've you been?"

"Upstairs," Nell says. Her antennae rise at her cousin's presence at the farm in the middle of the day. Shouldn't she be at her house in the Heights, or running after-school activities, or meeting clients in town for coaching? Nell wonders briefly if any of the Loulou lessons updated for a new century have made it into those sessions.

Pansy nods and goes directly to what she cares about. "Reema Patel called me."

Nell's face turns pink. She can't help feeling betrayed by Patel; then again, there's no confidential relationship between them, just savvy and politics.

"She told me a relative had just been to see her. Wanted to know if I knew anything about our family harboring a potentially stolen necklace of importance."

Stolen—really? Nell didn't peg Reema Patel as one for drama.

"Of course I had to cover," Pansy continues. "Had to pretend I knew all about it. That my family doesn't hide things from one another."

"There's no hiding. You saw it."

"Can I see it again?" Pansy asks, eyes on Nell's neck.

Nell wants to exercise another right as executor and say no. "You tried it on yesterday."

"Yeah." Pansy's palm is out flat, like "Hand it over." And some ancient authority Pansy has over her makes Nell untie it, then drag it over her head and off. For the second time today, she offers the jewel up for scrutiny.

"Reema said it was important," Pansy says, hefting it.

"How do you know Reema Patel?"

"One of her boys is in the same grade as Andrew. How'd you know to go to the museum with it?"

"You passed on it," Nell says, suddenly wary. "I thought the museum could shed some light."

"Well, it's a jewel, and yeah, I mean . . . You offered it to me. Still stand?"

Pansy laughs like this is a little joke, but it feels ominous to Nell. "Oh, look, it's exciting, okay?" Pansy says with a sparkle in her eye as she hands it back to Nell. "Can't I be excited?"

Pansy only has to throw her a bone and Nell starts considering letting go of skepticism and double thinking. The pull of going back to a time when they stood beside each other never quite leaves Nell. Even the slightest glimpse of lightness and Nell is willing to try again, is willing to believe that at least one Quincy could treat her like one of their own.

"It is nuts, isn't it?" Nell says.

"I think it's beautiful," Pansy gushes. "So unique. That's probably why Loulou never wore it. Probably thought it was too strange or unusual or something. You know how traditional she was."

They're standing there admiring it when the back screen door opens with a grinding squeak, as if someone is fit to rip the hinges off, and her uncle Baldwin strides in, a plastic grocery bag in his hand. "Brought an impromptu picnic," he says in a huff of exertion. "Nothing in this place." He turns to his daughter. "What are you doing here? I'm supposed to see you at the boys' lacrosse invitational this afternoon."

"But she did leave her jewels to me, you know," Pansy says. It's then Nell can see the argument, and it's not a bad one—sloppy drafting, mistaken intent, maybe a little dementia. Pansy wouldn't have a hard time getting an ambitious young attorney to take the case and make it for her—the potential upside might be huge, and there's publicity, getting known for a level head during a high-profile case, a connection to the Quincys. All boons whether they win or not. "You offered it to me," Pansy says, all lightness gone.

"She quite specifically left the jewels in the safe-deposit box to you," Nell answers, trying for reason. Neither of them provide context for Baldwin, but he doesn't seem to need it as he is rooting through cupboards for plates for the leftover fried chicken and grocery store potato salad he's brought. Like all Quincys, Baldwin's love of leftovers gave him a little puritanical thrill of thrift.

"You were trying to give it away."

Nell is aware that both of them have started self-consciously arguing in front of Baldwin as if they are in front of a judge.

"She's already taken it to the museum," Pansy addresses her father. All pretense of him being uninterested is gone.

"I was being responsible," Nell says.

"When were you going to tell us about it? After you found out what it's worth?" Pansy says.

"Clearly, we need a professional inventory," Baldwin says.

"I'll be ordering one soon as executor," Nell says, reminding them both of her role.

"Reema Patel called me," Pansy continues to her father, excluding Nell. "Told me some member of my family she'd never met before came down to the museum. She wanted to make sure everything was aboveboard." Pansy turns to

Nell. "Quite frankly, she wondered if you weren't some imposter trying to use the Quincy name."

Nell buries her sheepish feelings. Of course this is precisely how she'd felt. "As executor, I don't need to clear every move I make past you. And I'm not hiding anything." She opens one of Baldwin's grocery bags on the counter to focus on something to do.

"If you're going to be high-handed, this is going to get old fast," Pansy says.

"I'm not being high-handed."

"Why didn't you tell me what it was?" Pansy says, ramping up now. "Reema started angling for me to bring it in, made suggestions about getting it in the conservation lab. I'm sure she wants to get big donors down there with it, too."

"You wish," Nell says.

"Girls," Baldwin says, taking the bag of food out of Nell's hands. "I'm afraid I stand with Pansy on this one." As if he needs to say that he stands with his own daughter.

Nell wants to remind them that it's her gift and she is the executor, but politics win out.

"Come on." Baldwin gives Pansy a significant look, and a whole conversation passes between father and daughter. Then he ushers her out of the house, the two of them in close whispered conversation. Nell hears "Not now" and "Come to the house."

THE GYMKHANA

May lagged upstairs, ensuring they arrived late to the hunt club. Ethan drove onto the polo field and parked next to the other cars so they could "ride the bumper" as spectators. Loulou and Dicky and their friends tromped over the grass to shake hands and say hello. Some greeted Ambrose with forced cheer. Some waited to be reintroduced, as if they'd never met.

The hem of May's long white pleated dress dragged in the sodden grass above her saddle shoes. Loulou's friends reached in the neckline of May's blouse to lift the Indian necklace for inspection, touching it and stealing sideways glances at Ambrose.

When May joined him after her hellos, he couldn't resist. "It looks good on you." He nodded toward the lace collar of her white voile blouse.

"If you're going to comment every time I wear it, it's going to get tiresome." She crossed an arm over her waist.

"Why? Are you going to wear it every day?" He wanted it back, the way she used to be light with him.

He thought he'd embarrassed her. She ducked her head,

looking at the ground. Then she reached behind her neck to untie the gilded cords, returning the necklace on the spot.

"May . . ." Ambrose said. It hadn't been so easy to rile her before. Now, she reacted to his every word. "Don't." He reached out to stop her hands.

She flicked off his fingers. "Maybe I'll donate it to the cause." She continued struggling with the knots. Ambrose didn't dare touch her again.

Ethan came to her side then, gave her a puzzled look, and calmly put his good hand over hers on her neck. Then he turned to Ambrose as if he'd done nothing, his hand still on her nape, and said, "This is the end of the last chukka."

May didn't stop fiddling with the ties, and Ambrose could see Ethan's grip becoming tighter. "I thought we already decided this," Ethan said to her.

"It's mine, isn't it?" she said, dropping her hands to her side.

"What do you think?" Ethan turned to his brother. "Do you think she should give your gift away?"

There was no way for Ambrose to safely answer this, and so he remained silent. The half-undone knot trailing down May's back made Ambrose worry that the necklace would fall off. The horn sounded, ending the game to loud applause.

"Missed the whole thing," Ethan said as he steered May by the back of her neck around toward the terrace of the club for lunch.

Dicky and Loulou were already seated at their table in an exclusive tête-à-tête. Arabella was on their right. May had invited her. And next to Arabella, leaning into her face with aggressive cheer, was Declan O'Brennan, a young lawyer Ethan had recently hired.

The red-faced Irishman was sweating, despite sitting under the awnings, his dark suit too bulky and too businesslike for the day. He mopped his brow with a table napkin, grinning at one of Arabella's stories. His thick, well-groomed reddish mustache only made him look more sweltering and made his face more ruddy.

Ambrose thought the man looked like he belonged outside a west side speakeasy with a baseball bat in his hands, which Ambrose suspected provided some of the appeal for his brother. O'Brennan was younger than Ethan and a refreshing change from the ancient sages tenured in Israel's company. Most of those old wizards spent half the day dozing at their desks and the other half explaining how and why most things he wanted couldn't get done. Wanting a proxy and his own counsel, Ethan had gone out and hired the youngest and most ambitious lawyer he could find. Ethan said Declan was the only lawyer he'd ever met who'd find a way, who'd make it so, who said yes. O'Brennan had ensconced himself in the company with his decisive dealing with the Sandusky fire, and even Israel had been impressed. It reflected well on Ethan that he'd spotted talent in the outsider, and O'Brennan never forgot who had been his original benefactor. It meant O'Brennan was Ethan's eyes and ears at Israel's company now.

Somehow Ethan had twisted enough arms on the membership committee to get O'Brennan into the hunt club. It surprised Ambrose that a man like that would be interested in society, would be a joiner. Then again, Ambrose never needed to worry about joining anything. His invitations came by right.

Ambrose noted that throughout the afternoon May

wouldn't look at O'Brennan, and only addressed him when it was impossible not to, despite his many failed attempts to engage her—a pointed lack of sociability in the usually sparkling May. Even after the horse auction started and O'Brennan bought the first horse, a gelding called the Cad, May barely acknowledged him.

O'Brennan for his part was either impervious to these slights, or alternately too busy trying to recruit Arabella to his admiration society to notice. Arabella seemed a willing acolyte. She laughed at nearly everything O'Brennan said, her eyes locked on his face in rapt attention. Ambrose suspected Arabella wasn't genuinely interested in what he was saying, but was delighted by his gaucheness.

And examples of his gaucheness abounded. It was whispered among the guests that though the club was dry, O'Brennan "was doing something about it." Soon a generous silver flask circulated discreetly under the table-tops. And the man conducted his bidding with a flourish of crass bravado. He entered at the last moment, winning by a gasp-inducing, and unnecessary, one hundred dollars. And he spoke in an affected hush, as if he'd read somewhere that a gentleman was known by the low tenor of his voice. Chairs had to be rearranged to hear him.

Ambrose could feel the tension rising between May and Ethan as each successive horse was sold and Ethan's paddle never left the table, even for the horses Ambrose knew were a bargain. May fumbled with the necklace at her throat. When a lull of quiet settled over the table, Loulou, who never could stand silence, turned to Ambrose.

"So tell me," she said, "how much did you pay for that necklace?"

Ambrose thought the question rude, even among family. "Nothing. I stole it."

"Yes, you're very funny," Ethan said, jumping in, obviously interested in this topic. "Tell us."

"Why do you want to know?" Ambrose challenged his brother. "Feeling the need to pay me back?" Ethan had finally deposited the check for Ambrose's loan. Monetarily, they were even.

Ethan poured a nip from O'Brennan's flask into his cup. "Generous, extravagant," he said, replacing the cork. "Little strange, don't you think?"

"Well, you can't repay me," Ambrose said, and no one at the table failed to hear the defiance in his voice. "It didn't cost anything. I bartered for it."

"You didn't tell me that," May said, reaching for O'Brennan's flask for the first time all afternoon. Ethan pretended to ignore her and handed it back to its owner. O'Brennan brazenly leaned across the table to give it to May with a courtly air, glad to have May receive something of his.

"I was invited to a small dinner at a maharaja's palace, and after dinner his son, the prince, asked each of us to tell a story. He gave us gifts in appreciation, based on how well he liked the tale."

"You're like an epic Greek poet," Loulou said, too excited. Ambrose wanted to tell her to calm down.

"Guests performing like trained monkeys," Ethan said. "What will they think of next in the East? Harems, pleasure palaces . . ."

"What was the story?" May asked, kindly for once. The pleasure palace comment had displeased her.

"I think he planned on giving the gifts anyway, but I told a little story about a man who fell in love."

"So novel," May said flatly, and it didn't escape Ambrose's notice that Ethan glanced at her when she said it.

"Let's hear it," Ethan said, throwing down the gauntlet.

Ambrose began. "There was a young and penniless man who shared his last crust of bread with an old beggar woman shivering on the street. When the woman put the food in her mouth, she turned into a beautiful queen in flowing robes. She said, 'Because you have shown kindness to me when you had so little, I give you this golden key. It can open any lock. But use caution, for some locks are not meant to be opened.' The key itself was a beautiful thing, the bow inlaid with pearl and diamond and the bittings etched with ancient runes. When the young man looked up, the queen was gone.

"His first thought was to head directly to a bank, but on his way there he came across a bakery, closed for the night. With his stomach grumbling he used the key, his heart soaring when the lock tumbled and the door swung free. He ate his fill of pastries, leaving the rest and quietly locking the door behind him.

"In the days that followed he used his key, always at night and always taking only what he needed. He took a new suit from the tailor, new shoes from the cobbler, and a hat from the haberdasher. No one seemed to stop him with his new acquisitions during daylight, and so he became bolder. He took a bottle of fine wine, a box of cigars, and he even slipped into the museum one night and took his favorite painting straight off the wall."

"Don't you just wish?" May said, a little dreamily. "I know what I'd take."

"Well," Ambrose continued, a bit pointedly. "Having all he could want, the man had a thought for those who might benefit from his key. That first night he went into the bazaar and opened all the animal cages. The second night he went to the apothecary and unlocked all the medicines, placing them outside on the street for those in need. The third night he went to the jail and released all those who were falsely imprisoned."

"I wonder how he figured that out," Ethan said. "Sounds like one of those know-it-all types to me."

"The key called to him now." Ambrose ignored his brother. "He rarely passed a lock that he didn't feel compelled to open. And so one night, as he walked in the city beneath the moonlight, he spied a small wooden door, carved with vines and flowers, in the side of a tall stone building. Unlocking it, a flight of twisting stairs led him high until he reached a tiny chamber where a woman lay sleeping—a woman so beautiful that even the moon wondered at her beauty. Around her chest, three thick steel bands encased her heart. She awoke and they instantly fell in love."

"Isn't that how it always works?" asked Arabella.

"They lived in bliss, unlocking doors by night and sleeping in each other's arms by day. But gradually she began to complain that the metal binds around her heart were tight and constricting. She asked him to unlock them. He agreed, as the steel cage around her chest had begun to scrape him, too, cold and unyielding. When the man put the key in the lock he heard a loud crack, like the snap of something breaking. 'Don't mind it,' she said. 'It's only the old tumblers in the lock, unused to being opened.' But with the first turn of the key, the definite sound of steel snapping unnerved him. 'Go ahead,' she now begged. When finally he unlocked all three bands, the woman's face turned pale, but she smiled. She began to gasp for breath, yet joy lit her eyes. The man scrambled to reattach the steel bands, thinking she was dying, but it was no use. His love morphed before his eyes into a bird with scarlet plumage and a gold-feathered crest and flew away into the night without a look back. Bereft and heartbroken, he put the steel bands on himself, locked his heart tight, and threw the key into the river, where it lies even to this day."

"Oh bravo, most Gothic," Loulou said.

"That's it?" Ethan blurted. "I prefer happy endings."

"It was a happy ending," May said quietly.

To his embarrassment, Ambrose blushed. "Believe it or not, my story wasn't the worst one."

"Maybe we should do that next time I have a party," Arabella said. "Tell stories for prizes."

"His story wasn't that good," Ethan said.

"Kinda artsy," O'Brennan said, as if his review mattered.

"I'd have loved to have been there," May said. "To travel."

It was what Ambrose wished she'd said before he left, wished she'd agreed to when he'd asked. "You will," Ambrose said, trying to be expansive, but even he felt the weakness in this promise. He nodded toward his brother; including Ethan in the exchange seemed the best course. "You should take her."

"He doesn't take me places," May said. "I'll just have to go off. If I wait for him, it'll never happen."

Ethan seemed to come alive then. "I'm not sending my wife to India. The trip over there would have you in fits. I can just hear it now." He adopted a whiny, nasty imitation of a female voice. "Ethan, I've lost my tickets. Ethan, the maid has lost my dress. Ethan, they expect me to eat potted meat."

Ambrose craned his head around May to look at his brother full in the face. He thought the comments unwise.

It was then that the last horse was called to be auctioned, a heavyweight warmblood with a rampant lion brand named the Ragman.

The crowd, worn out from the bidding and with empty pockets, was bored and ready to move on to the afternoon dancing; plus, the horse looked powerful, a handful. In deference to her hostess, Arabella threw in a low-ball bid when the audience began to fidget. An uncomfortable shuffling and averting of eyes ruffled around the terrace as everyone wished the situation finished.

"Don't you dare," Ethan said under his breath to May, who was reaching for a paddle, but he was looking at Ambrose when he said it.

Ambrose thought he might dare. Ethan had been grating on him all afternoon. Ambrose might end the auction decently, he thought. He might please May by buying the horse and thereby donating to her cause. She seemed to be having a difficult time this afternoon. He might not want to borrow a horse from his brother ever again. He might not want to be in his brother's debt, even in the smallest way. Yes, he might dare.

When Ambrose raised his number, Arabella threw her napkin at his chest from across the table in mock outrage.

He was glad for this comic relief, as he'd entered the bidding directly against her. But her joke let him know she didn't mind being outbid, and she didn't raise her number again, either.

When the auctioneer called him as the winner, May smiled at him with warmth, a look of true fondness that took him back to other days. She understood his gesture. He'd understood what it would mean to make it. The crowd was on their feet after the gavel hit, intent on mixing after having sat for so long. May rose, and as Ethan took her arm, quickly and proprietarily Ambrose thought, she turned and mouthed the words "Thank you" at him over her shoulder.

THE INVITATION

After Baldwin and Pansy leave, Nell gnaws on a cold drumstick and drinks warm whiskey while listlessly poking through cupboards in the butler's pantry—lavish sets of china, complete with finger bowls, and stockpiled table linens with thick monograms she can't decipher. Someone's going to have to clean this place out, and like a sinking balloon she realizes it's going to be her.

She's done now with this trip back in time. And she's petulantly cursing her father for leaving so quickly. Pansy has Baldwin; who's in her corner?

She pulls herself up and reminds herself that she is a grown woman who no longer needs her daddy. During this trip, she's constantly had to remind herself that she's no longer a child. Her emotions keep flinging her back into the past. So much has happened since she arrived only days ago for the will meeting, and already she needs distance from it. Emerson left this morning. Lucky him.

She thinks back to shutting down Louis Morell's invitation to dinner. She'd been taken by surprise. Work

keeps her underwater, such that she can't remember the
last time she met someone interesting. The men she
knows in Oregon don't go on dinner dates. And then,
with her father there, there'd been no way to backpedal
and accept Louis's offer. Or perhaps she'd misread the
situation. Maybe it was just a work thing after all. He
must have someone. A man like that, of course he does.
She thinks maybe she'll call him. All she has is his office
number, and she leaves her name and number with the
assistant.

In less than a minute her phone rings with an unknown
number.

"Glad you called the office. I've got a bunch of voice
mails from Pansy."

She mentions that she took the necklace to the museum.

"So I've heard," he says.

Is nothing secret in this town? Nell thinks.

"I was meeting with a client out your way . . ." He
trails off.

There's something forced in his voice, and she's almost
sure this story is a ginned-up excuse to see her, the thought
both creepy and exciting.

"Stop by, why don't you?" she invites.

When he agrees, she hangs up and runs through the
house, throwing out the chicken and trying to decide if
she has enough time to brush her teeth but refreshing her
whiskey instead.

"Making the final call," she says in a mock solemn voice
as she opens the door, relieved to see someone, anyone,
who's not family. "Rewriting the will to jilt the third wife
and leave everything to the nubile nurse." She's feeling

the whiskey, feeling the release from the tension of the morning, feeling the relief it's not Pansy or Baldwin.

"Come on now, not everyone practices cutting-edge intellectual property law. Some of us are journeyman lawyers, serving the people."

"Or the dog? I love it when they leave everything to the Pekingese. And a tiny percentage of estates need lawyers, journeyman."

"Not all of us were on the law review, okay?"

"You've been researching me?"

"A lucky guess," he says.

He's already walking toward the flower room, leading her with that ease he has. He's not impressed by the house and not dismissive of it, either. His energy of competence with a soupçon of detachment makes her want to let him handle everything. Maybe this is why Loulou chose him, in addition to the nice view. He accepts a glass of whiskey, rolls up his sleeves, putting his veiny forearms on display, and settles on the droopy chintz sofa in the living room.

He sits silently across from her, like a priest or a therapist. His particular branch of their profession requires a combination of both.

A cloud passes over his face as she explains her museum meeting and that the Moon might be worth more than anyone anticipated, resulting in Pansy's not-so-veiled threats.

"They could make an argument that it's part of Pansy's jewelry and somehow got misplaced," Nell says, taking a sip of whiskey. "I mean, she basically did. Could also argue it's part of the contents."

He's nodding deeply. Does she imagine it, or does he

lean back from her? "It won't fly. I worded the provision to avoid a claim like that." He's become stiff, all business, and she worries that she's offended him, implied his drafting is Swiss cheese and subject to challenge.

"I'm not saying they'd win if they made a challenge," Nell says. "I'm saying they could make it hard for me."

"Of course they could," he says, while shaking his head no. "But it would cost them." They both know pride might have the Quincys shelling out for a grudge, but legal fees would have them standing down. "Cost them quite a bit, actually. Besides, anyone can contest the will, you know that."

"Still . . ." she says.

"Still." Louis inclines his head in agreement. "Vegas isn't even putting that one on the board. Also, now you have an ace up your sleeve."

When she doesn't react to his little quip, he says stiffly, "If you're worried about this, I can recommend outside counsel."

She realizes then he's taking offense, though he's trying not to look it as he loosens his tie. Every time he's been here she's had the impression that he belongs. He certainly feels comfortable enough settled back, ankle on knee, a convincing cover to the annoyance she hears in his voice.

"What ace?"

"Tax apportionment. Basically, the estate pays taxes on any specified gifts unless it's been stated otherwise. Loulou didn't specify, and I didn't push. There was no reason to since I didn't know the necklace was so valuable, hadn't seen it, no insurance policy on it."

Nell gets it right away. "So if I sold the necklace, the estate takes the tax hit."

"Even if you don't sell it. But now that we know what that thing likely is, the taxes on the sale would probably bankrupt Loulou's estate. A great place to negotiate from."

He's dropped by, but she's the one who took it as an invitation to talk shop. Perhaps he wanted to keep this all off the clock. Or perhaps he'll bill her. These are her concerns now that she's executor and keeping track of expenses. But it just felt so good to talk it through with someone.

"I've already taken up a good amount of your time," she says. "Thanks for coming so far out of your way." She'd like to make up for flubbing his prior invitation, would like to ask him to dinner. But now he might think her suggestion is a ploy to pump him for free advice.

"Why so formal?" he asks.

"I thought you might bill me."

"Wow," he deadpans. "Lawyers in Oregon must be cutthroat."

"I was the one who started talking shop."

"So maybe you should buy me dinner. You know, bartering."

She smiles, and she doesn't miss his pitch this time. "Big fancy firms accept meals as payment now?"

"You should know," he says with a delighted smile at her tacit invitation.

"It's your call. I don't know any restaurants here. I'm completely at your mercy."

"Excellent," he says with an exaggerated grin. "That's just how I like it."

THE CHARTREUSE ON ICE

After May publicly offered at the gymkhana to board the Ragman at the farm, Ethan had little choice but to go along. Ambrose fell into a pattern of taking the train between downtown and the farm on the weekends to ride with his brother, attend May's parties, and return to his father's house on Sunday night to spend his weeks working in town. Months ago, even a week or so, he wouldn't have been able to imagine such a schedule. And if he didn't think about it too hard, it felt like the most natural thing in the world.

Work was a dreary haze of what seemed like never-ending accounting books. Ambrose was most interested in the cleanup of the Sandusky fire and the aid fund for the families, but whenever he inquired he was told that the fund was in good hands and being distributed properly. The mine was shut and obviously not to be reopened. What was needed was time, his father said. There was really nothing more to be done.

After these weeks in town, weekends at May and Ethan's became what Ambrose most looked forward to.

Ethan, Ambrose noted, was never expected at the offices in town. He conducted most of his business out at the farm, sitting in the gunroom by the hour, loudly taking meetings down the telephone line and smoking cigars with the windows closed. May called it his Indian smoke house, and the ceiling was already turning gray. When Ambrose asked Israel about his brother's schedule, his father had looked at him from under his paled-out gray eyebrows and said simply, "Newlyweds." Ethan only came to town for board meetings.

This Friday, as Ambrose entered the farmhouse, he heard O'Brennan's familiar voice booming from the gunroom. Ambrose found May in the living room, sipping Chartreuse and ice. Three sets of large French doors were open to the scent of baking box hedges still in the sun and juniper bushes cooling in the afternoon shade of the house.

"Help yourself," she said, hooking a thumb back toward the flower room. "To whatever you can rummage up in there."

She fiddled with the jade Bakelite knobs on the radio next to her. "Lucky Lindy" followed him into the bright octagonal room with terrazzo floors and a fountain made out of Peeble tile set in a wall. The room was meant for flower arranging and other feminine country arts. Ambrose wasn't sure if Ethan had been anticipating a wife who enjoyed ladylike pastimes or if the room was simply what one expected in any fine country house. He doubted May used it for flowers. There were no cupboards full of vases, no clipping shears or gardening gloves left in casual disarray.

But there was Ethan's stash of hooch, hidden behind the recessed panels.

Ambrose fixed himself a small glass of gin, and joined May in the living room. As he lowered himself in the seat across from her, he felt the warring consciousness that dogged him nearly constantly now.

He wanted to be anyplace but here. There was no place else he'd rather be.

"Arabella's coming tonight," May said, as if she'd ordered his favorite dish for dinner. She organized a dinner party every Friday night, always with an eligible female acquaintance "rounding out the table." Ambrose noted that she'd not invited Arabella until now, one of the few girls he would have liked to see.

"Your sister, too." She rattled the ice in her glass, her drink nearly gone, and he wondered if it was her first or her third. She was sunk down in her chair, glum. He inquired about her week, and after a moment she leaned forward. "Do you think . . ." He could smell the herbaceous liquor on her breath from his seat, her voice low, as if afraid of being overheard. "Do you think there was anything Ethan could have done to prevent it?"

"Is that what they're talking about?" Ambrose's interest was piqued. His father would barely tell him a thing, had shut him out so completely from Sandusky, had claimed everything was in order. He should have known. Why else would O'Brennan travel all the way out here? Ambrose made to stand, to go in and insert himself in the business he wanted to be a part of.

But May stood and quickly grabbed his wrist. Her face showed true concern. She mentioned the fire in Sandusky every time he saw her now.

"Likely not," he answered truthfully, looking in her

eyes, though it was true he was only trying to placate her. "You can't prevent tragedy. It's all in how you deal with it afterward. That's all there is, really."

"You know he sealed them in there." She jerked her head toward the door. "He made O'Brennan do it. O'Brennan shouldn't have agreed, should have advised him against it. What good's an Irishman if he won't put up a fight when it's needed?"

Looking at May's face, he realized the source of her dislike of the lawyer—misplaced blame. "Ethan was acting on the best advice he had at the time. I'd be surprised if O'Brennan didn't try to find some other way around it. That's the recommendation with seam fires. They can damage the town if you're not careful. You don't think he'd do it callously?" he asked at the look on her face.

"He could have tried to save them. They managed to get Ethan out before they closed it."

"Well, you were here, not me, but I'd imagine he saved more lives than he didn't."

May only looked out the window. "You're right. He was here," she said.

In the intervening weeks, he'd expected the pull he felt toward May to lessen, to ease in her close proximity, the anesthetizing effect of familiarity.

But sometimes, at times like this, the urge to touch her rose in his body, unchecked. Those were the times he forgot she was his brother's wife. Times when he remembered that he'd known her first.

"They'll be a while," she said.

"Then come outside." He offered his hand casually, and when she didn't take it, he headed out the French doors.

He felt May follow, but then she overtook him, purposefully guiding them away from the pond and the tennis house, down a straight path mown through a hay field, dotted with blue chicory, goldenrod, and Queen Anne's lace, grown tall and not yet cut. A red-winged blackbird dove at their heads, clicking and shrieking, protecting a nearby nest in the grass.

He noted she'd refilled her glass before bringing it with her. He remembered a friend in college advising that one could tell when a person had trouble with drink by the way she held the glass like it didn't matter, but never let it out of her grasp.

"He killed those men for money," she finally said. The bright blue of the sky somehow mitigated the harshness of her words. As if in the open field of burnt hay and wildflowers even the ugliest things could be said and rendered bearable.

"May . . ." Her accusation was the beginning of making a case against Ethan, a convincing of herself.

"For convenience, then." Her turning against Ethan made him wary, but faintly hopeful.

"They were already dead. It was a sacrifice. Who's to say he didn't save more lives than if he hadn't . . ." His role as Ethan's defender was awkward, and he was embarrassed to realize it made him feel magnanimous.

"Sacrifice," she hummed over the word. "The ends justify the means. In the end it was for the best. That what you mean?"

"His arm . . ." Ambrose stated. "Surely you can't doubt his seriousness."

"His seriousness about what?"

"About saving people."

"People?" She turned to him with a blank, uncomprehending face. "He saved *me*."

Ambrose's vision narrowed, as if May were the only thing in the world.

"It's me who he saved," she continued.

Ambrose felt a confirmation of something glimpsed in his periphery since his return, half-seen in the way she unflinchingly took Ethan's damaged hand, in the way Ethan hovered behind her chair, in the way she turned the pages of his newspaper, in all their intricate rituals.

"But why? How were you even there?"

"The fire had been burning. I couldn't believe they were just going to sit there and wait for it to burn out. I couldn't believe they hadn't come up with anything to do to put it out." This was a familiar line of May's, and he was concerned she was about to veer off when she seemed to right herself. "Ethan had already gone with your father. I'd been sitting around, feeling useless, and so I took the train over. I thought at least I'd join the bucket brigade, talk to the women, something. And I was stupid. I was . . ." She stopped, controlling her breathing, fighting tears. "I can't look at you when I say this, but I was thinking of you. I was thinking of a way to make you understand that I was as adventurous as you, that I'm not some ineffectual . . . I don't know. They wouldn't let me near the fire, so I just grabbed a bucket and ran in.

"It was the stupidest thing I've ever done. Men were yelling at me to stop, but I thought they were being overly cautious. I wanted to help. But I didn't realize how dark it'd be inside. The smoke . . . I got confused. I couldn't get out. Someone told him I'd run in, and he came in after me. Pulled me in the right direction, but not before a beam collapsed on his arm."

Ambrose could barely understand what she said next. "I had to leave him, you understand? I ran out and four men went in and rescued him from under the burning timber. He was unconscious when he came out. I thought he was dead."

In that moment Ambrose felt the rushing knowledge of the silent organization and agreement of his family, who consistently edited this information out of all their dealings with him. They told him Ethan saved people, glossing over who and skipping ahead quickly to remark on his heroism. Ambrose had been washed away in a tide of agreement, praising his brother, never needling too hard on the particulars of a tender topic. How many did he save or who? These were obnoxious questions. What did it matter? A hero was a hero, whether he saved one or twenty, whether he saved a miner or May.

"I thought you knew." Her eyes were on the grass, tears on her lashes held back by a twisting mouth. "The reason he's like that is because of me."

What Ambrose had thought was pity was actually indebtedness. He'd seen his brother as manipulating her compassion as he recovered in his hospital bed, pulling her strings. He'd never understood why she'd succumbed. It made sense now. Ethan had literally put his life on the line to save hers. How much more can anyone ever ask?

"That's not how it works," he said.

"Isn't it?"

"He would have done it for anyone."

"That's what he says. I really don't think that makes it any better."

"He would have done it for anyone who's as important to me as you are."

"As I was," she said.

"As you are." And more quietly he added, "I would have done it, too."

She shoved one hand against his chest, surprisingly hard. "I never could resist you." She was breathing through her mouth, trying for control.

He smiled at that, enjoyed being irresistible, though she had been nothing but scrupulous. "No," he said.

"It's wrong," she said, and his heart skipped a beat at her thought process.

"Your definitions are small." It sounded flippant and joking, but he was serious. "Think broader."

When she turned back toward the house and stormed off down the field, he didn't follow her.

THE SPEAKEASY

Louis drives Nell downtown to a former speakeasy where the twenty-dollar cocktails are crafted by attractive ladies with full-sleeve tattoos and pin-up makeup.

"Slice of the Northwest, right here in the Midwest," Nell says when they sit facing the burl-wood vintage bar.

"The lumberjack trope is actually quite close to the steelworker cliché. Brothers from another mother," he says.

"Sisters from a different mister."

"Both of which have become mythic recently, right? I had a feeling the lady doesn't like beer."

"The lady does not," Nell says, and orders a sidecar from the leather-bound bar tome.

They're halfway through the usual date questions, questions about where they went to school and where they've been living, where they've traveled and where they're going.

"So this apportionment thing," Nell says, "I'm thinking it might cut both ways, right? If she knew what it was, she would have planned out the taxes, insured it. Since she didn't do that, they can make an argument that she didn't know what it was or what she was doing."

"I forget you're smart," he says, hooking his foot under her bar stool and dragging her closer. She notes he's finished his cocktail. "Because a civilian in your position would be terrified right now."

"Having drinks with an attractive attorney? Didn't know that was military-grade risky."

"I like that word, 'attractive,'" he says, before ordering another drink. "But I just meant she knew what she was doing. I kept asking her if I could see the thing, if she could find the necklace for me. Don't know if you know, but she played dotty fairly well. 'I misplaced it.' 'I'm looking for it.' I should have known. She knew what it was. It was up there with her the whole time. Maybe not specifically what it was worth in today's dollars, but she knew."

"It's just so out of character. On so many levels."

"Tax apportionment is a card for you to play. Also, it doesn't really matter, because everything I draft is watertight."

"Like a ship?"

"Like a friggin' battleship."

She smiles as his second drink arrives, further loosening his tongue. "It occurs to me that I might have some reporting duty," she says. "It is stolen, after all."

"You don't know it's stolen. You don't even know for sure if it's the Moon of Nizam."

"I saw it on Reema Patel's screen," Nell says.

"Who cares? Doesn't mean that's what you have. I'd bet you have a good amount of gray area to play with here. To figure out what's what before anyone else gets involved."

"Patel could be calling in the cavalry—UNESCO, Interpol, Homeland Security."

"Did you just say Interpol to me right now? Like this is *Mission: Impossible* or something?"

She shrugs her shoulder over into his then, in the middle of the crowded bar, her mind full of squirrelly thoughts. When he shifts his weight into hers in response, with even a little more force, she wants to grin.

"Patel wouldn't do that. She wants to get her hands all over it as much as you do," he says with a roguish grin. "Let me look into it for you."

Really, men are so easy. A slight pressure on the shoulder, a slight something they can fix, a way they can finagle being needed, and it's on.

There's a moment before his lips touch hers, before they start down this path, when she thinks maybe the anticipation is enough. The tension. She considers bailing out. And as if reading her mind he says, "It's good, right? The buildup?"

She kisses him then, because it's too perfect not to. And it's a perfect sort of kiss—soft and open and overwhelming in a way that sends blood racing through her body.

Louis leans away from her on his bar stool. "This was stupid," he says. "I shouldn't get involved with a client."

"There's going to be involvement?" To her delight he actually blushes, and it's a heady thing to have this man, all sinew and smarts, a little flustered. "I'm not your client," she says, thrilled and powerful.

"Technically, as executor, you are," he says pedantically, eyes on her mouth.

She moves in close, going slowly, but the moment still feels fast. And she has a thought for whether she's reading this situation correctly, whether this whole trip hasn't been a brewing pot of emotion now about to boil over. When their lips touch again, he tastes as good as he smells.

With closed eyes he simply says, "Come home with me."

No pretense and no apology, no ramp-up or side winding. She can't match his bluntness; they'd barrel on with no brakes. Then again, they both know where this is going.

"I think I promised to feed you," she says.

"Not hungry," he replies.

"I'm staying out at the farm," she tries, a lame obstacle.

"Stay with me," he says, coming in to kiss her again.

"Why so bossy?"

"Why so tempting?"

"I like that word, 'tempting,'" she says.

"You are. So come," he says, sliding his keys across the bar toward her, acknowledging her half-drunk cocktail next to his second. "With me."

THE DUCK HUNTING

Ambrose was in the bathroom gargling water and bicarbonate of soda when his brother appeared in the doorway. Ambrose startled, swallowed half, and choked on the other.

"Not expecting me?" Ethan asked.

Ambrose braced both hands on the pedestal sink as he sputtered and coughed, clearing his throat. "You're silent," he said.

"Are you ill?" Ethan asked, with genuine interest.

"A bug, I think." Ambrose shouldered past Ethan, feeling seedy and horrifically guilty, which made him annoyed and angry. The twisted bed linen and general odor of a distillery gave away the true nature of his illness.

"Shall I ring for another egg yolk?" Ethan asked, glancing out of the side of his eye.

Dinner with O'Brennan last night had been a tense affair, lightened only temporarily by Arabella's arrival. But Ambrose had watched as she sailed in on silk and pearls and slowly deflated as she sat at a table that became as leaden as the gluey attempt at Vichyssoise Glacée the cook sent out for the first course.

The atmosphere at the table set May on edge. Ambrose could see it. O'Brennan tried to engage her in society gossip. But she was distracted, stepping on the buzzer set in the floor to send back the soup and asking the maid to fill the already full water glasses.

Loulou arrived late and sat down as they were clearing the soup. Her excuses were both weak and flustered, as if she'd been summoned at the last minute.

Ambrose couldn't get what May had said in the field out of his mind. She couldn't resist him. He'd felt elated, then abashed, next angry, and finally bewildered, wondering how this entire scenario had actually happened, him eating at May and Ethan's table as a guest. Ambrose tried to keep up his side of the conversation, but nearly everything that came out of his mouth was flat. O'Brennan couldn't engage any of them, not for lack of trying, as he lit up a volley of failed topics that flared over the silver candlesticks and then flamed out. Loulou faded into the walls with her watchful, silent air. Even Arabella was quiet, no doubt feeling the tension eddying around the table.

As a result Ambrose drank quite a bit more than usual. By the time May excused herself before dessert was served, claiming a headache, he was quite drunk.

The moment she left the room, Ethan and O'Brennan rose, saying they'd have rye in the gunroom. Both O'Brennan and Ethan had avoided any mention of what they'd been talking about that afternoon. Ambrose thought it was Ethan's good manners—no business at the table—but it dawned on him that this censoriousness was in deference to May.

When Ambrose followed them, Ethan stopped him at the door.

"You're being rude. Go talk to Arabella." Ethan's unscarred hand pushed at Ambrose's chest with finality, and then he shut the gunroom door in Ambrose's face.

How expertly his brother had maneuvered things. Ambrose would have to knock on the door like a pitiable outsider to gain entrance, and Ambrose refused to beg.

He'd had to draw himself up before heading into the living room where Arabella and Loulou sat in superficial conversation, trying to skim over the disaster of the dinner with small talk about Arabella's new dogs.

Arabella rose when she saw him and told him she'd be leaving with a knowing little pat on his arm. She'd managed a conspiratorial eye roll toward the closed gunroom door on her way out, which made him feel better. But his initial spark of anger flared when he came back in the room and saw Loulou sitting up straight, as if she had news to deliver.

"You have to stop," she said.

"You're right. I probably should." He put down the half-full decanter he'd brought into the room.

"I don't mean that," she said nodding her head. "But it's a good idea, too. I meant you have to stop this whole charade."

Ambrose was quiet, both relieved and on the defensive to be caught out. "I don't know what you're talking about."

She sighed. "I hate this pretending. We both know

what you're doing. You're pretending you're back here to, I don't know, be brothers. Anyone who sat at that dinner table tonight knows what you're doing."

"I'm not doing anything."

"Yet." Loulou got up then and went straight for the decanter, where she poured a generous dram but only managed a small sip and a grimace.

"I love you," she said. "You're my brother, but so is he. It's killing me watching you two. This isn't our family. This isn't how we do things."

"What do you know about how this family does things?" Such sentiments always raised Ambrose's ire.

"I saw you," Loulou says. "I saw you and May head down to the pond at your going-away party. You think I'm still some naïve little girl, but I know those feelings don't just disappear. And really, how could they?" She abandoned her drink next to the decanter. "I understand. I really do. But you made your choice. Now it's time to live with it." She turned to face him. "I think you should leave."

"Father's house is not going to help me. I know that much."

"Leave town," she said. "Leave the state. I know how you can be, and you're just going to cause heartache."

"Gee, thanks, Lou." He was trying for levity.

Loulou was in earnest. "It was better when you weren't there. For everyone."

Ambrose picked up the decanter, pondering the heavy lead crystal stopper, thinking how satisfying it would be to throw it through the window. Loulou turning against him, pushing him away, stung.

But he turned for the stairs instead and Loulou's silence as she watched him, not calling him back, not trying to reassure him, made his spirits sink deeper. He'd paused at the top of the stairs. Listening for what, he didn't know exactly. Loulou to call him back and apologize, to tell him they would all be okay. If he'd heard May, he would have gone to her, but still silence greeted him, and he turned for his room.

Now, in the morning light, Ambrose turned his back on his brother, picked up his trousers off the floor, and buttoned them on. "What can I do for you?" he asked, tensed for a confrontation, but doubting one all the same. Ethan wasn't like Loulou. He was rarely direct.

Ethan perched on the foot of a chaise longue, the only place in the room not covered with clothes, books open and breaking the spines, and brimming ashtrays. He was staring at Ambrose's bare chest, his arms, and then he looked away. "You've made yourself a little nest up here." He picked up a shoehorn and slapped it against his thigh.

"You've been kind."

His brother inclined his head in acknowledgment. "You should build out here. Calvin Van Alstyne has a pretty parcel he wants to sell."

Ambrose hadn't seen the Van Alstynes since that night in Mandalay when he'd sat next to them on the riverfront, drinking champagne. Calvin Van Alstyne had since bought a thousand acres of land next to Ethan's farm. May was the reason the area was becoming fashionable.

Ambrose didn't miss the implication in his brother's comment—get your own place. "Where?" he asked.

"Next to the duck pond. Good for shooting. Know how you love it."

Ambrose could think of few things more dreary than shooting harmless mallards on a tiny pond next to his brother for the rest of his life. His enjoyment of the hunt, of almost anything really, was related to the dangerousness of the quarry. The desire to leave rose up in him again. Maybe Loulou was right. Maybe he should leave. He willed himself into silence, to wait for Ethan to get to the point. Perhaps Ethan had noticed something, perhaps he had accusations. Well, if he wanted a confrontation, Ambrose found he had a few accusations of his own.

He was sure now that May still loved him, had never stopped, and had only married Ethan out of duty and pity. And Ethan had calculated on that pity when he'd asked her to marry him. Ambrose wondered, for the first time since he'd seen them dance together at his party those years ago, if Ethan loved her or if he merely wanted what Ambrose had. Ethan never could resist besting him. He'd done it in business, by emulating their father, and now by stealing May. If Ethan wanted to address any of this, Ambrose was ready. Was looking forward to it, actually.

"Father's been called to testify about the fire," Ethan said.

Ambrose slumped back into his bed, felled by the unexpected. "Columbus?" He realized then that the telephone had been ringing in the background all morning. He'd thought that'd been typical.

"Washington. We're taking the train this afternoon."

Ambrose pushed himself up on his elbows, lodging three pillows behind his head.

And in that moment he felt an inkling of that long-lost affection for his brother. A kinship that he hadn't felt since before he'd left. The command that Ambrose help work through a crisis—how could Ambrose say no? Though he'd be working for his father.

"I'll get up." A wave of nausea crashed over him. He lay back in bed, knowing another hour or two of sleep would cure him.

His brother tapped the shoehorn on the nearly empty decanter from last night, ringing the crystal. "I just spoke with Father and he asked . . . well, we agreed . . . you need to look after things from here." At Ambrose's face he added, "In town."

When the light stopped pulsing behind his eyes, Ambrose said, "I'll feel better after a bath, just give me a minute."

"There are going to be decisions. We need someone here. We need someone downtown at the offices." His brother's saying "we" rang in Ambrose's head. Ethan was hiding behind "we" all the time now.

Ethan was scratching his scarred, lifeless hand with the edge of the shoehorn. "Father's been patient. And generous, too. What do you plan to do here if you're not interested in making a contribution?"

"Right," Ambrose said, sitting up. "That's why I should go with you."

"You need to do what's asked of you. I know . . ." And

here he looked off, something catching his eye at the window. "I know that's not your strong suit."

Ambrose felt the indignity rising in him. He felt sure his brother was referring to May, to her request those years ago that he stay. And he saw again the shifting of alliances, a glimpse of the close familiarities between husband and wife.

"I want to help," Ambrose said. But the rest of his brother's statement lay unanswered between them.

It had become a rare thing in his life now to feel guilt. Yet since he'd been home, he was presented with it nearly constantly—a feeling almost as sickening as his hangover.

In the silence, Ethan stood and walked to the window overlooking the driveway. He deftly drew up the sash one-handed, letting in the clean morning air and a cacophony of birdcalls. A breeze moved over the sheets, a reprieve from the close smell of the room. Ambrose sat up, scrubbing his face.

His brother seemed distracted, watching something in the front. And then he angled his face toward the sunlight, warming himself like a cat.

"Why don't I come with you to the train station? We can go into town and talk about who'll go on," Ambrose said, finding his clothes in the bureau next to the bed and taking them into the bathroom with shaking hands. "Father has plenty of people who can stay behind," he called. After quickly shaving and dressing, he lit a cigarette and emerged a few minutes later to find the room empty, his brother gone.

When he went downstairs, the maid told him that his brother had just left in Mr. O'Brennan's car. Mr. O'Brennan had arrived about five minutes ago and hadn't even gotten out of his car before Mr. Ethan joined him and they drove off, she said.

THE CARRIER PIGEONS

To: Cornelia Q. Merrihew, Esq.
From: Louis S. Morrell
Re: Notice of Letter

Ms. Merrihew:

I'm in receipt of a letter from your cousin putting me (and you) on notice that she intends to pursue claims concerning your bequest. I am copied on the original and I would like to confirm your receipt of same.

Additionally, you left your underwear in my bed. Shall I FedEx it to you, care of your office?

He's been sending her emails all week. They've been falling off her screen amid an avalanche of work, but she can't avoid this one.

To: Louis S. Morrell
From: Cornelia Q. Merrihew
Re: re: Notice of Letter

Mr. Morrell—You are mistaken. I am in possession of all my undergarments. Perhaps you should query your other bedmates. And in the future, please contact me via private text to discuss personal matters.

This email acknowledges that I am in receipt of my cousin's letter.

She's not surprised when her phone pings almost immediately.

> **Louis:** Bedmates! You didn't leave anything, as you rightly point out, but I had to say something to get your attention. You've been ignoring my emails. I'm not the greatest at being ignored.

As if anyone could ignore him. That night of the speakeasy, under the pretense of a tour of his house, he'd shown her almost directly to his bedroom. Before she'd had a chance to take in the particulars, he'd already started unbuttoning his shirt. She's getting used to Mr. No Pretense now, but that night she couldn't help but stare at his chest, a leaned-out flex of muscle from neck to wrist, from shoulder to belt buckle. A spare body with a honed mind to match; "gristly," you might call it at his age. "Oh, but it looks good on you, Mr. Morrell," she'd wanted to say.

"My eyes are up here," he'd said, tipping her chin up toward him.

"That's usually my line," she'd said.

"Should I ask what color they are?"

She'd snapped her eyes shut. "Blue. Mine?"

When he'd paused too long, she'd opened them.

"Green. I always hate that game."

"Always, huh?"

"You," he'd said, coming close and reaching inside the neckline of her blouse to slip her bra strap down her arm, "are trouble."

Nell: Apologies. Wasn't ignoring. Work is insane. I'm supposed to believe this phantom underwear was a ruse to get me to pay attention to you? You could also be covering your ass. Confusing me with that other person, the one who can't remember to put on her clothes.

Louis: There's no one else, silly. And I'm not using lady things to cover my ass. Not my type of thing. No judgment on dudes who are into that. After your last night here, you should know what I'm into. I can't stop thinking about it or you. When are you coming back?

He'd been silly and sly that night before she'd left, with an appealing gleam in his eye. She'd like to see him again.

Nell: Might be coming back soon, given the
letter. Would be lovely to see you.

Louis: Lovely? What every man wants to hear.
I think it'd be a little more than lovely.
Shall I come out there first? Exchange
upcoming Cleveland snow for rain.
In this case, I'll take the swap. Also, I
have info for you on duties. Good news
is—no prison for you. Bad news is—I've
always wanted to hike Mt. Rainier. Even
in the rain.

Nell smiles at this. She's already done enough of her
own preliminary research to know that until the Moon is
verified and authenticated she has very few worries about
legalities.

Nell: Top of Rainier is a technical climb
involving crampons and ice axes, but by
all means lace up your Adidas and grab
a water bottle. I'll be working. The case
I'm on does not appear to be settling.

Louis: Is your stiff-arming serious? Or do you
like a little chase?

He'd been straightforward that night, too.
"I'm not drunk," he'd said. "But if you are . . ."
"No," she'd said. "I know what I'm doing."
He'd waited then—appealing and desirous, but never

forcing. When she'd reached forward for a belt loop, pulling him close, that had been all the confirmation he'd needed.

Nell: Apologies. You're lovely. I don't mean to stiff-arm at all. I'm just unused to this.

Louis: No more apologies. And no more with the "lovely." I don't have time to mess around. I like you. When I like something I go right after it.

Nell: I'm an it? How about handsome?

Louis: Better. Don't forget virile, strong, smart, and good at chess, both literal and metaphorical. You could never be an "it," so don't pretend like I'm making you out to be a thing.

Nell: So bossy.

Louis: Seriously, I don't want to tip the scales over into pest, and lovely is rather wan.

Nell: But you really are. Lovely that is. You're a man who uses the word wan. If you come right now, I won't have time to see you. But hold please, for further updates.

Louis: Fine. We can do this the old-fashioned way—letters/texts/whatever. Carrier pigeon, I don't care. I don't know if you know, but I'm very charming.

Nell: Yes, I'm aware.

Louis: And determined.

Nell: Clearly.

THE RAGMAN

Ambrose thought of following Ethan and O'Brennan, of ordering a car to take him to the train station, of not letting them shut him out again, of not letting them close another door in his face. But that was the weak move, wasn't it? Trailing after them like a puppy?

His neck started to itch, close to the surface under his chin where he'd nicked himself shaving, and around the back toward his hairline.

Some movement was needed, some sort of action. After a quick change out of the traveling clothes he'd put on anticipating a train ride, he was out the front door. He crunched down the gravel lane between the high summer grass soon to be baled and headed for Ethan's stables—a large complex of shingled barns a good half mile from the house. His itchiness subsided as he strode.

Ambrose stomped into the barn, but the scent of horse manure and hay mixed with leather soap and liniment transported him out of his thoughts with the promise of exercise, motion, and fresh air. He consciously calmed himself when the stable hand, not more than a boy, led the

Ragman to him. The horse was wary, and reading Ambrose's energy, the animal shied. Poor beast, none of this was his fault. Though he had a pitiable name, the Ragman was a black nearly eighteen hands. Some lineage from Holland, Ambrose had been told the day at the auction. Ambrose ordered a black saddle and black tack along with his own black britches and boots. He figured if he was going to be the ne'er-do-well brother, he might as well go all the way.

He was looking forward to his ride now. But the stableboy wouldn't meet his eye, and paranoid thoughts raced through Ambrose's mind—some help in the house had overheard him and May, someone had seen Ethan and O'Brennan leave him behind—everyone knew how servants talked.

"I hear Mr. Van Alstyne is up on the mountain," the boy said shyly. Ambrose adjusted his thoughts. The boy was just a young farmhand, deferential to the owner's brother. "New horse, too. Thoroughbred, so I've heard. Fast." Ambrose looked forward to seeing his contented friend Van Alstyne. No surprise he'd be riding a racehorse off track. He had a penchant for horses he could hardly handle. "But fragile in the legs, I'm told," the boy said.

Ambrose approached the mounting block.

"My sister works over there," the hand explained as Ambrose threw a leg over. "At the Van Alstyne place."

"I'll keep an eye out for him," Ambrose said, and clicked his tongue to get the Ragman moving.

The boy tipped his cap.

Ambrose guided the horse up the small trail to the side of the "mountain," really not more than a tree-covered hill. The stable smell gave way to dirt and leaf mold and a carpet of green ferns. A slight wind at the tops of the trees frothed everything up, including his spirits. Cured from this morning's mess, and filled with pure air, Ambrose started to feel solid again, clear and vital.

He was nearing the top of the hill when he heard the dull, thudding hooves of another rider and saw a chestnut streak moving through the trees. The rider took a jump over three neatly stacked logs wedged in between a locust and a tulip tree. After a sound landing, the horse slowed and pranced, dancing back toward the beginning of the run-up, wanting more. It was then that Van Alstyne turned and raised a hand.

He dismounted, throwing the reins loosely over his arm like a cloak, and walked over to Ambrose with the other hand outstretched. Ambrose had the feeling then that Van Alstyne had timed the jump for maximum effect.

"Ambrose, my boy." He was only a few years Ambrose's senior, and this avuncular tone was new. Ambrose made the man reach up to shake hands, leaning over only as far as was polite.

"Get down off that beast and help me put another log on this jump," Van Alstyne ordered.

Ambrose dismounted and tied the Ragman's reins to a nearby maple sapling. The horse didn't need to be fully restrained, just needed to think he was.

He walked over to where Van Alstyne was stooping down to lift one end of a log. "Grab that and pull it over here," he said.

The two men grunted and heaved the log up and on top of the stack of tree trunks, wedged between saplings so they wouldn't roll.

"Surprised to find you up here," Van Alstyne said, wiping mud on his haunches, mindless of his expensive riding kit. "With all your family has on its hands right now."

Ambrose kicked the logs to make sure they were secure. "Ethan's the one heading to DC, then?"

Ambrose assumed the hearings must be in the papers already. There was something about the fire, the investigation, and the affected families nearly every day now. He knew Ethan had taken to hiding the papers from May, but she just demanded them from the maids.

"I'm back here to man the ship. Really, they're going to need a lot of counsel from home."

"I'm sure," Van Alstyne said, rather too heartily. In a change of topic he said, "But your brother's becoming quite the land baron, isn't he? Vivian says he's crazy about land." Somehow Van Alstyne had become the type of man who attributed his thoughts to his wife. Whether he was in perpetual surety of her agreement, or afraid to express his views as his own, Ambrose suspected the verbal tic was the former. The Van Alstynes had always been enviously well suited. Ambrose wanted to ask him about it, wanted to ask how it was maintained, and if it was as easy and blissful as it looked from the outside. He didn't know if he'd be relieved or disappointed if their union required compromise and hard labor. Ambrose hoped there was at least one easy love story in the world, but he couldn't pry into the unknowable privacy of someone else's marriage.

"I don't know about crazy," Ambrose said.

"Made me an offer on that duck pond at the far end of my property. Pretty little thing, but I wasn't thinking of parting with it. He named quite a generous sum."

Ambrose's ears burned. Was Ethan trying to best him again, make him want something, and then get it first? Or did he intend to gift it to Ambrose, as an act of charity? Either way, it was enraging. Why had he suggested it to Ambrose this morning? His brother's actions were never clear to him. Was this an act of keeping his brother close, or an enemy closer?

"Frankly, I was surprised," Van Alstyne was saying. "Ethan's never really been the sportsman, has he? And now, well . . ." He trailed off, embarrassed by even this tangential mention of Ethan's handicap that made it impossible for him to shoot. "Makes Vivian think he's out to buy up half the county. Maybe he'd let you shoot over there. I'm sure you're quite the marksman after your travels."

They continued, with Van Alstyne asking many detailed questions about Ambrose's itinerary after Mandalay and Ambrose asking many detailed questions about the construction of the Van Alstyne manse next door.

"Now, you tell Ethan to call me when he gets back. Tell him to come see me about that duck pond," Van Alstyne said, clicking the chestnut racehorse into a walk down the opposite path.

Ambrose continued toward the top of the little mountain, a strange hill that made him feel like he'd ridden back in time. As he rode along the north side of the rise, the views spread all the way to Lake Erie and then across to Canada. The vast horizon made him feel that if he kept riding he would meet water and then perhaps a boat to take him off into all that blue.

He thought of that night on the riverfront in Mandalay with the Van Alstynes, when they should have been at the ball but instead sat getting tipsy and telling stories. The blithe ease that radiated from the couple and enfolded all in their close company focused Ambrose's mind, and something that had been just in his peripheral vision came into full view.

He could take May. They could leave.

He hadn't let himself think of it, hadn't let his mind even consider it. Van Alstyne's comments had also left a panicky tightness in Ambrose's chest at the thought of living next to Ethan and May for the rest of his life. But the breeze and the trees began to clear this, began to make him feel expansive, as if anything were possible.

Ethan knew as well as anyone that Ambrose wasn't going to be content in the middle of the country playing at baron. His brother wanted to keep him close, that much was clear. He probably feared that if Ambrose left, May would go with him. And really, what did Ethan expect? He'd married her under the most precarious circumstances. Ethan was nervous about Ambrose's return home, that much was clear. Didn't that nervousness prove there was something wrong with the match?

He heard hooves turning up the trail behind him and, assuming it was Van Alstyne again, he continued toward the ridge.

But it was May who came up beside him on her petite Arabian gray, Blueskin, who daintily sidestepped young trees, keeping tight to the deer path. May was astride. She only rode sidesaddle for show now. Dressed in Ethan's worn riding clothes, she breathed hard from riding to catch up. The necklace sparkled on her skin.

"Lucky that thing's sturdy," he said, pointing with a gloved hand.

"She's sturdy enough to get me up here at a full canter, though it's probably not good for her," May said, purposefully misunderstanding, but Ambrose let it go.

When she was abreast of him, she said, "I love it up here. It's where we come." She leaned down and patted her horse's neck. "Don't we?"

"You were following me."

"I was already out. But I did see Calvin. He told me you were here."

Ambrose leaned over to grab Blueskin's bridle near the bit, feeling the Ragman sway and prance as Ambrose reined the horses neck and neck. He leaned over then to whisper something in May's ear, something about them going away, about the expanses before them, the day and the energy of the ride having gone to his head. But she turned toward him at the last minute, and he caught her lips instead and kissed her.

For only a moment he thought of his brother. But thought was replaced by sensation coupled with the deep knowing that life was short. Then the smell of her perfume and a lingering scent of violets overwhelmed him until every thought left his head except for rightness and the opening of memory. When they parted he knew she was his. She belonged with him.

He scrabbled with the reins and the bridle, awkwardly trying to get an arm around her, to bring her closer when her little horse stepped away.

"Why'd you have to do that?" she asked, turning to look at the view ahead, avoiding his eyes.

"You know why." He pulled her horse in again, but Blueskin stepped back. Ambrose loosened the reins, never wanting to force, but watching May's face closely.

She looked down, defeated.

He swung off the saddle, coming next to her. "Come down," he said, patting her horse.

She didn't move from her position.

"I can't talk to you if you're up there."

She slid off the saddle, ignoring his arms waiting to help her.

"I'm down," she said.

He took a breath. The timing felt fateful. "I love you. I always have. I was an idiot to leave."

"Go to hell," she whispered, and started to walk away, Blueskin following.

He clambered after her, leading the Ragman. "I'm already in hell. You think this is easy for me?" He wanted to stop her, to talk face-to-face, but she wouldn't look at him.

"Love is an action, you know?" she said. "It's not something preserved in glass."

"Seems to me you took some actions yourself." He reached out, trying to get them both to stop.

"Would you let go of her?" May swatted at his arm.

He wasn't about to let go without saying what needed to be said. He put an arm around May, but she balked, shrugging him off and walking toward the view.

"Look, I don't understand why you did what you did," he said, following her. She turned at that and he faltered. "I mean, I do and I don't. I made mistakes, one huge mistake, but so did you, and I don't know how to make it right. But I know what matters now. I swear, you're the only thing that ever has."

There were tears in her eyes. "God, you're an ass."

Anger rose. "I'm serious. Don't pretend that you don't

know exactly what I'm talking about. You married my brother out of some sense of duty."

There, he'd said it. He watched her face, but she neither flinched nor denied it. He suspected that whatever alchemy lay between her and Ethan, it had never transformed into all-out passion. "You can't live your life based on some misplaced notion of duty, May. Don't you see that?"

"You were always trying to get me to see that."

She'd always be the girl she'd been on that afternoon at his brother's house. Even if lately her eyes were more shadowed. Even if a bright diamond and a thin band shone on her left hand, likely even when her hair shone with gray. He'd still see her as she was at the party.

"The trouble is, you thought we had time. You still think we do," she said.

"You're right. We don't have endless time. Let's fix it right now. Let's not waste another minute."

"Let's just ride off into the horizon?"

Ambrose looked forward, contemplating Lake Erie. It wasn't that far off from what he'd been thinking.

He took her hand, turned it up, and pressed a kiss in her rough palm—the smell of leather, the taste of salt, and the feel of one rough callous, as she refused to wear gloves.

She snatched her hand back, turning to lead her horse back down the hill.

"May, come on," he said, but didn't follow her.

"You're impossible," she called. "That was always the problem."

THE FOX HEADS

Nell has only just flown back into town and drives straight to the hunt club in a stuffy rental car. Though the air outside is still chilly, it holds a warm trace of earliest spring. She fumbles with the temperature controls. She's agreed to meet Pansy for dinner, and she's curious as to what her cousin's going to say.

She'd flown home to Portland after the wake, after her meeting at the museum with Reema Patel, after Pansy had cornered her, after Louis had taken her for drinks, taken her home, and taken her apart. She'd wanted to leave the necklace in a safe-deposit box, but thought better of it. It was irrational, but she felt it might somehow be misinterpreted as Pansy's if she did that, might cause confusion that strengthened Pansy's claim. In the end, Nell decided that the only way to keep it safe was to wear it, especially when she traveled.

In Portland work had descended on her like a tsunami, drowning her holidays. She managed to forget the farm, the will, Louis, the whole thing, for hours at a time, parts of whole days, until the heavy necklace brought those thoughts back.

She'd been in her office with the door closed, head down in the new year, when the letter arrived—heavy bond paper with lengthy letterhead at the top, sent from the local office of one of the largest and most expensive law firms in the country. They wrote on behalf of Pansy with a lot of stern language about the fiduciary duties of executors and veiled queries about the legitimacy of certain provisions in the will. The letter requested Nell's presence at a meeting to begin discussing dividing the contents of the farm.

Directness is in Nell's training, and so after the letter had hit her desk, she'd called Pansy.

"Hey," Nell had said, with no preamble. "Got your letter."

"Oh God, that letter," Pansy had said, clearly flustered by Nell's directness. "I saw it when you did. I had no idea they'd actually send it."

This, Nell knew, was bullshit. "You forget I'm a lawyer."

"Believe me, none of us forget that," Pansy had said, and then she'd rambled on quickly to cover. "I'm not like you. I don't know what I'm doing."

Pansy in the part of the baby bunny would have been amusing if it hadn't been such a familiar tactic in her arsenal.

"I need someone to look out for my interests," she'd said. "Well, not just mine, everyone's." Nell didn't mention that this is effectively her job as executor. She let Pansy talk. "To make sure it's really fair, but now they're firing off letters. I wanted a second set of eyes, you know? I mean, how much do we really know about Louis? I had no idea they'd be so aggressive. I'm sorry. I don't know how to stop this."

But Nell didn't buy the airhead routine. "So you didn't tell them to write it?"

"I don't tell them what to do."

"You didn't tell them to send it?"

"This isn't a deposition."

If only, thought Nell. Then I could compel you to give me a straight answer.

"I had one meeting with them," Pansy continued. "And now they're firing off letters. Maybe it's better if you deal with them directly."

So she wants to hide behind a lawyer. So fine, thought Nell.

"But I think a meeting would be a good idea. Before this all spirals out of control. You need to be back here. Things need to be dealt with that can't be done remotely. You can't just walk away from this, Nell. Much as I know you'd like to."

Pansy's spin on Nell's attempt at treading lightly rankled again, as if Nell wanted to shirk her duty, the outsider always.

A mere twenty minutes after she'd hung up, Emerson called and politely offered to deal with the contents of the farm on her behalf and at her direction. Vlad's background and position at the Met would be an invaluable help in sorting the treasures from the trash. She shouldn't have been surprised that the mechanics of the Quincys worked just that fast. The coolness in Emerson's tone let her know that he's been designated the one to deal with her, the one who can handle her. Actually, it was quite generous of Emerson to step into that mess. Both she and Pansy trust him implicitly, as does Baldwin. He had some good ideas for conducting a division, and so she'd agreed to come this weekend and start.

Louis's subsequent texts had only encouraged her decision for a visit. She's enjoyed his repartee, the slow getting to know each other through email and texts over the last few months. She's been hiding behind work, but he hasn't forced her. That patience is appealing, sexy even. She hasn't seen him since that night at his place.

The first spring slush is melting in the streets when Nell pulls up at the white clapboard clubhouse of the hunt club next to the river, relatively small for the size of the membership and definitely discreet. Quincys have been members since the founding. The hunt is now a drag, and the polo is long gone, but the stables are still filled with the members' horses.

She opens the front door, black lacquer with a brass fox-head knocker. Inside, a huge ginger jar filled with flowering quince branches sits on an austere Federalist table. The threadbare-but-still-good rugs are supposed to make you feel like you're visiting Grandma's. Silver horse trophies rest next to a curated collection of magazines on the side table—the most recent *Town & Country* and *Country Life* are fanned out next to today's *Financial Times* and the *Wall Street Journal*.

Nell's surprised to see Reema Patel leaning forward, in her myopic way, examining an old framed photograph of a man on horseback, who is leaning down with a fond smile to talk to a woman in a diaphanous white skirt and saddle shoes.

"How are you?" Nell asks, extending a hand. Patel is wearing a chic navy silk dress and seems not at all surprised to be meeting here.

Instead of shaking hands, Patel points to the caption and reads aloud, "Mr. Ambrose Quincy on the Ragman."

"They say he was a natural seat," Nell says.

"No name for her, though . . ." Patel trails off, waiting for Nell to supply detail.

"Typical," Nell says, hoping for some sisterhood.

Patel straightens, her detached eye inspecting Nell as if she's an artifact, and then her eyes get wide. "Are you actually wearing—" She stops herself.

"I thought it was safest on me," Nell says, and because things are getting awkward, she points to the taxidermy on either side of the fireplace—a half-dozen snarling fox heads on small plaques labeled with dates. "My mom's actually responsible for one of these."

The closest head unfurls its black tongue, desiccated and turning to dust. She remembers her mother averting her eyes from them when they'd come here during summer visits. She'd told Nell that when she went on her first hunt, after the hounds caught the fox and killed it, her mother was bloodied in keeping with tradition. An oldster huntsman had wrangled the carcass from the dogs and then smeared the blood of the fox on her cheeks and forehead to signal she was part of the group now. She'd almost vomited. Nell had asked her mother which fox head it was, but her mother couldn't bear to look at them too closely. Nell can't imagine her mother, a fan of Greenpeace and PETA, riding out for the hunt. Though perhaps this was the catalyst for her affinity for animals. Nell has to admit she got an uneasy thrill from the sadistic glamour of the story. Her mother had been a different person at one point in her life, submitting to incongruous dark rites in the name of all things Quincy.

Nell's just about to tell Patel about the tradition when Pansy comes out of a recessed door set into a panel next to the chimney.

"In here, you two," she says cheerily, and turns around, certain Nell and Patel will follow.

In the small paneled nook lined with dingy volumes detailing horse bloodlines, Baldwin sits at a small table set for five with a white tablecloth. When she sees there are no other tables in the library, Nell's stomach sinks. With Patel following and Baldwin already here, this has the whiff of an ambush.

Baldwin rises to hug her and usher her into the seat next to him, holding out her chair. She doesn't want to sit next to him, but she has no choice. Patel sits and unfurls her napkin, unimpressed by the preppy surroundings.

"Do I need counsel?" Nell asks, trying to sound light as Baldwin scoots her chair in behind her, nearly taking her out at the knees.

"Last I checked, you *are* a lawyer," Baldwin says, re-seating himself.

"A lawyer who represents herself has a fool for a client. Isn't that the old chestnut?" she asks.

"I believe that's attributed to Abraham Lincoln," says a big man straight out of a toothpaste ad. "Charles Walker. You must be Cornelia," he says, entering the room, hand outstretched, beaming around his gleaming teeth. "Or is Nell okay? Sorry to be late. We're merging right now, don't know if you know." He says this directly to Pansy, as if they all should be up on law firm happenings. "I'm wearing so many hats right now, I'm like a Jamaican."

Nell checks her retort while Walker shakes her uncle's hand. Starting off by making an enemy is not the best plan.

"Baldwin, a pleasure," Walker is saying. Then he introduces himself to Patel with a hearty handshake and a "Nice to put a face with a voice on the phone."

Nell sips her sweating ice water, hoping it will calm the knot grinding in her stomach. The knot telling her that this is an inside job.

"Such a great old club," Walker says, sitting down heavily in the only leather armchair at the table.

Nell feels the unseen wheels that have been turning while she's been away.

Pansy settles herself, looking spookily like a hip, black-clad version of Loulou—the pearls, the tasteful makeup, the hidden agenda, and the air of entitlement.

The menus, bound in green leather, feature offerings unchanged for generations—shrimp salad in half an avocado to start, Welsh rarebit, and lobster bisque. Pansy snaps hers shut and orders sole meunière.

There's a pause after the waitress leaves. All eyes are on Pansy, waiting for her to speak, and it's then Nell realizes the depth of the setup, because it's Charles Walker, the lawyer, who goes first.

"As you know, my client . . ." The word makes Nell sit up straighter in her chair, mentally donning her work armor. Perhaps she should have lawyered up like Pansy. How have things escalated while she wasn't looking? ". . . has some concerns centering on the Moon of Nizam and the frankly unclear drafting of some of the will provisions."

Just then, a commotion in the foyer precedes Louis Morrell walking into the library—a small phalanx of waitstaff following behind him with a spare chair and menu. She'd mentioned this dinner in passing when texting with him about her trip. She didn't expect him to show up. He's saying "Thank you so much," and "I'll be fine," and "Something simple, so I don't hold them up." She feels a jolt of electricity from his entrance, from his appealing smile, from the private way he looks at her as if they share a secret. Feeling his actual energy in the room after months of correspondence sends a buzz through her. Within minutes, he's wedged himself between Nell and Baldwin as the waitress lays his place setting and efficiently takes his order. "Whatever Ms. Merrihew is having, order me that," he says, adjusting his knife and fork. "Sorry I'm late." Nell checks Pansy's face, so surprised she hasn't been able to hide it yet.

"Louis, there's really no need for you to be here," Walker is saying.

"Then you won't mind if I sit in." He closes both eyes at Nell with a silent nod, as if to say "I got this."

She's shocked that he's crashed the dinner. Walker is right. As estate lawyer, he's not technically required at this meeting. She feels a little thrill curl up her spine, the thrill of having someone in her corner.

Walker pauses, considering how far to take his objections, and whether he's going to cause a scene, but he decides to pick up where he left off. "I think we can all agree that the testator's intent was to leave her jewelry to Pansy here."

"The jewelry in the safe-deposit box, yes," Louis says in a measured tone, jumping in right away. "Except for the one clearly enumerated and specifically bequeathed gift, which goes to Nell."

"Well, I think leaving an item of this importance in a whiskey bag shoved in the back of her dressing table, where anyone might find it, even nurses or maids, shows that the testator could have become reckless toward the end, even impaired, which doesn't go against her intent to leave all jewels, both secured and unsecured, to Pansy. Certainly if she'd treat an item of this importance this cavalierly, perhaps she hadn't all her faculties when she was changing will provisions."

Pansy is looking out the window, watching a horse being lunged in a nearby paddock in the twilight, her face serene, as if she has nothing to do with the scene unfolding before her.

Reema Patel is fascinated by the melba toast on her bread plate as she breaks off a miniscule piece and thoroughly butters it.

Baldwin stares right at Nell, gauging her reaction.

Louis puts his elbows on the table, leaning forward.

Nell knows this Walker lawyer is blowing smoke if he's showing his hand so early, trying to best her easily while testing the effectiveness of his argument. He's hoping an early agreement will avoid a lot of heavy legal lifting later.

There's a pause while they're served wine. When the waiter leaves with a quiet click of the door, Walker starts up again.

"Look, we all know there are some issues here. Sorry, Louis, but there are. And we don't want anything dragged out. My letter was to put you on notice that we believe my client has a significant claim to that necklace," he says, nodding toward Nell's chest. Nell tries to tuck the Moon in her shirt, but this only draws attention.

"A claim you intend to pursue through the courts?" Nell asks, finding her voice. This affects her most of all. She doesn't need Louis speaking for her.

"Well, there's no need to start worrying about things that haven't happened yet."

That's right, Nell thinks. Back off.

"We're just here for a discussion," Walker says.

"But in talking with Pansy and Baldwin"—Nell looks at her uncle; no surprise he's in on Pansy's plans—"we had an idea that might sidestep all of this unpleasantness, and that's why I've asked Reema to be here with us today," he says, gesturing toward Patel, who holds up a hand while chewing. "I thought she might outline some of the benefits of collaboration with the museum."

"Collaboration," a euphemism for donation, and it's then Nell sees the play they're making.

"It would be significant," Patel starts. "A piece like this would make an incredible anchor to the Southeast Asia collection. A calling-card piece, if you will. As I touched on briefly when you came to see me, it needs to be authenticated and researched, not only for verification, but for historical importance and meaning. Additionally, and I think Charles could speak more to this than I could, I believe there are beneficial tax implications for the estate."

"Which is also where your job as a fiduciary comes in," Baldwin admonishes, as if Nell isn't a lawyer, as if she hasn't put the obvious together.

Patel continues. "It would be in the most careful of caretaking hands. We could ensure preservation and, of course, allow it to be viewed to increase understanding of Mughal culture. A gift to scholars, to the public, really. And we would ensure that it would be on continuous display in the most sophisticated exhibit, surrounded by appropriate pieces to tell its story and give it context."

Nell's silent, giving nothing away.

"After you left, I did some preliminary research," Patel continues. "Curiosity and the cat and all. The maharaja, the Mahj, you remember, I told you about him . . ."

Nell does remember, and she'd done a bit of her own Internet searching. The twelfth maharaja of Baroda, known to the paparazzi as the Mahj, lives in London and is fond of Eastern European models, Bugattis, and the tiki bar Prince Harry favors. Surprisingly, he also fancies himself a bit of an activist and has been known to disrupt auctions for important Indian antiquities by bidding the price sky-high and then refusing to pay.

"I don't get how he hasn't been caught," Nell says to Patel now. "That's a binding contract the moment he becomes the high bidder."

"What's this?" Baldwin asks.

"Legally, yes. But he makes a huge stink in the press. The auction houses can try to go after him, but they won't since it just gives his cause airtime. He gets to wax poetic about stolen culture. He's actually a pretty good speaker. The optics on the whole thing are a nightmare. Plus they'd be getting a judgment in US court and then they'd have to enforce it in India against a popular royal. His bids are way out of whack with any rational valuation, and so they've quietly negotiated sales to the next highest bidder. But buyers are reluctant because they've been up against a shill, and the price has to be unnaturally deflated for sale. I know they've had to finesse those sales for a lot less than the original reserve."

"Would you guys please fill us in?" Pansy whines, and Patel brings the rest of the table up to speed.

"So?" Pansy asks when she's done.

"So the position of the Baroda family is that the Moon of Nizam was stolen." By Patel's tone, it's clear Pansy's managed to irk her. Good, thinks Nell. "After a party in the 1920s," Patel continues.

"Wait. What now?" Baldwin asks.

"Most of this information is online," Patel says.

"Hold on," Baldwin says, drawing himself up straight. "Ambrose Quincy didn't steal things. Why, there isn't a Quincy in the world who was a thief. I can assure you."

"I think it's kind of badass," Pansy says. And she would, probably imagining James Bond or Indiana Jones instead of a sneaky guest pilfering during a dinner party. "Weren't there stories that Ambrose ran out of money over there?"

Patel looks at Pansy, stymied for a full minute by this comment, and then turns to Baldwin. "No one's accusing anyone of anything. And it wouldn't have to have been a Quincy who stole it. Maybe he bought it from the thief. These things are rarely clear-cut. And I should restate," she says, looking at Pansy. "The necklace hasn't actually been authenticated as the Moon."

Nell notes Patel's use of the gray area.

"Yet," Pansy says, and Nell notes her proprietary tone.

"If it were," Patel says, "we'd predict extensive negotiations with the country of origin, but similar negotiations have been successful in the past without repatriation. The Toledo Museum of Art just concluded a successful negotiation with Syria, right before everything began over there. It was in the news. Then again, we just had to return an important tenth-century statue of Hanuman to Cambodia, so I should tell you that these things are never assured."

"I don't think you'd have a hard time getting the rest of the family to agree to a donation," Walker interjects. "As Reema here just laid out for us, you might have a harder time if you pursue other venues."

"Last I checked, I don't need the rest of the family to agree to anything," Nell says.

"A legacy from the Quincy family," Baldwin says.

"Wouldn't that be the Merrihew family?" Nell says.

Baldwin clears his throat and squirms in his chair. "It was bought by Quincys. It's coming from Quincys. It should have the Quincy family name on it."

Nell leaves it unsaid that it would be gifted by a Merrihew.

Nell views the complicated mechanics that have gone on while she's been immersed in her own life and work. In those few months, Pansy has lawyered up, Reema Patel has started strategizing, and Baldwin has claimed naming rights.

"Well." Nell looks straight at Pansy. If it's an ambush, then now is the time to fire back. "As your lawyer"—Nell waves a hand at Walker—"has probably explained to you, my claim on the Moon is absolute. And it's not something

I'll be relinquishing. Pursuing litigation would be entirely your decision and, as I am sure you can explain to her," she says to Walker, "entirely your loss."

"Now, calm down," Walker says, palms flat on the table, as if stabilizing it. This of course makes Nell feel the opposite of calm, as it is meant to. "There's no need . . ."

"As for any specious claims the twelfth maharaja may have to the piece," Nell interrupts, turning to Patel, "I doubt they're as clear as you're portraying them. Have they reported it stolen until now, almost a century later?" Nell knew enough from her Internet searching that they hadn't ever made a formal claim. "Even if they did, that family would have little standing in a US court and any interference on their part would be actionable, potentially tortious, if you want to go that way."

It's then that Pansy takes a break from picking at the remnants of her fish to look up. "There's no need to get nasty, Nell."

"May I speak with you?" Nell rises and leaves the room, fully expecting Pansy to follow.

Nell walks with purpose, despite being afraid Pansy will just stay seated, and she is relieved when Pansy follows her into the ladies' room, as big as Nell's living room with a full vanity and four flounced seats before a dressing table and a matching fainting couch. Pansy does a quick check of her clothes in the full-length mirror and then looks under the doors of the stalls, ensuring no eavesdroppers, before she faces Nell.

"I told them you'd be reasonable," Pansy starts. "I figured when we laid it out for you, you'd see it's the right thing to do."

"Is anyone asking Emerson to donate his painting?" Nell questions.

Pansy turns back to the mirror, calmly leaning in to check her undetectable lipstick. "I always said I'd want you on my side in a fight."

"Who's fighting?"

"This is all just information for you. I know this is so new to you, I wanted to expose you to some options."

"I'm aware of my options." Nell fiddles with the hand sanitizer on the dressing table.

"I know you don't want things to get unsavory, either, but you know as well as I do that the necklace isn't really yours. And the right thing to do would be to donate it," Pansy says in a chummy tone of complicity. "Granny Lou was going a little nuts at the end, I guess. Living out there with nurses. Strangers, really. Giving things away out of the family. She gave away almost all of the silver." Pansy nods at Nell's raised eyebrow. "Yes, even that nice little piece of Paul Revere. She gave it to some physical therapist who came to the house once. I had to track down her address, go visit her, and have a little talk." Nell gives a shudder, thinking of that hardworking home health aide opening her front door to a righteous Pansy. "Luckily she had no clue what it was. Thought it was pewter and gave it back. That's when we put everything on lockdown."

And all the good jewels in the safe, thinks Nell. Nell wonders then if they'd found the Moon, whether they'd have put it downtown in Pansy's safe-deposit box. Then things would have been much messier.

"Not that you're not family," Pansy is saying. "But let's be real. You're not *really* family, either. I mean, you certainly won't have to worry about an undue influence claim or anything. You hadn't seen her in years." It both stings and illuminates. Pansy has been pursuing all her legal arguments. "You're very much your mom's child. And Daddy was the one who had the bond with her."

"You're being nuts."

"What's nuts is you're back here trying to pretend you're a part of this. For you to be in charge of something so monumental and not have the family involved in what happens to it. Don't you think it's confusing?" she asks. "Confusing" is Pansy's evasive word for infuriating. "I can't imagine what she was thinking, but there's no way she knew how valuable it is. And you wouldn't know this, but she would have wanted it donated. Philanthropy was huge with her." Pansy rises, smoothing down her black layers. "We should get back. Just listen, would you? I think you might come down the same way we all do."

As Pansy swings open the door, she leans back long enough to say, "I'd be so sad if this caused a rift between us."

When they return to the room, Nell overhears Patel saying, "That's all premature until it's authenticated. And I mean, I'll be going to other institutions, but I'm going to bring in the main freelance curators as well. Then we'll make a determination once we know what's what."

The men all stand when they come back, something Nell never sees on the West Coast, and then they are all seated again.

"We'd love to get this dealt with and put to bed before you leave again," Walker is saying, scooting his chair in, as if Nell isn't completely accessible on the West Coast, like they rely on the Pony Express or something.

"Why the pressure?" Louis asks.

Patel ignores him and turns to Nell. "If you're at all inclined to go this way, I'd really encourage you to let us get the ball rolling. And if I may," she says, squaring her shoulders, "I'd like to make the case for discouraging you from pursuing the auction route. I know that's always attractive, and I'm sure you'll look into it at some point. But firstly, the sapphire will likely be put in a vault if it's sold privately, and no one will see it again—a huge loss. And that's the best-case scenario. The worst case is the sapphire is dug out and resold. At that point it becomes a pure commodity based on weight and other metrics. Any art value is lost. It'd likely be slammed into a modern setting, too, but that's neither here nor there. The cultural value is destroyed—historical, ethnographic, archaeological. Forgive me for being dramatic, but I see it as not unlike the dynamiting of the Buddhas of Bamiyan. Lost forever. And we really would be able to properly handle it for you, not to mention we'd want to celebrate it with you. And I don't have to tell you that prices are never guaranteed at auction." She says the last part unflinchingly, holding Nell's eye.

"Is the museum thinking of ponying up?" Nell asks.

Baldwin winces.

"We'd need to understand the context," Patel says smoothly. "But I'll remind you that the Cleveland Museum of Art has one of the largest acquisition budgets in the nation, up there with the Getty and the Met."

"I'd like her to have time to consult with outside experts," Louis says, jumping in on Nell's behalf.

"She's a sophisticated attorney," Walker says, as if Nell

isn't there. "There's been more than enough time for her to understand all the implications. Plus she's had a private meeting with the curator of an internationally renowned museum, she's had a few months back home to think about it, and most important, she is a magna cum laude graduate of Stanford Law School and a partner at one of the leading firms practicing intellectual property litigation on the West Coast. It's not like she's overwhelmed in negotiations about her great-aunt's will."

"You understand I'm sitting right here," Nell says.

"Just like your mom," Baldwin says with a sickly smile. "Making your presence known."

THE MOONLIGHT

Ambrose didn't see May for the rest of the day after their ride. She'd beat him back to the house and disappeared. When he came down for dinner, the maid told him May had a headache and had asked for a tray in her room.

Message received, he thought. And over dinner by himself, he decided he'd leave in the morning, on the first train. He was outraged at her for avoiding him as he sat in the dining room alone eating cold ham and country biscuits. He promised himself, in earnest this time, that he would move on with his life. He'd leave now. Not to follow his brother and father; he wouldn't be going to DC. First to Chicago or even farther west—a man could lose himself out there. He could start anew—palm trees and Santa Barbara, maybe even Hollywood.

Upstairs he packed his small weekend bag. The books and assorted things he'd brought from town, as if he were living out here, living with them. Looking at it now, he realized what a sham it'd been. He'd been waiting, testing, and it'd finally happened. May had given her answer, once and for all. Ambrose supposed he'd had to come back and see it, feel it, before he could know it. Everything was over.

He'd leave his books here for May, let her sort through them if she wanted. He'd leave the Ragman, too.

When he finished, having tidied everything and now lying in bed, he was about to finally let go, to slip under to unconsciousness, his grip loosening on the day, on his expectations, on May. The door creaked open.

May slipped into his room in her white nightgown, which shone nearly pale blue in the moonlight streaming through the windows. He reached for the bedside lamp.

"No," she said. "Don't turn it on."

His pulse hammered in his ears as she crossed the room. Anger morphed into excitement; adrenaline serving both. And then she slipped under the thin linen, her body a warm delight next to his.

He stilled himself, as if a bird had landed on his shoulder. If he'd learned anything today, it was that he couldn't force her. He waited, exhilarated but not grasping, sure now. Why else would she walk down the hall to him?

Her lips came tentatively at first, tiny kisses at his neck, her hand traveling across his bare chest, and then her lips to his—the spark of connection. He restrained himself from grabbing her.

Under the cover of night she was both braver and more demanding than he. The feel of her hands passing over his heart raised chill shivers up his neck. Her insistence bordered on blind determination, and he knew she was shutting down her doubts. He'd seen her do that before. He'd watched as she cast her lot—for pleasure, for desire, for him—that day before he'd left on his trip.

He slipped a hand high up her thigh, thinking he might; he could; it was possible. It was impossible.

But desire won out, and she felt warm under his fingertips, and so soft, and when she finally slipped him home he could feel her open mouth against his neck.

"You," she said.

He knew in that moment that he never should have left. Or he should have taken her with him. Or she should have waited. Something should have been different. Starting now it would have to be *made* different, some things destroyed and others made new. He would see to that.

The smell of her around him, the feel of her crushed against him, drove him toward some elemental rivalry that in the moment, before he could check it, he had to know.

"Was it like this? Before. Was it ever like this?"

She shook her head and he breathed into her asking, "Ever? It was never like us?"

Her hair fell against his mouth as she shook her head. "No, never like us."

THE VICTORIAN

After Charles Walker's attempt at strong-armed rush-ing, and Pansy's attempt at blatant coercion, Nell's had enough of dinner. She'd chew glass before she stayed for coffee and those sticky coconut macaroons they served at the hunt club. She gathers her things, quickly shaking everyone's hand like a grown-up, while she steams on the inside. She heads out to her car fast enough that no one can collect themselves to come after her.

She jumps a little when the passenger-side door opens and Louis leans in.

"We're going to need to talk," he says.

Nell's so relieved it's him and not Baldwin or Pansy or Charles Walker that she starts up the car and merely asks, "Where to?"

He directs her downtown. Putting miles between them and the scene at dinner calms her. While she drives, Louis keeps up a reassuring patter of small talk, avoiding anything of substance, letting her calm down.

When he directs her to the exit next to City Hall, Nell remembers the way to the boxy Victorian with flaking white paint. The lawn is still in the need of a cut, as it was the last time she was here.

In the kitchen there's a fridge with some beer inside and little else. Louis offers her one, but quickly pulls it back. "Oh, right," he says to himself, and that sends him rifling through the cupboards, which turns up an ancient bottle of warm white wine.

"I'm good, really," she says, but he opens the bottle and pours some over ice anyway.

She takes a sip; it's sour, corked.

"To Chuck Walker," he says.

Nell almost snorts her drink through her nose. It's such a perfect name for that aging good old boy.

"Really?"

"All his life," Louis says. "Took an iron hand and the determination of a beaver for him to get everyone to call him Charles. But my sister went to college with him and he was Chuck all the way until law school. Every once in a while someone from his past calls or visits and 'Chuck' gets out, then he has to enact a reign of terror all over again to stuff it back in its box."

"That's so perfect. It makes me think God's on his cloud throne and all's right with the world. He's a total Chuck."

"Isn't he, though?"

"But smart," she says. Walker may have been an ass, but he hadn't been stupid.

"Decently."

She follows Louis to the sofa in the living room. The only furniture besides an elaborate television setup; she remembers this from before. The house is mostly bare, with clean floors and white walls, cut up into dinky rooms. The fixtures are cheap, likely replaced in the sixties. He told her last time that he'd bought it as an investment, a fixer-upper in a gentrifying neighborhood. The place has the air of the unfinished about it, the bachelor, the workaholic. There are no photos on the walls.

"But I don't think they'll make it difficult for you now that we know why they're pushing so hard for you to donate," Louis says, sitting down. "I didn't get it at first, but as I sat there I realized they must know they're not going to have a real basis for a challenge, not legally. So maybe this is their way to control it."

"And look like big shots all over town."

"There is that."

"If that's the worst of it, I can handle it," she says.

"If you donate it, the tax apportionment issue would go away, too. I'm sure Chuck explained that to them. Another reason they'd be keen to have you give it away. I should have sewed it up during drafting, but it wasn't important at the time. These things have a way of biting you in the ass."

There's zing in this throwaway line; it comes out of his mouth with intent.

"God, that sounded weirdly . . ." To her delight, his ears turn red. "Literal."

She waves off his discomfort as she fiddles with her glass, glad to have him on the back foot for once.

His beer is finished, and he tips it toward her, as if to ask, "Want another?"

Her sour wine is forgotten, left on the floor, as there's no coffee table. Right now she knows what she wants, and it's not another drink.

She'd been hesitant to see him, wondering if it would be

awkward in person after weeks of writing. But her doubts disappear when he stands, offers her a hand, and leads her upstairs with no hesitation.

His bedroom is as spartan as the rest of the house. The bed is on a basic metal frame, smack in the middle of the room, and sex immediately comes to her mind. Plain white sheets smell like clean laundry and him.

"You're going to stay," he says with a cheeky smile. They both know she's staying.

"Tonight?"

"Yeah, or, you know, forever. Whichever you want."

He's charming, yes, but there's something in this senti-ment that irks her. He's all intensity and certainty, which is flattering, but the unspoken is that she will stay here with him. She will fit into his world. And Nell is sick of trying to fit in.

But she lets it go. She's been looking forward to this.

"Maybe I should keep you here as my captive. Never let you go back." He's teasing, of course, playful, and not at all serious. It would have been a turn-on before, but it frays the same nerve now. She's not some damsel. He's not some knight.

She checks herself, again. She hasn't been with anyone since the last time with him, and she's feeling pent-up, ready for a night of sense pleasure, if he'd just stop talking.

But he's not reading her silence correctly, probably thinking she's nervous.

"'Cause I could, you know. Keep you here with me, keep you all to myself."

Three strikes and you're out, she thinks. She's fully annoyed now.

"You know, I really should be getting back," she says.

"Wait, what?" he asks, shrugging his shirt back on. "What just happened?"

"I need to go back to the farm." Let's see if he can be accommodating, she thinks. "You could come with me," she says.

"But we're here. You don't need to go."

"I do."

"Let's not leave."

"Look," she says, sighing, realizing the truth. "We both know this is impossible."

Stunned, he says, "Impossible?"

"Well, I mean, you won't even come out to the farm. Are you going to move?" At the look on his face, she says, "Right. It's not like you're going to move across the country, and so it's going to be me who's going to have to uproot her life. And frankly I'm too old and too good at what I do for that. So really, what is the point of this? You're not keeping me here. I'm not staying back here. My parents left for a reason and they never came back. We don't come back."

He freezes and then says, "You just did a whole thing in your head."

"Maybe. Doesn't mean I'm wrong."

"Do I get a say in any of this?"

"You have something to say, say it."

When he's silent, she turns to gather up her stuff and go.

"Wait. I'm thinking," he says. "You're so damned fast."

But Nell wants to leave, to move, to put miles between herself and this. She's not coming back here. She doesn't belong here. It's instinct—certainty without thinking—that urge to flee. Nevertheless, at the look on Louis's face she pauses, waiting.

"This is some bullshit," he says. "Marry me."

"What? You're not serious."

He comes to her then, takes her in his arms. "As a heart attack."

"You're ridiculous."

"So? I know what I want. Why wait?"

"Even the way you said it, I marry you. Why isn't it you who marries me?"

"Okay," he says quickly.

"Be real."

He kisses her then, a most persuasive argument. "I love you. I knew it that night. We've gotten to know each other all long-distance and chaste-like. I know who you are, and I don't want to wait or be without you. I was coming out there to get you."

"You were coming to *get* me?"

"Yeah. That's where this is all going anyway. It's where you went in your head just now. You feel it, too, don't you? So why draw it out? Why not do the romantic thing? The impractical thing. The impossible?"

"You can't propose to get me to spend the night with you. You can't coerce me like that." It's a blatant attempt to manipulate her with the brass ring every woman supposedly wants. His proposal is infuriating, but it's also enticing. She's never been that woman, pining to be a bride, but she isn't immune to a brash and handsome man either.

Nell wonders at his confidence, his outrageousness. Does he really feel this way, or is he merely throwing out a proposal he knows she won't accept? And what if she did? What if she called his bluff? He'd likely backpedal. Or he might book tickets on the next plane to Vegas. She wouldn't put it past him. And this thought softens her a bit.

"Stay. Let me convince you how right we are for each other."

She has a thought for staying, for one more night of his particular brand of escape, a way to forget about the world. She'd like to forget again.

He is energy and optimism, competence and calm, and she just wants to feel him pressed up against her skin. "You're going to convince me?"

"Just need one more night," he says with a playful smile.

"One night, then," she says, looking forward to a getaway from the mundane.

"Excellent," he says as he kisses her, his hands in her hair, backing her up toward his bed. "I can work with one night."

THE LEATHER JOURNAL

Days passed in a haze for Ambrose. He and May spent most of their time outdoors to avoid the staff. Riding to secluded spots, he would coax her off Blueskin and down next to him on saddle blankets he'd take from the barns and spread on the grass. They did things that apparently frightened the horses, who both managed to slip their leads and take off at a pace for the stables. Ambrose and May dressed and ambled after them, straggling back in rumpled clothes, to the raised eyebrow of the barn manager.

Down at the pond, Ambrose dared her to climb up on the top of the bathhouse and jump. She'd done it and come up laughing, complaining that her feet hit mud when she leapt from that height. They'd wasted afternoons in the humid sun and the mossy water.

They ate together in the dining room at night, small dinners à deux, with furtive clasped hands under the table and whispered plans that stopped when the maids would come in with more champagne or to clear plates. Ambrose rarely let May out of his sight; he was so absorbed by her and the real physicality of her after so many daydreams

243

that he couldn't think about anything else. But when she was in her bath or riding alone or discussing things with the cook, when he had even a moment by himself, he was silently plotting their escape and a return. Ambrose wanted it, and he'd create it—the chance to begin again, to go back and make a decision differently, for the both of them. And he didn't care now which one of them should have chosen differently, if the fault lay with him for trying to jump May through a set of hoops or with May for marrying while he was gone. It didn't move anything forward to look back like that.

Each night before dinner he brought her violets from the greenhouses, though she didn't wear flowers in her hair anymore, which he thought a pity.

Each night after dinner she tiptoed down to his room in her long white nightgown, returning back to her end of the house before morning, lest the help talked.

This morning she'd announced the need for a walk, alone. Though it made his stomach sink, Ambrose smiled, wary of seeming overbearing. Continually beating under any moment that May wasn't with him was the desire to just take her away, to convince her to leave before Ethan came back and go where no one would be able to find them. He sat in the living room, fumbling over a leather-bound journal, trying for calm. He was inspired, as he hadn't been since India, to try writing verse. His frustrated scribbling and many crossed-out words showcased his inability to capture the moment.

He worked, hoping to have something to give her by the time she was back. When he heard the front door creak, thinking it was she, he called out, "Darling."

Heavy footfalls alerted him that it wasn't May, and Ethan entered the room, his face placid.

Ambrose rose, willing himself not to blush, and hoped his "Darling" sounded casual, like an offhand, teasing thing between a hostess and her long-standing houseguest.

"You're back. How'd it go?" Ambrose regretted it the minute he said it. He'd kept in little contact with his father's office, making only a few halfhearted phone calls, during which he'd been told all was under control and there was nothing for him to do, no decisions to be made. They'd call if he was needed, they assured him. Ambrose suspected that they were glad to have him out of the way, and he'd been only too happy to oblige. There'd been telegrams from Ethan, and letters, too, which Ambrose had left unopened on a never-used table in the library.

He felt it then, the fragile bubble he'd been living in with May, and seeing the look on Ethan's face, Ambrose felt it pop.

"Drink?" Ambrose asked, searching for something to do, something to offer.

When Ethan had his glass and was settled, the sound of the front door silenced the brothers. Ambrose tried to think of some way to warn May as her boots clacked across the hall. "There you are," she said, coming in the room with a wide, fond smile. "You were right, I feel so much . . ." She turned then, seeing the look on Ambrose's face.

"Surprise," Ethan said flatly.

She looked so young, her hair a shiny curve at her cheek, baggy jodhpurs with a rip at the knee and an old tuxedo shirt of Ambrose's, wrapped so she didn't need studs. She'd been on the mountain, and mud was splashed up the leg of her britches—a wild thing wearing a small fortune from a maharaja around her neck while tromping through the woods. It was the sort of careless thing that attracted him to May, and he knew his brother was attracted to it, too, knew Ethan would have had no quarrel with it if the jewels had been from him.

"I wasn't expecting you," she said.

"I know you weren't," Ethan said evenly. "I didn't want to waste time telephoning, so I just came on the train as quickly as I could." But Ambrose knew this was not why Ethan had surprised them. He'd wanted to catch them unawares.

"Is everything all right?" May asked with genuine concern. Ambrose couldn't help it. Even that small amount of gentleness from May kindled jealousy.

Ethan slumped down in his chair while May stood in front of the cold fireplace.

"As good as it can be, I guess." He turned toward Ambrose. "It was hard for Father. Quite a strain. He seems to feel . . ."

Ambrose could imagine their pious father's mood.

"I didn't realize how responsible he feels," Ethan continued. "You know how he is." Ambrose did know how Israel could be—absolute, certain, bleak, and uncompromising.

"Once he's made something into a moral issue—" Ethan raised his glass for a long draw. "It becomes quite black-and-white for him. Frankly, given his morose state of mind, I'm a bit worried."

"Worried how?"

"He kept talking about man's duty to man and the nature of sin." He looked at his brother then. "Maybe you and your philosophers got to him. He was constantly reading his Bible. Even on the train."

They sat one full beat, letting this sink in. Though he knew his father was religious, he couldn't imagine him reading his Bible on a public train. Ethan continued, "In any case, I think he needs company now. You should head into town. For some reason, I feel like he shouldn't be alone."

It riled Ambrose, this demonstration of how easily Ethan could kick him out of the house if he wanted.

May piped in then. "But we're going to Arabella Rensselaer's dog-racing party." At Ethan's blank face, May continued. "You'll have to come now. She's showing off those new little Italian dogs of hers. Skinny things—whippets, they're called. I told her you were gone, but now you're back."

"I'm not going to a party. Besides, I'm sure Ambrose will have a better time with his ladylove if we're not there." Ethan watched his brother's face as he said this.

"I hear she's going around with your man O'Brennan now," Ambrose said, meeting his brother's gaze.

"Well, I want to go; if you don't want to . . ." May trailed off.

"You wouldn't go without me, would you dear? Not after I've been gone."

She rose then. "I'm going to rest and have a bath," she said. "And then we're *all* going to the party."

Ethan rose to meet her. And Ambrose watched as Ethan took her in his arms. Ambrose felt only slight vindication that she looked stiff even from across the room.

"A kiss for your husband," Ethan said, seeming to linger on the last word.

She kissed him quickly, a fast, closed-mouth peck against his lips, but he wouldn't let her go. His right arm locked around her until she yielded and kissed him properly. Ambrose looked away. Then she headed for the stairs, her gait only slightly under a run.

THE STEAMER TRUNKS

In the morning Nell tries to slip out with no good-byes. Not that she's running away from Louis's place, exactly, but she'd like to stay thought-free a little longer. If she has to turn her brain on, and get out of this delicious haze, then she wants space to think. Alone. They'd discarded his proposal, along with their clothes on the floor. But she's dressed now, and she's almost made it to the door when she remembers the Moon on the windowsill in his bedroom and stealthily turns around.

"Such a sneaker," Louis says, opening one eye when she reenters the scene from last night. "Are you actually tiptoeing?"

She has her phone out; it's already vibrating with incoming emails and texts. One from her assistant, late last night on West Coast time; something from Chuck the lawyer at five o'clock this morning; more from clients; and a text from Pansy—formal and deferential with no abbreviations or emojis—giving notice that she'll be out at the farm with Emerson today putting their names on the pieces of furniture they want. Nell walks over to the bed and holds it up for Louis to read, blue light reflecting off his calm, intelligent eyes.

"If you go out there, I'm coming with you," he says, sitting up and scrubbing his face.

"No need."

"My car's still at the hunt club. You'll drop me off, and then we'll head over caravan style. We'll need food first." Despite having just woken up, he's neatly organized her day and inserted himself in the middle of it as he heads to the kitchen to make breakfast. "You need a neutral third party with you. Not that I'm neutral," he says, checking over his shoulder that she's still there, that she isn't objecting to his bossiness. "But I am a third party."

"You'd do all that for me?" she says, mock-touched, and heads for the mirror in the bathroom to put the Moon back on.

"I think it's pretty clear after last night that I'll do anything you want."

A contractor's Dumpster, forty cubic yards, sits in the farm's driveway, blocking the front door. Whoever ordered it knew the size of the job ahead.

Inside the house, little packing tags with Emerson's or Pansy's name on them are tied to the legs of chairs and placed on top of tables. To Nell's eye there looks to be a lot of them, and it gives her pause. She wonders for a moment just what her ancestors would think of this, of Emerson and Pansy and Nell dividing up everything from the linens to the Limoges. Would they be pleased at the frugality, the appearance of respect for legacy? Or would they be appalled that this was all that was left of a formerly vast empire?

Louis's calling through the house for the cousins, and Nell's relieved she'll have the place to herself for a moment. She's interrupted, though, by a knock on the door.

Two of the oldest members of the farm crew come in. Both in their sixties, they've each worked on the place since they were young men. Combined, they know more about the ins and outs of Quincy family politics than Nell does. One has a five-gallon bucket in each hand, filled with green blocks. The other carries a cardboard box.

"Saw the car. We've been waiting to do this." The buckets, Nell now realizes, are filled with blocks of rat poison.

"Is that all going in here?"

"Some goes in the attics, most goes in the basement. Just getting on fall now, and that's when the little furry guys start looking for a place to spend the winter."

Nell doesn't want to add poison to the house. Doesn't it make dust? She feels it's one of the few things she and Pansy might agree on right now. No more toxins.

"Do we have to?" she asks. There's an awkward silence, and she realizes they're wondering if she has the authority to stop them.

"You don't *have* to," says the shorter one, setting a cardboard box down on the first stair step. "But it's gonna look like a New York City subway station in here if you don't. Rats everywhere."

"No, they're field mice," says the other. "Pretty cute, I guess."

"You know, maybe today's not the right day, fellas,"

Louis says stepping in. "We were going to take a crack at the attics."

"Thought you might," the shorter one says, nodding toward the box.

She sees now that it's filled with dust masks, black contractor's trash bags, and latex gloves.

"That's really nice of you," Nell says.

"You're gonna stir up a lot of crud," he says with a shrug.

Mission complete, they head out the door, load the poison into the bed of the pickup, and each take a Swisher Sweet out of the pack on the dashboard.

"You call us when you're done, now, and we'll come put it in," the shorter one says. He nods toward her, starts up the ancient farm truck, and rattles off.

When they've left Louis says, "Starting in the attic isn't a bad idea, you know. Since it's all leftover crap anyway, it's probably filled with the easiest decisions. Bet you fill that thing in a day or two." He nods toward the Dumpster.

Nell is grateful he's here with his clear-sighted counsel and his calm demeanor. He's probably advised loads of families on cleaning out an old place.

She changes into jeans, and with thoughts of Pansy lurking, keeps the Moon fastened and tucked inside her T-shirt. Then, taking Louis's advice, she heads for the attics. They won't be able to call her a flake or a shirker now.

The door to the attic off the third-floor dormitory creaks open, and she's filled with trepidation, as if breaching a tomb. Dust sparkles in shafts of sunlight and she silently thanks the old architects who deemed huge dormer windows a necessity in an attic.

She pulls the dust mask over her mouth, dons gloves, and grabs a black contractor bag, feeling like she's suiting up for a biohazard. And she kind of is—she read somewhere that dust is 90 percent human skin. She will be breathing in her ancestors.

She stumbles over a tower of crumbling cardboard boxes from a long-defunct department store twice tied with twine. She'll have to tackle those rotting mysteries at some point. Along the back wall is an uninterrupted line of closets, and she decides to start there.

Opening the first closet takes some muscle, but when she succeeds, she finds it's lined in cedar and surprisingly clean. Craftsmen being what they were back in the day, the door's joints are so tight that no dust has reached inside. Hangers present a jumbled mishmash of slipcovers for furniture that no longer exists, a hint of netting, and sequins from faded gowns in tatters, but mostly it's old uniforms for nurses and maids. Nell fills a trash bag quickly and hefts it onto the landing.

She loses track of time amid old bedpans, broken cribs, and Christmas decorations with dubious wiring. Louis is running bulging bags down to the Dumpster, bringing her water, bringing her a broom, but mostly staying out of her way. She removes one igneous layer of attic accumulation and then comes to a corner she's been avoiding.

At least twenty disintegrating leather steamer trunks are huddled in this corner. They are substantial, with cracked leather strapping, tarnished brass hardware, and faded monograms of Quincys long dead and stamps from voyages never to be taken again. They're beautiful. They're filthy with mold. They're heavy as hell. She despairs at the thought of their bulk going in the Dumpster and then taking up space in a landfill.

They were made for a time when one didn't touch one's bags when traveling, didn't even pack them. She tests a few and finds them locked, but more are open or the locks are busted, the contents already ransacked. Quincys have nothing on Egyptian tomb raiders. Nell knows the attic has been picked clean of the real loot, so it's with resignation that she heaves open the hinged tops and finds the trunks are lined in fitted trays. Usually about six of them, dovetail joints tighter than her dining room furniture back home. She imagines the trays filled with clothes wrapped in scented tissue paper, and gives a rueful thought to her recent flight, where she was crammed in a germy seat, her things stuffed in the overhead bin or on the grimy floor under the seat in front of her.

The empty trunks are easy to deal with, and Louis helps haul them down. By now she's dusty, thirsty, and a little dispirited. Despite working through lunch and filling nearly half the Dumpster, it doesn't look like she's done a thing up here, hasn't made a dent. She wants food and a shower, or maybe the shower first, preferably with Louis. So with the idea of getting one last thing done before she quits for the day, she hoists open a trunk. It's buff leather, and lighter straps give it a feminine feel. If a trunk can be gender specific, this one is.

Opening it, she finds the drawers have been removed, and it's as if someone has dumped a river of letters into the trunk. The entire interior is filled to the brim with a jumble of envelopes—flowing script in faded brown fountain ink on yellowed envelopes. She can't resist, and she reaches a gloved hand in, hoping there's nothing nesting inside, and lets them fall through her hands.

Nell sifts through the letters, dry and crumbling at the edges, and she uncovers a dark object nestled in the corner. It's a leather journal, tooled with art nouveau flowers and vines. When she lifts it, the natural crease falls open to the last page with writing. A masculine, pointy scrawl in sepia ink.

May, my darling—You've gone off to ride and so I'm left with my thoughts. I must get them out, I must tell someone, and so I'll set them down here. Never have my days meant more to me, has life seemed brighter or sweeter than now. Is it only because of the secretive nature of this? No, I think it can't be. It is the universe realigned, the planet set right on its axis, and we are together. I finally have a taste of what it's like to have everything I've wanted. You've left me now, only for moments, and to have that feeling diminished throws my purpose into high relief. My head is filled only with how to solve this. It is my task, as I'm the one who initially set things on this course. How to take us away?

I love seeing my jewel on you. I know it's barbaric, but I wish the other thing you wear every day were off your finger. I haven't dared ask you not to wear it. And so I am satisfied that you wear mine near to your heart. Jewels and gems have been on my mind. You are my treasure. I realize that now.

I feel compelled to write in a way I haven't in a very long time.

Within my mouth rich jewels bloom,
Cabochons, orient pearls of price.

Around my neck and over my heart
Her shimmering golden cord wraps tight.
Her lips that my soul dies for
Her eyes that ever speak true
Her small hands on me, enticing
My skin aflame, the thrill renewed.

There's more, but I feel out of practice. All my writing
dropped off so dramatically after I stopped writing to you.

When I first saw the necklace, I knew it belonged with
you. The maharani was showing it off as she danced, and
she refused to part with it. But she was a born negotiator,
because in the end I offered such an exorbitant price that she
was persuaded. Literally a king's ransom for you. I had to
tell Ethan it was a gift. He'd have wondered at my spending
money like that. He'd have wanted to repay me for it, and I
didn't want that. I initially thought it would cut my trip short
for lack of funds. Then he paid me to continue only so he
could take something that was mine. Though I shouldn't judge
his motivations; I'd do anything for you, too. I bought the
necklace only with the thought that I'd see you wear it as mine.

Under very different circumstances.

I have been haunted by the what ifs, the choices that I
could have made differently. I can hardly sleep for thinking.
But then I've hardly let you sleep, either. If only I hadn't
been so young then. If only I'd seen what was in front of
me. It was more than hesitation or cold feet before destiny.
It was something I felt I had to do, leaving. But we pay for
these things for such a long time, don't we? That's what I've
learned. That the worst mistakes aren't the ones that hurt
you, yourself, though I have been hurt, as I'm sure you can

see. The worst mistakes are the ones that hurt the ones you love. And when that happens, if there's a way to rectify it at all—then you must. You must even if others will be tangentially hurt in the end. If it is in service to your greater fate. Our greater fate. We must

Here the entry ends, and there are no other writings in the journal.

She turns the page to a photograph lodged in the spine. Ripped in many pieces and then stuck together on the back with yellowed tape, thin and brittle, it shows a young Indian woman in profile, tucking a lock of hair behind her ear and back into her thick braid.

And even though she is in profile, she is very clearly wearing the Moon of Nizam around her neck.

With the picture in hand, Nell rereads that last entry. And then every one before it. Written on the corner of the title page, in the same faded ink, is "Ambrose S. Quincy." Next to it, a pressed violet still retains a trace of its color.

She's sure, even with her hazy knowledge of auction house rules, that this will make a pretty package with the necklace, and that it will help prove proper provenance.

She hears tread on the stairs. "You won't believe . . ." she starts, the journal still in her hands.

She shoves it behind her back when she sees that it's Pansy on the staircase.

"Won't believe what?" Pansy asks, eyeing Nell.

Nell starts to panic. She wants time to think through how to play this, and here Pansy is with her ancient totalitarian presence. "Where's Louis?" Nell asks. "I thought you were Louis."

"He's digging around in the garden shed for buckets or something. What have you got there?" Pansy leans around Nell, trying to see.

"Nothing." Nell feels like a child.

"For real?" Pansy says, putting her palm out. She's wearing a gold bracelet covered in scrolling vines.

When Nell doesn't move, Pansy steps closer. "Grow up," she says.

Nell reluctantly hands it over. What else is she supposed to do, exactly? Is she really going to play a game of keep-away?

After scanning it, Pansy looks up. "Of course this means nothing for anything."

"It's everything. And you know it."

"Because it proves he bought it, I guess? You know the argument based on him stealing it was a loser."

"Because they had an affair," Nell says, trying to will Pansy to give the journal back to her.

"I highly doubt it."

"Did we not just read the same thing?"

"I'm sure it was a very chaste, unrequited sort of thing. It was the twenties."

"Judging from that, I'm pretty sure people had sex in the twenties," Nell says.

"But not her type of people. I mean, there wasn't even birth control, I don't think. Or it was illegal or something. You know what you're saying? That she . . . that she would . . ."

"There was birth control, but people had sex before birth control." As Nell says it, they both stop before she says what is finally so plain. Her mother's theory supported and justified—history reassembling and dissembling before them both. Nell doesn't even need to say it. Between the two of them it's become fact—Ambrose was her mother's true father, Nell's grandfather.

Pansy moves her hand toward the top of the book as if she's going to rip the page out of the journal. Nell puts her hand out, trying to stop her, but Pansy blocks and turns away. Nell doesn't want to force the conclusion. Footsteps ring on the stairs amid their tussle.

"What are we doing?" Louis's heavy tread on the stairs stops and his big grin that accompanies his silly use of the royal "we" fades. Reading the energy, he says, "Are we doing something we shouldn't be doing?"

Pansy puts the journal behind her back, just like Nell did, but Louis just reaches around her.

He fumbles as he puts one arm around Nell's waist, holding her close into his side, reading. "You know what this means, right?" He's nodding toward the page as Nell looks on. She can feel Pansy watching them, wide-eyed. Then he's digging in his pocket for his phone, calling an associate, and walking away as he's updating, already discussing angles and strategies. She hears him say "contemporaneous record" and "authenticated purchase."

When he hangs up, he looks at Nell. "Did you know?"

"My mom did, but she never had proof. My dad, too, I mean, he's the one who told me. She only suspected it because of the family resemblance, but that can be chalked up to anything. This is real proof. I wish she were still here. I wish I could show it to her. She was right."

"I still don't see how any of this makes any difference," says Pansy, nodding toward Louis's hands, which are securely wrapped around the brittle leather.

"No, you wouldn't, but it makes all the difference in the world for that," Louis says, nodding toward Nell's neckline and the Moon.

THE GOLD BANGLE

Ambrose approached the closed door to the bedroom and knocked softly. When he didn't hear anything, he slowly pushed in.

She was lying across the big tester bed, facedown, wearing a kimono of deepest blue. One arm rested flat on the bed above her head, the wrist encircled by a gold bangle etched with scrolling vines. She didn't look up when he came in.

"Mayfair," he said, reaching down and gripping her bare ankle.

"Don't call me that," she said into the bedding without moving.

"May-the-fair-one." Ambrose came and sat next to her on the bed. "You have to come down," he said softly.

She rolled over, revealing wet eyes and a red nose, her hair a dark slice at her cheekbone. It was childish, he knew, but he noted that the necklace remained at her throat. He wondered, idly, if she'd bathed in it. A flash of her in the bath clad only in his jewel came to his mind so vividly, it was as if she had. "I'm a mess," she said.

261

He reached in his pocket and handed her his hand-kerchief. "It's clean."

This made her smile, and she sat up among the pillows, wiping her eyes. "You'd give me a used one?" When she'd caught her breath she said, "I'll claim headache."

Ambrose nodded. "You can't."

"Doesn't your being up here checking on me confirm everything?"

"Came upstairs to get my cigarettes. He's yelling down the line to town."

May walked into her dressing room and sat down behind her dressing table, fiddling with crystal pots and silver boxes.

"You must come down," he said again, gently. "We have to."

"I know," she said with irritation, leaning forward to dab something under her eyes. Gaining composure, she said, "You saw him when I walked in. He already suspects." Despite her efforts at cover-up, tears rolled down her face. "I can't do this." She ripped a tissue from the box at her elbow. "I made a mistake. You *absolutely* made a mistake. But I don't cheat." Ambrose checked himself from pointing out the obvious. They had both already cheated. "It's all a hideous lie. And I'm not a liar."

"Then we face it and undo it," he said.

"Listen to yourself. I can't just undo this. I'm married to him. I can't switch brothers like musical chairs."

Ambrose closed his eyes. May could be blunt. He knew this. "There's a lot of history here. Things you don't understand," he said.

"I thought it would change. I thought when we got married there would be a feeling, I guess. I thought I'd forget. That it wouldn't matter. That he and I could make something more." He remained silent at this glimpse into her thinking. She was open, and he knew it was time to make his case.

"Did it never occur to you that he knew you'd feel indebted when he asked you to marry him? That he was playing on your sympathies?"

"I can't believe you just said that." She closed her eyes, as if in pain. "And yes, the thought had crossed my mind." With a resigned exhale, she said, "You were gone for so long. Are you trying to say he doesn't really love me?"

Ambrose was silent.

"I do love him, you know. I can never hurt him," she said.

Ambrose's throat shut down, hearing her say she loved another.

"But not the way I love you. Never the way I loved you."

Relief washed over him. He gathered her up in his arms. "We have to be honorable. We can't deceive him. It will hurt a bit, but in the long run it's better. It's best we tell him as soon as possible. It's kinder. Sooner is better."

"God, listen to you."

"We're going to hurt people. What else can we do?"

She took a deep breath.

"It's time to be brave," he continued. "I asked you to do that once, and you wouldn't. It's time to do that now."

"I won't be unfaithful."

He kissed her, the scent of violets filling his head. "Then we won't." And those negatives were their beginning.

He took a deep breath. "We'll leave."

"Where will we go?"

"We'll go west. Santa Barbara, maybe Hollywood."

May slumped. Now that he'd said it, he couldn't see her on the West Coast, either.

"Running away, that's your solution to things, isn't it?"

She could be biting. He'd learned this, too. But he released the sting of her comment. "You wanted to go away. I mean far away. We'll leave and let things blow over." May sat up a little straighter then. "A year or two at least. See every place you've ever wanted to see in Europe. Give everyone a chance to calm down, and then we'll come back. They'll have no choice but to accept us."

"Like we're on the lam or something?" she said.

"It's a big world, May. Come get lost in it with me. Once everyone has calmed down, they'll see how right we are for each other, how serious we are. No one will be able to deny us. After a while, it'll be fact. Let's do it right this time."

"You have a plan?"

"I know where to go."

"No one's ever denied you anything, have they? That's what it means to be the favorite son, I guess."

"Ethan's the favorite. Father disapproves of almost everything I do."

"He loves you because you do all the shocking things he won't."

"Father doesn't want to be like me."

"But you always get your way," she said, giving him a halfhearted shove.

"You should remember that. Now fix yourself up and come down before this becomes a scandal," he said, pulling her up.

May wiped her eyes and headed for her bathroom. "Becomes a scandal?" she murmured.

THE GOLD IPHONE

Nell sent the auction house the journal entry, and they'd made the Moon of Nizam the centerpiece of the fall jewelry auction. They'd put the gem on the cover of the fancy catalog, overlaid on an image of Ambrose's poem, which was being offered as part of the lot. The romance of it had attracted media interest. Unprecedented, the gleeful jewelry specialist told Nell after a *New York Times* interview. They'd tallied up more registered bidders than they'd ever had at one of these sales.

Nell had been concerned about the publicity, but after Louis made a few calls to the legal department on her behalf, he was satisfied that a sale would go through. They'd heard nothing from the government of India, and word from a trusted source at the embassy assured them that the Indian government wasn't interested in stopping the sale. It was all too tenuous for Nell, but Louis told her not to question good fortune.

He's been guiding her through the legalities of the estate. She's needed his precise expertise. They've spent the last six months flying back and forth, under the pretense of estate business, but really stealing time together. They'd both let his proposal drop. It was a relief, but also a validation of her annoyance. He had been using it as a ploy, a manipulation to get her to stay that night and nothing more, or else why give up so easily? But she'll give him a pass. She's not looking to rekindle the offer and accept, so why reopen it?

Pansy and Baldwin aren't speaking to Nell or to the press. Their complete silence is an indication of the depth of their disgust. Partly over the supposed "controversy" this sheds on May Quincy's relationship with her brother-in-law. Partly over the public way it's been latched onto and dragged through the press. A researcher from Kenyon College had called them all, trying to gain access to the journal. After that, Baldwin sent Nell a curt email filled with words like "unacceptable," "scandal," and "Kardashian-esque." The last one had made Nell smile. Baldwin does keep up with the times.

Though she suspects it's the windfall coming her way that is unacceptable to Baldwin.

The jewelry auction is held every fall, allowing plenty of time for Russian oligarch buyers and threadbare British aristo sellers to make their respective transactions before the holidays. They use these auctions as if they are their own personal eBay—a tidy transfer of assets from the land-poor to the newly flush. She's been told there's likely museum interest in the Moon.

She's ensconced in a luxe little conference room reserved for VIP consignors overlooking the auction floor, when the head of the jewelry department knocks on the door and peeks her head in. Today she is wearing a shroud of black layers from her chin to her flat boot–clad feet. Her pale, almost-white hair is tied back with a leather strap, and she has no makeup on her grave Flemish angel face except for a glowy sheen high on her cheekbones.

She hands Nell the glossy catalog; it's a luxurious hard-cover coffee table book, a first for her department, and she asks if Nell needs anything, clearly juggling a long to-do list.

Just a new stomach to deal with her nerves and a high bidder, Nell thinks.

She'd been encouraged to stay home by nearly everyone, including the Flemish angel, but in the end it was her father who convinced her to come to New York, making the once-in-a-lifetime argument. Of course he'd insisted on meeting her here; she suspects he couldn't resist the glamour of the event. Louis is here, too, claiming he was needed in his role as estate attorney, but she suspects he also wanted to witness the spectacle as much as she did.

Nell had reintroduced them over dinner last night, and she was relieved when they'd discovered a common affection for Cleveland sports teams and red wine.

They're side by side, hidden behind the skybox's one-way glass window, looking down on the crowd, scanning. She feels the sharp crackle between her and Louis, heightened by the energy coming off the room. She knows he's looking for the Mahj, too.

Nell actually points, hitting glass, when she sees Reema Patel walk in. Being a curator at a museum with one of the largest endowments in the country means she's recognized on auction floors the world over. She's greeted by a small clutch of attendees—air-kisses and handshakes all around.

Right behind her, a young, slick-looking Indian man in large aviator sunglasses enters, talking on a gold-plated cell phone. His wrinkled suit looks expensive, as do his scuffed loafers and tousled hair with manicured stubble. He's handsome enough to be a Bollywood star, but his artful dishevelment marks him out as living in the West. The Indian men she's previously encountered have been meticulously groomed.

"Gotta be," Louis says, chin up once sharply.

Just last week her father had forwarded her a link about the Mahj gate-crashing the Royal Enclosure at Ascot and being denied by security, yet another confirmation of his nostalgic tendencies despite his youth.

Nevertheless, his playboy habits and ability to attract the paparazzi have made him something of a media darling. Many in the crowd unashamedly take pictures of him with their cell phones, and a few lean in for selfies.

He's been banned from the big auction houses and has taken to enlisting proxies and aliases. So it's with some confusion that Nell watches the head of the jewelry department, the Flemish angel, rush across the room to shake the Mahj's hand, as excited as a six-year-old meeting Santa. The Mahj is off his phone, and he removes his sunglasses with a courtly flourish as Reema Patel formally introduces him. The department head, uncharacteristically red-faced with excitement, shows them both to prime seats located side by side in the front row.

"The hell?" Louis says.

Reema Patel is scanning the room. When she looks up at the bank of skybox windows, she smiles, assured and only slightly frosty. Nell reminds herself that Patel can't see through the one-way glass, because it'd been awkward when Nell had told her the Moon was going to auction. Patel had been professional and formal, but clearly disappointed and disapproving. Nell notes a slightly triumphant swish of that black hair as Patel now takes her seat next to royalty.

Nell wants to call the Flemish angel back and ask what's going on.

But there's no time, as the auction begins right away. Lesser modern lots go for over their estimates. Bidding's energetic on the floor and topped up by the phones and the Internet.

When the white-gloved auction house assistant brings the Moon of Nizam onto the stage, a hush falls over the room. On a large screen behind the auctioneer, a projection of Ambrose's journal entry looms over them all. The portions pertaining to Ambrose buying the piece from the maharani are highlighted, his old-fashioned fountain pen script as romantic as the pressed violet Nell had found next to his name.

The auctioneer is droning on about the gemological specifications of the necklace, carats and clarity. And when it comes to provenance, he says, "Former property of May Quincy, wife of industrialist Ethan Quincy, as given to her by her brother-in-law, Ambrose Quincy, and consigned by their granddaughter."

It's then that Nell really feels the truth of it. For of course the auctioneer meant that Nell is Ethan and May's granddaughter, but all she hears is that she is May and Ambrose's.

"Shhh." Louis hip-checks her, his nose practically against the window.

"I didn't say anything."

Bidding has started at one million and is ramping up in hundred-thousand-dollar increments.

There's an out-of-time feeling. And Nell knows then that when Loulou wrote her will, she made a very specific choice.

"We're at the reserve now," Louis says, his eyes never leaving the crowd. "It's going for sure." He jostles her elbow.

This wasn't a mistake. She believes it then. It wasn't a dotty, demented old lady with too much stuff on her hands. And Nell's known all along it wasn't an oversight or sloppiness on Louis's part. It's an apology, an offer of restitution, an attempt at absolution, and a chance to right a wrong. And as Nell watches the price increase on the floor, she knows it was meant to be a debt repaid.

The auctioneer has close to ten million on the floor. The Internet bidders have dropped off. The phone bidders have gone silent.

Loulou had to have known more than anyone what was between May and Ambrose and exactly where Nell's mother, their daughter, fell in the course of it. Loulou had been the repository of not only the heirlooms, but of the secrets, too.

It's then that the Mahj raises his paddle.

"Would you pay attention?" Louis gestures toward the floor.

"And we have a new bidder in the mix." The unflappable auctioneer, who's built his career on friendly froideur, lets a crack of excitement show as the Mahj and one last bidder take up the game in a back-and-forth, rising higher until only the Mahj is left.

"Going once at twelve million." The auctioneer is gesturing to the room. "All done at twelve million." His voice has a questioning lilt as he hesitates only a moment before bringing the compact gavel down with a crisp bang. "Sold to the gentleman in the front row for twelve million dollars."

Assistants are rushing to see the official bidding number. There's clapping and handshakes, and it takes a few minutes for the crowd to quiet enough to pay attention to the next lot.

"I believe it now," Nell says to her father, watching as the Moon is whisked out of the room.

Louis hugs her. "You just made twelve million dollars!"

Her father raises his eyebrows at this.

"Did I?" The entire thing feels like a dream.

The jewelry department head barges into the room, breathless from rushing upstairs to congratulate her.

But Louis steps forward, as protective as ever. "You might have a very specific problem on your hands," he says to the department head. "Even allowing him on the floor is suspect."

"Oh, no need to start barking at me, Mr. Morrell." The Flemish angel practically pushes Louis aside to get to Nell. "I can't go into specifics, you understand, but having one of the largest museums in the country involved helped his case." She's shaking Nell's hand so vigorously, it's like she's shaking Nell bodily. All professional distance is gone. The woman is full of unabashed excitement. "Also, the Indian government let it be known they approved. Knew there was a better shot than not that it might be coming back home. There are international interests as well, you understand," she says to Nell. "And of course certain funds were held in escrow, that's all I'll say." She holds up a hand in warning. "Please don't quote me. But I do feel it's only fair to tell you, given the unique circumstances." She turns to Louis. "You've no worries on the surety front. Please rest assured."

As much as Nell's excited, the money feels unreal. The whole scene feels as if she's underwater, and it's then she knows what she wants.

"Can I meet him?" Nell asks. "I want to meet the maharaja."

The department head's mouth twists down in a little moue. "Of course," she says, faux brightly in a way Nell knows means the opposite. "I don't see why not."

THE BUCKEYE

"I want to drive," May insisted when they walked out the front door. The chauffeur had left the Packard four-seater in front of the house, the roof tucked and folded. Already, the seats looked hot.

"Have you been crying?" Ethan asked with ill-disguised disgust now that they were outside in the sunlight.

"Hay fever," she said, though she had no history of it. She crunched across the gravel, but Ethan held his grip on the keys. "Can't I do one thing? Besides, you're drunk."

Ambrose was alert, and he knew defiance was not the way to handle Ethan right now. Ambrose had noted the glass in his brother's hand in the gunroom, though Ethan seemed the same, straight Ethan in spite of it. Only the slight slurring together of words suggested that mixing whiskey and his pain pills might be more than Ethan could handle. They'd waited for May in stilted silence as Ethan refreshed his drink and drank a second whiskey straight down.

Out front, Ethan kept his grip on his keys. Not that Ambrose could blame him; handing May the keys would be akin to handing over his manhood.

Ambrose climbed over the door and plopped himself down in the back seat, waiting for them to finish their brinkmanship.

"I won't get in," May said, crossing her arms over her chest, and Ambrose had to admit, the stance was unattractive.

But Ethan seemed to know when she wouldn't be moved. He handed the keys over to her, without looking at her face, and then silently walked around to the passenger side.

With a little stamp of her foot May then hopped behind the wheel, and Ambrose realized her satisfaction at being in control—of anything.

May started the car and as they accelerated, Ambrose noted that she kept continual watch on Ethan out of the corner of her eye. He thought he saw Ethan mouth something to her, but he couldn't make out what it was.

"Eyes on the road," Ethan said over the wind.

"My eyes are on the road. If you hadn't been drinking, you'd see that," May said primly.

"I haven't been drinking," Ethan said. Typical Ethan, Ambrose thought sourly. He never would own up to his questionable behavior.

She turned down a dirt lane connecting the Shaw farm and the Van Alstynes' new place. She picked up speed on the straightaway.

"Slow down," Ethan said.

She laughed. "Don't be such an old woman." She continued to accelerate the car.

"You know, darling," Ethan said, his eyes on the road. "Don't you think it's a little much to be wearing that necklace today?"

May's hand was instantly at her throat. "I wear it every day."

"Just like your wedding ring," he said, turning fully sideways to face her.

Dry dust from the road rose around Ambrose, mixing with the hot day and coating all the leaves on the trees. And then his brother said, "You think I'm stupid."

Ambrose leaned over the driver's seat then, his hand on May's shoulder.

"I think you're stupid drunk," May said, eyes facing front.

"You think I don't know what's happening right in my own house?" Ethan said.

"What's happening in *your* house, Ethan?" May said, drawing out the "your."

Ambrose's hand slipped in front of May's chest, pressing her back into her seat protectively. "Watch the road," he said in her ear, willing her to keep them safe.

"You don't tell her what to do," Ethan said, turning fully toward the back seat.

"Neither do you," May said. Ambrose wanted to tell her to quit it, to get along, but that had never been May's way.

Turning to May, Ethan said, "I want it off." His voice was loud and dangerous. Then, in a flash Ambrose couldn't have anticipated, Ethan swiped his right arm, his good arm, across the car toward May's throat.

Ambrose blocked him.

"I'm driving." A nervous little chuckle arose out of her as her hand fiddled at her neck. "I'll take it off when we stop." That she acquiesced so easily meant she recognized the danger in the situation.

"I want it off!" Ethan yelled, lunging toward May again. The car swerved, and Ambrose fell back as Ethan reached for the necklace, gaining purchase. He gripped the side of the delicate cording and dug his fingers in, wrapping around the silk, and then he tugged—hard.

"Ethan, stop," May said in a garbled voice. One hand grabbed for the wheel and one hand scrabbled at her throat as Ethan pulled her head toward him. "You're hurting me."

But Ethan pulled harder until Ambrose could see the cording imbedding in the opposite side of her neck. He rose up between the seats again and hit his brother's arm, trying to sever his grip. The car swerved, but Ethan didn't let go.

"For God's sake, let go!" Ambrose shouted over the wind. "You've lost your mind!"

The car swerved and skittered. Ethan's grip slackened a bit as he looked back to the road, giving May a chance to right the car.

May swatted at his hand. Ambrose tried to get leverage over the seats, almost crawling in between the two of them. Finally, the cord snapped. The necklace and May's head flung to the left. Ethan flew to the side of the car as May jerked the steering wheel to the right. The car lurched toward the rutted ditch at the side of the road.

It seemed an instant that the buckeye tree loomed in front of them. Ambrose leaned from the back to brace May into her seat with all the protective force he could muster, and then it was the sound of steel crumpling and the hot smell of burning leather and grease.

THE EARL GREY

The interloper's doorbell rings at the farm, and Nell
expects an entourage, or at least Reema Patel acting
as the Mahj's handler, much like she did those months
ago at the auction. But when Nell opens the door to the
handsome and elegantly scruffy young man she remembers, she's a bit relieved it will be just the two of them
today. She has questions to ask, and she doesn't want an
audience.

The Mahj is sharply dressed in an Italian playboy's idea
of country clothes, though spring mud is likely doing a
number on his delicate cognac boots. His waxed hacking
jacket is too clean to be anything but brand-new. His
frayed corduroy trousers are too heavy for the unexpected
jump into the sixties today, but they'll be just right for the
fall back down into the thirties tonight.

"Mrs. Quincy," he says, and she wouldn't be surprised
if he bowed. "This is a pleasure."

The incorrect name doesn't faze her anymore. Throughout this process she's been addressed this way. "Call me
Nell, please."

She's waiting for him to reciprocate, to tell her what to call him. Your highness, Maharaja, Mahj? When he doesn't offer, she tries not to address him by name.

When Nell had received an invitation to the museum reception, sent to her in Oregon, she had called Reema Patel, who'd been hard to get on the phone. Not that Nell minds; the woman is working on the show of her career, titled "From Partition to Pride: The Artistic Jewelry Traditions of India." The centerpiece is, of course, the Moon of Nizam, on generous loan from its new owner, the Mahj.

Nell had chatted up Patel in anticipation of asking her for a favor, patiently listening to her litany of busyness as she got together a marquee exhibition in half the usual time. Patel's been friendlier since she gained possession of the Moon, and she recounts how she's been calling in every favor due her in a prestigious career to get accompanying jewelry and miniature paintings for the exhibit in order to tell the story of the Moon, its place in Mughal history, and its importance to Indian patrimony. The insurance for the exhibit is exorbitant, she'd complained. Security is a nightmare, she'd confided. When Nell had finally asked if Patel would help set up a meeting, Patel had agreed; she'd been enthusiastic about it even.

Now, Nell leads the Mahj in to the flower room. She's set up tea on the massive marble table that's always acted as a bar. Moving this monster will be a considerable undertaking, one Emerson hasn't puzzled out yet. He and Vlad have been staying out here supervising the cleanout for the last week, but they've made themselves scarce today. She'd held her breath weeks ago when she'd asked Em for this favor, sidestepping Baldwin, who's still not speaking to her, despite her decision to pay the taxes on the Moon. She'd decided it was the right thing to do, but Baldwin wasn't mollified. Her decision was met with silence, though she'd spared them all a headache and saved the Quincys a bundle. But Emerson had thanked her and when she'd asked for this favor, he'd said "Sure, Nell-bell. I'm sure G-Lou would approve of royalty visiting the place."

She'd fretted over the menu and given up on the idea of serving chai altogether. She's made a pot of Earl Grey and placed it next to a bottle of champagne chilling in a silver bucket. When he sees it, the Mahj grabs the bottle up by the neck, unasked.

"I see you're familiar with my TMZ headlines. You're thinking I'm drinking champagne morning, noon, and night." Before she can protest or apologize, worried that she's offended him, he expertly uncorks the bottle with only the slightest sigh and pours them both a coupe. "Why not be civilized?" he says, and toasts her without touching the rims of the wide bowls. She's glad she snagged the old-school glasses out of a box and washed them. Vlad had packed them up, deeming them vintage kitsch, not worth much and bound for a bric-a-brac guy in town unless someone in the family wanted them.

They load up delicate plates with little cakes. The Mahj picks up a meethi she'd managed to find in a suburban Indian grocery. "You've gone to an awful lot of trouble," he says with a smile. She leads him into the chilly living room. The heat was turned down for the winter and the spring thaw has yet to reach the interior, making her wish he'd chosen the tea. Her shoes click on the bare floors. Most of the furniture has been divided up or sold, including all the fairly good rugs. She'd worried over what the Mahj would think of the place with the air of a yard sale about it. But if the Mahj notices, she can't tell. He's reflexively gracious, with ingrained manners that mark a royal trained from birth.

Emerson's had the place scrupulously cleaned, but it just shows the shabbiness even more and somehow makes the house feel colder. The Canaletto is gone. The bright outline of its former place on the wall makes the rest of the room look gray. The blackbuck mount is gone, too, already donated to the natural history museum. Emerson has sent her a precise and detailed accounting of it all, but it's different seeing it in person.

They settle themselves in two awkward, brocade-covered tiny chairs in front of the cold fireplace. Emerson has set them up—likely from a bedroom upstairs—and she smiles at her cousin's thoughtfulness. Niceties about the Mahj's trip and questions about his stay are exchanged while they balance their plates on their laps and put the champagne on the floor like a picnic. Emerson overlooked providing them with a table.

"My trip," the Mahj says, "is really full of lovely surprises. I must say I am loving these flowering trees." It's not until he's fetched the champagne bottle from the other room and poured them both a second glass despite the chill that they fall silent.

"Thank you for indulging my curiosity. I couldn't get much out of anyone other than this," he says as he brings the journal entry out of his pocket, folded up and creased. She'd spent a good amount of time agonizing over whether to include the entire journal and the photo with the lot, and she's glad she decided against it. Who knows what he would have done with it if he's carrying this around in his pocket?

She has the journal at the ready in the library and gets up to fetch it.

"This fell out of the entry when I found it," she says, coming back in the room and handing him the photo placed on top.

"That was my grandmother. They told you?"

They had told her. The maharani of Baroda, second of four wives to the maharaja and known as the Indian Wallis Simpson for her glamour and divisiveness. She'd ransacked the maharaja's jewels, reset some more to her liking, which included having the biggest and most famous strands of rubies remade into anklets that she wore daily. That kind of effortless middle finger to the world made Coco Chanel call her a kindred spirit when they'd met once in Paris.

"I have many pictures of her dressed like this," he says, unimpressed. "Dressing like this was her escape, you understand?"

Nell gives a little shake of her head. "No, sorry."

"They observed *ghoonghat*—like purdah? At least the fancier you were, the more the women were kept separate. It was popular among my family at the time—obviously not anymore. Dressing like a peasant was her release. She had a little *haveli*, too, her Petit Trianon, if you will. Lined completely in mirrors, where she'd go and pretend she was a dancing girl." He's pointing to the background of the picture. "This was taken there. It was where she used to have rendezvous."

At Nell's silence, he continues, "Trysts, you understand. With foreigners, mainly," he says, as if reading her mind.

"She was educated, which was unheard of, but she was a great favorite of her father's and her mother was ambitious. She spoke nearly perfect French, I'm told." He's examining the picture. "I've heard before that she took lovers. My great-grandfather took four wives, so I suppose it's fair. So he . . ." The Mahj flicks Ambrose's journal with a gentle tap of his buffed nail. ". . . I'm sorry to say, was not the only one." Instead of being embarrassed and blushing, like a Quincy, he seems to wear this as a point of pride. Nell remembers that he's been educated abroad, and she can't help but admire his progressive ways.

"I don't think they were lovers," she says.

He looks smug. "Mrs. Quincy, Nell. This is actually a conversation I've had more than once, if you can believe it. I'm not at all squeamish about talking about my grandmother's love life. You shouldn't be, either. They were people." He takes a sip from his coupe.

"No, I mean, I'm fine with it. I just don't think they were because he was in love with someone else."

"He was in love with this May?" he asks, skimming the journal entries.

"She was his sister-in-law," Nell says.

The Mahj pauses, eyebrows raised, and Nell pushes on. "His friend was with your grandmother." She shows him the letter from Ambrose to May describing Dicky's dancing girl. Shows him the picture of Dicky from the scrapbooks Loulou kept.

"So I see," the Mahj says, politely, but he is most interested in the photograph of his grandmother wearing the necklace.

"She was very beautiful," Nell offers as he studies it. "You look quite a bit like her."

He ducks his head because, of course, good looks run in the family.

"She was a great favorite of the people," he says. "I still run across shrines to her when I'm in the countryside back home." Nell gives silent thanks that there are no shrines to Quincys, just the one she'd created in her own mind. The one she has almost completely dismantled.

After another sip from her glass Nell decides it's time to ask. "But why did she sell it?"

"Do you know the Hindi word *'stridhan'*?" At Nell's shake of the head he continues. "It's like a cross between an insurance policy and a dowry. Jewels were meant to be stridhan for women, a security to be sold when they needed cash. It wasn't all that unusual for my grandmother to sell her jewels. My grandfather was extravagant, loved polo ponies."

"Is that why it was never reported stolen?"

Louis comes through the door then, without knocking or ringing. He knows Quincy ways now. She's been staying with him in town on this trip before the opening of the exhibition. The cross-country thing they've been doing remains delicious if undefined, but she's come to know a few of his quirks, such as timing his entrances perfectly.

After introductions, Nell assures the Mahj he can speak freely in front of Louis, as he's the estate lawyer.

"Oh, I'm sorry, you're not together?" the Mahj asks.

Neither of them says anything. Louis's proposal remains dropped between them. Nell hasn't mentioned it, and Louis has kept quiet—a pride-off between them.

The Mahj smirks. "You Americans, so touchy, so puritanical. I am learning this about you. I thought it was a stereotype. But to answer your question, Nell, I think my grandfather knew what happened to the Moon, that she'd sold it," the Mahj says. "Her father-in-law gave it to her before the wedding fire. And frankly I think my grandfather was relieved to have the thing done. By that time he knew government changes were inevitable—tax increases and land reform. He was a smart man, and he was probably glad to have the money."

"So why did you want to shell out for it?" Nell asks. They've drunk nearly the whole bottle of champagne. Louis's presence at her side gives her courage.

"Obviously you'd let the government know it'd be coming home," Louis says. "That's why we didn't have any problems."

The Mahj inclines his head. "I don't know if you know, but bringing back Indian heritage is something I feel rather strongly about."

"So why didn't you just make an offer privately?" Louis asks.

"Once I heard you had evidence that the thing had been legitimately bought, wasn't stolen as we thought, well, I was advised that my claim wasn't strong and international antiquity law is hard to enforce anyway, as you know," he says, gesturing to Louis.

"And you must forgive me here if I do not get the nuance right, but we weren't at all sure who you were." For the first time all afternoon he seems flustered and actually blushes.

"I'm sorry?" Nell says.

"We weren't sure what you'd do if you knew a maharaja was interested in the necklace. Where your negotiations would wind up." And Nell does see: they were afraid she'd try to gouge them and they'd decided to take their chances at a public auction.

"Please know this is not personal to you," he says. "But I have had the experience in the past of people assuming all sorts of things, most of them wrong, when I am involved in a sale. Some of it is my own fault, yes," he says, acknowledging his past faux bidding. "And we lost a piece I dearly wanted by being too direct in our approach. With the Moon, quite frankly, I couldn't let that happen again. So a public sale by a third party was the best way."

He slips the patched and faded photograph of his great-grandmother into his jacket pocket, unasked, sips the last of his champagne, and stands. "I should be going." But not before he empties the last of the bottle into Nell's glass. "I think you'll enjoy seeing the restoration of the Moon. I helped them bring in artisans from one of the famous workshops in Jaipur. The rumor is that back in the day, that very shop was the court jeweler for some of the Mughal emperors. They rewove the cording and shined it up properly. They'll actually be at the party tonight." He's heading for the front hall, saying, "I'll be looking forward to seeing you at the opening." He bows a little to Louis. "You both, I hope."

Nell had debated going to the reception even though she'd be less on display than the Moon or the Mahj, and she has no fear of overshadowing either. The Mahj can clearly hold his own, and no one can outshine the Moon. Patel had told her Baldwin and Pansy, all the Quincys in fact, had RSVP'ed right away. Those old familiar twinges of the imposter, the pretender, had gripped her, making her want to stay away. She was never a true owner of the

Moon; it had passed through her possession quickly. She'd merely been acting as a placeholder in a drama bigger than her. The universe had paid her well for this, yes, and that should be her consolation.

But Nell is done with hiding, done with molding herself, done with monuments and shrines. She is ready to be seen for exactly who she is now in the midst of this. She is done with nostalgia.

Besides, Patel had been charmingly tenacious, which made Nell feel welcomed, and Louis has promised to be her wingman.

When he's at the door, the Mahj turns and asks, "So she left him for his brother? The love letter. Buying her the necklace. A scandal, I'm sure."

"I'm afraid not, actually. Ambrose died in a car crash. They were all in the car when it happened."

"Oh, how tragic."

"Yes."

"My grandmother May died in childbirth later that year and Ethan Quincy drowned."

"Drowned?"

"Some thought it suicide. There was a mine fire, an industrial accident, and some say he felt responsible for it. Some think he was depressed for other reasons."

The Mahj squints closely at her, sizing up the color of her hair, the point of her chin, the light color of her eyes.

"Do you know the Hindi word '*jaraja*'?"

She shakes her head.

"Forgive me, it's not a nice word. I don't know you well, but let's say it means 'love child,' essentially. The resemblance is uncanny."

"Yes," she says, blushing. "My mother had her suspicions."

"So you find that to be true?"

"I'll never know, but given the letters, I believe so. Many in the family find it shocking. I suppose that makes them scandalous, a little immoral."

The Mahj is shaking his head. "No," he says with a smile and his hand over his heart like a romantic balladeer. "I think that makes them human."

THE DIVING BOARD

After the Mahj leaves, Nell needs to get outside. Despite counseling herself to caution, he was such a charmer that she drank more champagne than she wanted and now she's jangly, face flushed and wanting cold air. She changes into wellies and pulls on an abandoned anorak from the hall closet that's two sizes too big—a hodgepodge with the red wool dress she's wearing, chosen to try to look chic for the Mahj. Louis takes her hand as they walk down a muddy path, the tall weed trees just starting to bud green. The borders of the field are soggy with last fall's cut, but this trail is old and worn so deep into the land that it will never disappear.

The pond houses still stand, though the foundations on the men's side look like they need attention. The diving board, a single plank of locust polished smooth by generations of wet feet, still gives a mighty spring into water that is thawing and patchy with ice.

"Think we could make something of this?" Louis asks, walking into the little clapboard house and patting the river rock of the fireplace. There's a tentative grin on his face. Is he dreaming about living at the farm? Has he had his eye turned by Quincy grandeur? She supposes she shouldn't judge him if he has. She's been susceptible to it her whole life.

"That's assuming we could get our hands on the property. Pretty sure Baldwin owns all the way down to the pond now," she says.

"Not this," he says. "This." He waves back and forth at the space between them. "I feel bad that I haven't seriously asked you," he says, and in a moment she's in a kiss that erases everything, all the doubts, leaving only connection and certainty.

When they part, this huge man, all six feet of conviction, folds himself down with one knee on the clear pine floor.

Her pulse storms in her head, flying on champagne and the traditional words, though he doesn't need to say them. Everything is plain on his face. This is no joke proposal or manipulation.

She can't deny that nagging questions have dogged her about how much of his attraction to her is because she's now so well set up after the sale of the Moon. She admonishes herself that it's uncharitable to think that of him. They'd been attracted to each other before anything with the Moon happened. He'd proposed, even—such as it was. But where will they live? Who will move for whom?

But in the moment when he asks, she savors; she breathes before this moment speeds into the past.

A compromise, a meeting halfway, that's what's often advised in a romance, but it hardly ever works to make half a commitment and keep half safe. It would be so easy to keep a piece of herself back. She's been doing that for months. But she's coming to understand that what is required is making herself vulnerable, moving fully and completely to a place that's not safe or comfortable. He hangs then, waiting for a response. She knows when it comes, it can't be halfway. If it is, they'll never meet. She must come all the way over, exposing, rendering herself vulnerable, being clear.

From the poem and the Moon, Nell knows that a pair who were meant to be together were not. Though who moved or failed to move, who had courage and who was a coward, will remain forever obscured to her.

And the things she has been looking to belong to, to fit herself into, seemingly for her whole life, fall away as she looks at Louis at her feet, his eyes lit with a fierce faith.

"See, this is why people have a ring," he says, misreading her silence. "You have doubts, that's fine. I'll be certain for both of us. I thought this might take a little convincing. Forget what people will say, I know you feel it, too . . ."

It's then she kneels down to stop him, comes to his level to kiss him, with everything—with love and hope and the feeling of ultimate belonging—and then on an exhale she says, "Yes."

ACKNOWLEDGMENTS

Though the Moon of Nizam is a fictional jewel, it was inspired in part by the Patiala Necklace. Created by the House of Cartier in the 1920s for Maharaja Bhupinder Singh, the Patiala Necklace included the seventh-largest diamond in the world, amid a setting of 2,930 diamonds and rubies. The entire necklace went missing in 1946. The main diamond came up for auction by an anonymous seller in Geneva in 1982, and it was bought by the De Beers Company and renamed on their behalf. In 1998, a representative of Cartier found the remnants of the setting in a secondhand jewelry shop in London. In addition to the missing De Beers diamond, most of the significant stones, including several important Burmese rubies, were also missing and have yet to resurface publicly. The House of Cartier has restored the ransacked necklace by replacing the missing gems with synthetic stones, and they have kept it for their archives and traveling display.

The Maharani of Baroda is a creation of fiction. But for a deeper understanding of *ghoonghat* and *stridhan*, as well as the North Indian life of a maharani as it was lived,

I recommend Maharani Gayatri Devi's autobiography, *A Princess Remembers*. As the fourth maharani of Jaipur, Devi was known as the "Indian Jackie Kennedy" for her beauty and style. Indeed, Jackie Kennedy was the maharani's guest in Jaipur during Kennedy's famous tour of India in 1962. Devi was elected to the Indian Parliament and served as the representative for Jaipur.

The character of Ambrose Quincy and his many indiscretions and charms are fictional. However, I am indebted to the travel journals Amasa Stone Mather kept during his trip around the world in 1907. These volumes were privately published by his father, Samuel Mather, and 150 copies were gifted to friends in 1910. They became very dear to his family after Amasa died of influenza in 1920. I am thankful to this primary source for providing inspiration for Ambrose's letters.

The story Ambrose retells at the gymkhana owes a debt to the Brothers Grimm tale *The Frog Prince*.

I was aided by a small army of experts while writing this book, but any mistakes or inaccuracies are entirely my own.

Many thanks to my friend Grosvie Cooley for facilitating my connection to the Western Reserve Historical Society.

Particular thanks to Ann Sindelar of the Cleveland History Center, who provided me with my many requested boxes of issues of *Town Topics* and *The Bystander*, the *People* and *Us Weekly* magazines of 1920s Cleveland.

Special gratitude to Patty Edmondson and Danielle Peck of the Cleveland History Center, who allowed me access to the costume collection archives, where I spent a day in the vault amidst 1920s splendor.

Many thanks to Dr. Jim Edmonson of the Dittrick Medical History Museum at Case Western Reserve University, where I spent time down in the stacks learning about burn treatments, pain management, and crush injury protocol in the 1920s.

Grateful thanks to Stephen Josh Knerly, Esq., who schooled me in provenance law and the ethical guidelines surrounding potentially stolen antiquities.

Legal ninja and estate expert Jennifer Savage, Esq., patiently answered my many questions, asked through a hazy recollection of my wills and estates class in law school. Many thanks for her kindness and generosity.

Appreciation and thanks to the charming Sonya Rhie Quintanilla, who thoroughly answered my many prying questions about her job as curator of Indian and Southeast Asian Art at the Cleveland Museum of Art.

Additionally, I'm blessed with accomplished friends, on whom I leaned shamelessly, though any errors are solely my own.

Britt Frome, orthopedic surgeon and horsewoman extraordinaire, guided me through horse bloodlines and the ramifications of crush injury with equal expertise. Susan Jarros gifted me with an invaluable crash course in the history of provenance law and served as a trusted resource. Abigail Shapard brought her knowledge to the auction chapter and made it brighter and more accurate. Grateful thanks to these impressive women of many talents.

I offer sincere thanks to the selection committee for the Edith Wharton Writer-in-Residence program, the board of trustees, and the incredible staff at The Mount, Edith Wharton's home in Lenox, Massachusetts. I spent two weeks in 2016 working through edits for this book in Edith Wharton's very bedroom, where she did her writing. There are few more productive or magical places.

Humble thanks and love to dear friends and generous prereaders Halley Moore and Irina Reyn, who gave me the great gifts of their time, attention, and insights from their fine minds and saved me from myself in multiple ways.

Elizabeth Kaplan is an insightful reader and advisor, as well as my stellar agent. Many thanks to her for all her efforts on behalf of this book and my writing in general.

Trish Todd is my excellent editor, whose careful, guiding eye made this book better and stronger than it was. Grateful thanks to her and her team for all they do, especially Kaitlin Olson, Jessica Roth, and Meredith Vilarello.

Purest love and gratitude in abundance to Mac and Flora—for you guys, I would.

And true love and devotion to Sandy, who hands me the matches and keeps the spark. I'm grateful for that and for so much more. Thank you.

A SELECTION OF SOURCES

Devi, Gayatri (Maharani of Jaipur). *A Princess Remembers: The Memoirs of the Maharani of Jaipur*. New Delhi: Rupa & Co., 1995.

Ghoshray, Saby. "Repatriation of the Kohinoor Diamond: Expanding on the Legal Paradigm for Cultural Heritage." *Fordham International Law Journal* 31, no. 3 (2007): 739–780.

Greenfield, Jeanette. *The Return of Cultural Treasures*. Cambridge: Cambridge University Press, 1996.

Haidar, Navina Najat and Courtney Ann Stewart. *Treasures from India: Jewels from the Al-Thani Collection*. New York: The Metropolitan Museum of Art, 2014.

Herford, Oliver. *The Deb's Dictionary: The Essential A to Z Guide for the Aspiring Debutante*. New York: J. B. Lippincott Company, 1931.

Krishnan, Usha R. Bala and Meera Sushil Kumar. *Indian Jewellry: Dance of the Peacock*. Mumbai: India Book House Limited, 2001.

Laubner, Ellie. *Fashions of the Roaring '20s: Economics and Legal Relationships*. Atglen, PA: Schiffer Publishing, 1996.

Makley, Kathryn L. *Samuel Mather, First Citizen of Cleveland*. Edited by Joan Levinson. N.p.: Tasora Books, 2013.

Mather, Amasa Stone. *Extracts from Letters, Diary, and Note Books of Amasa Stone Mather, Volumes 1 and 2*. Cleveland, OH: Arthur H. Clark Company, 1910.

Mather, Amasa Stone. *The Occasional Impromptu Verses and Songs of Amasa Stone Mather, 1884–1920*. Cleveland, OH: Printing Press, 1920.

Waxman, Sharon. *Loot: The Battle Over the Stolen Treasures of the Ancient World*. New York: Henry Holt and Company, 2009.

Wick, Warren Corning. *My Recollections of Old Cleveland: Manners, Mansions, Mischief*. Edited by Joanne M. Lewis. Cleveland, OH: Publix Book Mart, 1979.

ABOUT THE AUTHOR

Claire McMillan is the author of *Gilded Age* and *The Necklace*. She grew up in Pasadena, California, and now lives on her husband's family farm outside of Cleveland, Ohio, with their two children. She practiced law until 2003 and then received her MFA in creative writing from Bennington College.